A Fo

Magill had the taxi c
his bag. Before M
Carter had propelled
the door, and was pushing money at the driver. It was an American hundred-dollar bill.

'*A l'Orly. Vite.*'

Magill shouted a countermand, but the driver ignored it. The taxi shot out into the traffic. Magill reached for the door on his side. Carter grinned at him. 'It will be awfully messy.'

Magill sank back into the seat and glared. Carter's whole personality was suddenly different. He was in charge. To underline the fact, his right hand was tucked inside his coat and there was an ominous bulge pointing at Magill's chest.

'What the hell do you think you're doing?'

'Kidnapping you.'

[illegible]ngle in North

[illegible] open. The porters threw in
[illegible]ughly could close the door,
[illegible] himself into the taxi, slammed

LEONARD ST CLAIR

A Fortune in Death

MAGNUM BOOKS
Methuen Paperbacks Ltd

A Magnum Book

A FORTUNE IN DEATH
ISBN 0 417 02130 5

First published 1976
by Constable & Company Ltd
Magnum edition published 1978

Magnum Books are published
by Methuen Paperbacks Ltd
11 New Fetter Lane, London, EC4P 4EE

Made and printed in Great Britain
by Richard Clay (The Chaucer Press) Ltd
Bungay, Suffolk

To Catherine
for so many reasons

I

The jeep lurched and slammed along the dirt road. Tumbleweed bounced and swirled in its wake. Now and then, the jeep plowed into a stretch of alkali which would spume up behind in a cloud of choking white. The driver glanced only occasionally at the ruts racing toward him, then disappearing beneath the radiator. His eyes, shaded by the brim of a metal work-helmet, stared through dusty goggles at a point on the horizon, at a steel finger aimed into the California sky.

Something was wrong at the rig. There ought to be steam rising from the boilers. The air was still, a windless 110°. The smoke and steam ought to be rising in columns visible for five miles or more. But there was nothing.

The jeep jerked to a stop a few yards from the drilling platform. Dave Magill cut the engine and noted a second ominous sign. The silence. There was no apocalyptic roar, no gut-shaking vibration. The drill stem was dead in its housing. Magill clambered out of the jeep and slapped the dust from his khaki trousers and shirt. He strode to the drilling platform and climbed the iron ladder. He stared at the knot of bare-chested workmen who were crouched around the drill stem. Two of the men turned grease-streaked faces toward Magill; they smiled uneasily and looked away. He paced slowly around the platform. He kicked a boot at a box wrench. He stared up into the rig; he counted the lengths of pipe strung overhead which waited to be lowered into the hole. What was the foul-up this time? Damn it to hell, from the hour of spudding in, it had been a jinx well. At twenty-one hundred feet the number-two boiler had exploded. At thirty-nine hundred, a man had fallen from the crown-block, suffering a broken back. At fifty-seven hundred, the drill stem had snapped. And again at sixty-six hundred.

Without another glance at the workmen, Magill turned and climbed down the ladder and trudged toward the house trailer which served as the field office and bunk-house. He saw Barney O'Brien, his foreman, appear in the doorway.

'I was just going to town to tell you,' O'Brien began, then hesitated.

Magill pushed his helmet to the back of his head, took off his goggles, and wiped the sweat from his forehead. His dark blue eyes squinted thoughtfully at the gray-haired man with the bull neck and the ham-hands, the foreman he had inherited from his dead father.

Barney shifted uneasily and spat a stream of tobacco juice into the sand. 'We oughta put a radio-telephone in the trailer. Then you wouldn't have to keep coming out.'

Magill jerked his head toward the rig. 'What's our depth?'

'It's 7110. I told the boys not to use too much power, and they didn't. It wasn't like last time.'

'Stem crystalize?'

'Yep. Damned basalt is hard as the drill.' Barney paused to make another arc of tobacco juice. 'I figure we can fish it up in a couple of days.'

'If we're lucky.'

'If we're lucky.'

'And if we're not?'

'Christ, let's not think about it!'

'I've got to, Barney. Look. We've wasted enough time fishing drill pipe out of this hole. Let's plug back and slant-drill.'

'Leave the diamond drill down there? My God, Dave, the cost!'

'Time is a cost, too.'

O'Brien sighed, then repeated what had become an article of faith to both men. 'The oil's down there, God damn it! It's got to be!'

'If it isn't, *I'll* soon be working for *you*.'

The two men stared silently at the rig. Over three hundred and twenty thousand dollars had been poured down that hole in the ground. Some of it had come from mullets, small investors outside the oil industry. Three hundred and twenty thousand dollars. And now this latest complication. Magill calculated rapidly; his savings account contained enough to cover the cost of a new diamond drill, enough for the payroll for another two or three weeks. If nothing else went wrong. But after that . . .

Barney O'Brien sensed his thoughts. 'You suppose you could sell off another piece? Maybe two or three percent?'

'Where?'

'Maybe Texas?'

Magill shook his head. He had had trouble getting that last fifty thousand in Texas. Most of the longhorn mullets had been tapped by their local promoters. As for New York—he remembered the ache in his buttocks from a week of sitting in club cars bound for New Haven and Hartford. He had played gin and downed liquor with every mother's son who might have a thousand to gamble or who might have a wife with a rich uncle or an inheritance. He had found most of his mullets in San Francisco along Montgomery Street and right here in the San Joaquin Valley.

He had spent a year on this project. The first money, his own, had gone for seismographic testing of the area, for lease bonuses to the landowners, for attorneys' fees in drawing up the leases, then for the hiring of a drilling contractor and his crew. He had delayed selling off percentages in his well until he had examined the first cores. They held promise. They were encouraging. The first mullets had been easy sells—after that, not so easy. The people in the San Joaquin Valley began to watch his well; enthusiasm turned to nervousness. Everybody began to remind himself of the grim odds in wildcatting—only one well out of ten ever found oil.

Magill stared across the sagebrush. A few yards away a big slate-colored jackrabbit hopped out of a clump of sage, blinked at the two men, then raised one hind leg and began to scratch its side. Magill picked up a pebble. He nudged his foreman.

'That jack. Five bucks he runs to the left.'

O'Brien grinned. This was the old Dave Magill. 'You're on. Five he goes to the right.'

Magill threw. The jackrabbit rose straight up, pivoted in the air, and streaked away to the left. O'Brien laughed and reached into his pocket.

Magill shook his head. 'Save it, Barney. I'll take it out of your bonus when the well comes in.'

He slapped O'Brien on the shoulder and walked back to the jeep.

It was too early for the regulars in the Polo Lounge. Most of the guests at the Beverly Hills Hotel were still on the tennis courts, or changing out of their swim trunks and bikinis in the pool dressing rooms, or starting the duel of the freeways on the way back from television and motion picture studios. In the lounge, the mirrors behind the bar still reflected the late afternoon sunlight which filtered in from the tropic garden. There were only two other couples in the booths besides Magill and Louise.

Louise was a handsome, athletic thirty. Her eyes were medium brown. Her hair, also brown, was cut short with bangs. Her mouth was wide and pleasant. She sipped her whiskey sour and glanced around the room.

'We had some good times here,' she said. 'Good times and good friends.'

Magill nodded and finished his straight scotch. 'I've been figuring just how long it's been. One year and four months.'

'Since the divorce was final? Yes. Two years, eight months, from the time I filed.'

'And you're happy now?'

'I'm sure you didn't invite me here just to ask.' She paused thoughtfully. 'Yes, I'm happy. *Content* might be a better word. Carl and I have a different kind of life. It's—organized.'

Magill winced. This woman beside him had touched the sore spot. No. More than that. She had pulled the sutures out of the unhealed wound. He signaled the waiter for a second round.

'Well, Dave?'

'Yes?'

'What is it?'

He told her. About the new well, his hopes for it, the probable size of the production, the number of acres he held under lease. And the broken drill stem. And the little money left.

She chewed her lower lip as he talked, and when he had finished, she said, 'So it couldn't be worse, hmm?'

'No! It's just a little sticky right now. It will work out. I'm going to bring in a damned good producer.'

She smiled tightly. 'If I lend you the money. That's it, isn't it?'

He sighed. She was always ahead of him. He had paid her seventy-five thousand in the divorce settlement. If, he explained, she could invest fifty thousand of that money, he would sign over one-half of his remaining percentage.

'So I was right. It's really bad.'

'No, Lou! No!'

'You've never come to me before, and you wouldn't be offering so big a percentage.'

'I'd rather you made the money than a stranger.'

'Or I lose it than a stranger.' She laughed quickly. 'I didn't mean that. No, darling, I've gambled enough. My three years with you was it. No more chances.' The waiter came with the drinks. After he had picked up the empty glasses and returned to the bar, Louise went on. 'Dave, you just aren't thinking. You used to have some good contacts here in town. Talk to them. Beverly Hills is loaded with money.'

Magill snorted. 'Beverly Hills! I know all about Beverly Hills dollars. Ten cents in cash and ninety cents horse-shit!' He glared. 'Times have changed, anyway. Used to be, every two-bit movie producer, every TV star, wanted a piece of an oil well. It was classy, it was status. They went to parties and talked about *their* wells, making like Murchison's and J. Paul Getty's. But the first dry hole, and they screamed holy murder and bugged out. They weren't investors, they weren't even gamblers. They were just chickenshits! They bought percentages the same way they bought cars or cigarettes or vacations—as symbols of masculinity or adventure or sexual conquest!'

Louise leaned back in the booth and stared at her former husband. 'You've certainly learned to be articulate.' She broke off and thought for a moment. 'Dave, let me talk to Carl. He's got a business manager who has lots of big clients.'

'Oh, Lou, how many times did we go through that routine? Another business manager! Some rat-eyed book-keeper who invites me to a cozy little dinner so he can get the big picture, the feel of the thing—meaning the size of the cut off the top before he talks to his clients. And across the table sits his ever-loving with her toes in my crotch!'

She laughed. 'There was plenty of that.'

'Lou, I never—'

'You think I imagined it all? Look over there.' She nodded toward a booth across the lounge. A brunette, alone, wearing a shade too much makeup and a cocktail dress an hour too early, had seated herself during the conversation. She was watching Magill with interest.

Magill sniffed. 'She doesn't count. She's a hooker.'

'She's a woman. And she likes what she sees. Don't forget, most women think with their vaginas and act with their ovaries.'

He looked at her sharply. 'You never talked like that before.'

'I'm married to a doctor. Remember?'

He did not want to remember. 'Lou, why did you come here?'

'I was curious.'

'And now you're satisfied.'

'Not in the least. I had hoped you might be different.'

'In what way?'

'That you had stopped being a romantic about oil wells. In a way, it may be a very good thing if this well bankrupts you. No, no! Let me finish. It's better if you can't raise the money. Then you'll *have* to forget wildcatting. You'll *have* to join one of the big companies. They can afford your dreams. You can't. And they'll break their backs to get someone as good as you.'

He looked at her sadly. 'We haven't changed, have we? Either of us.'

'No, dear. We haven't.' She glanced at her wristwatch. 'Oh, God, I've got to get home. Carl and I are having dinner with one of his associates.'

'I wish you a dull evening.'

She laughed. 'Thank you. It will be.' She rose from the table, kissed him lightly on one cheek, and walked quickly toward the lobby.

Magill watched her until she disappeared. It was hard to think of her going home to another man. Suddenly he felt tired. What was the matter with him? Disappointment? Of course. Loneliness? That was nothing so terribly new. He took a gulp of scotch. No. It was more than that. *It may be a very good thing if this well bankrupts you.* What a lousy thing to say. Suppose it happened. Really happened. He wouldn't be the first wildcatter to end up a toolie, a roustabout. Rupturing his guts for somebody else, going to town on Saturday nights and drinking his pay-check. A few years of that . . .

Magill shuddered. This was a hell of a time to get the hee-haws. He tossed down the last of his scotch and glanced across the room at the brunette professional. A tall man in bulky tweed was sliding down into the booth beside her. Magill heard him call a greeting to the bartender in an English accent. Magill hummed to himself. English. Likable people. Lovely country. There might be something to think about. He nodded to the waiter, who was hovering with the bill. Magill would have another scotch and a deck of playing cards.

He broke the seal on the package of cards and began to shuffle. So he was a romantic about oil wells. Hell, he wasn't ashamed of it. Never would be. He would never lose his awe of the miracle of petroleum and natural gas. Man, a weak and clumsy biped, roams the earth and pokes holes through thousands of feet of shale and sucks up the memories of life existing billions of years ago. The liquified remains of trillions upon trillions of mammals and birds and fishes are pumped up to the twentieth century and converted into energy and light, used as power for factories and automobiles and ships and aircraft, metabolized into chemicals and plastics and medicines. Romantic? Poetic? Christ, yes!

Black Knave on Red Queen. Red Ten on Black Knave. He glanced across the room again. He could see the brunette's knees under the table; they were tightly crossed, barring the Englishman's hand. The price was still under debate.

Red Seven on Black Eight. Black Six on Red Seven. Magill tapped the edge of a card against his lower lip. English. It was an idea. It was a very good idea. As he considered it, tested it, weighed the odds, he became conscious of a familiar empty feeling in his stomach. The feeling he always had before an important gamble. The same queasiness that went with the first bite of earth at a new well. It would be a gamble, all right. An expensive one. A nervy play to save the whole play. But if it worked . . .

Magill stuffed the deck of cards into a coat pocket. He peeled off a bill for the waiter, got up and strolled to the patio doorway and into the tropical garden and the warm California dusk. He inhaled deeply. He felt wonderfully alive.

2

Magill seated himself next to a window in the airport bus. Not that he'd view the scenery on the drive into London, but rather he'd try to read, in the fading daylight, the *Times* he had bought at Heathrow Terminal. He glanced casually at the headlines on the first page, then turned to a section titled *The Business World.* Yes, there it was. Three columns on the opening day's proceedings of the International Petroleum Congress, now convened in London. The marketing chairman predicted a rise of six percent in world consumption for the coming year. They always predicted six percent. The producers' committee viewed with alarm the new royalty demands of the Arabs and Venezuelans. They always viewed with alarm. Magill's eyes coasted down the page. 'Oil World's Tragic Loss. List Of Air Victims Given Out.' He remembered a headline at Kennedy Airport about a plane explosion. Now the subtitle amplified. 'Anglo-Tex Engineers Lost in Explosion Over Red Sea.' Anglo-Tex. The name stirred in Magill's memory. Who was it who had joined that outfit? He ran down the casualty list. Ralph Beardsley. British. Carter Denfield. British. Marius Schippers. Dutch. Ward Farren. American. Magill's eyes locked on the name. His throat tightened.

'The first rule of business, Davey boy. The secret of all success. Just three little words: Don't get caught!'

Ward Farren stretched out in his bunk in the men's dorm. Twelve years before. Ward with the left hip smashed in a football scrimmage. Even with the cast off, he spent most of his time on his back—talking, talking, talking. And emptying cans of beer which were paid for by David Magill.

'Pioneers never get rich. That's another verse to remember. It's the smart bastard who comes in right after the fathead pioneer. The guy with the angle. He gets the gravy. He gets the yachts. He gets the dames. Everything! All it takes is an angle.'

'And you've figured your angle?'

'Not yet. But the first step is to hook up with one of the big outfits, just to smell out what's rotten in the setup.'

'Everything isn't rotten, Ward. That's sick talk.'

'Davey, you've just given me a picture of yourself thirty years from now. There you are, still stumbling around in some frigging patch of sagebrush or some slimy jungle. Still plugging down dry holes, sweating the payroll, beating your suppliers' bills, and telling yourself: "Everything isn't rotten."—Okay! Laugh, you dumb son of a bitch! But look at your dad. Fifty years old and busted!'

'At the moment. He's been busted lots of times and loaded lots of times. That's the oil game.'

'Not my little old oil game!'

When had he last seen Ward Farren? Argentina? Canada? No. Earlier than that. Louisiana. That was it. Louisiana Offshore. They had apprenticed themselves to different majors. Both field engineers learning their trade. It must have been a Saturday night because they had run into each other in a bar. Ward still talked grandly of finding his angle; still limped with the old football injury; still laughed at Magill's idealism. A lifetime ago and a world away. After that meeting, there had been a few postcards, and Magill had read a line or two about Ward in the *Oil World Journal*. Various overseas operations. Then he had signed on with Anglo-Tex. Still a field engineer. And now he was dead. He had found his angle.

The airport bus stopped at the Hilton Hotel, and Magill transferred to a mini-cab. It was dusk and raining in a halfhearted fashion. Before going on to his hotel, Magill told the cabby, he wanted a quick refresher on some of his favorite London locales.

The cabby grinned; a sentimental American meant a generous tip.

The Thames at Waterloo Bridge, the Houses of Parliament and Big Ben. Magill peered through the rain-steamed window at Whitehall and Trafalgar Square and the maelstrom of Piccadilly Circus. He took it all in with steadily mounting excitement. London. One of his favorite cities. Where he and Louise had spent the happiest period of their honeymoon. Where he was determined to be happy again. And successful. Now along Piccadilly and up New Bond Street. Into Grosvenor Street and finally a quiet square with high plane trees. The Carlos Tower faced into the square with the dignity of a Victorian matron gazing into her private garden.

Magill noticed a clump of men and women huddled under their black brollies on either side of the hotel entrance. He nudged the cabby. 'Why all the people?'

'Waitin' for aut'graphs, mate. Here's where the big uns stay.'

Magill smiled to himself. His inquiries in New York were paying off. The big ones. The international film stars, directors, producers and money men. Not a tourist hotel; small, intimate, clublike, very expensive. The right address for an important California oil man. And for mullets.

The assistant manager escorted Magill along the hallway. Ahead of them, two waiters wheeled carts laden with canapés and champagne bottles. They knocked at a door, which opened with a blast of music and women's laughter. The hotel man frowned at Magill, as if to imply this was a serious breach of house rules. He unlocked a door and ushered Magill into his suite. The sitting-room was hotel-French—rose satin draperies framing the balcony window, rose satin divan, a marquetry coffee table with a bouquet of white chrysanthemums, tapestried side chairs, writing desk with boulle-work dribbling down the legs. The bedroom was more rose satin and inlaid woods. All a bit too feminine, Magill remarked, but he would accept it. The assistant manager bowed; he would have the bellman up with the bags.

Magill walked to the floor-length french windows and stared out at the skyline. Skyscrapers fingered the night in every direction. The Shell Tower, the British Petroleum, the Hilton Hotel, the GPO Tower. London certainly gave no indication that the nation was teetering on the verge of bankruptcy. There was a lot of life left in the old girl yet. She would live, Magill thought, so long as she could trade; so long as she controlled so much of the world's oil. That was Britain's real secret, not the gold or lack of it in Britain's vaults. The real secret was the faraway well pumping oil into a pipeline, pouring it into the hold of a tanker. Oil into synthetic rubber, into fertilizers, into medicines, into plastics. Magill smiled out into the night. Yes, coming to London had been the right move.

He went to the telephone, which was atop the writing desk, and gave room service his order for dinner. A bottle of Blanc de Blancs, hors d'oeuvres *variés*, lobster Cayetana, green salad, cognac—at least forty years old—and a half-dozen Pride of Havana maduro panatellas. He grinned to himself; that should alert the hotel. First impressions were important. The appearance of money would attract money.

The bellman came with his bags and a cablegram which had been awaiting Magill's arrival.

NUMBER ONE BOILER GONE. REPLACEMENT FOUR DAYS. DEPTH 7140 VEDDER SANDS NO SHOWS. ANY LUCK YOUR END. BARNEY.

Magill grimaced. Another boiler. He *would* pick a contract driller with beat-up equipment. He flipped open his billfold and found the slip of paper on which he had written a telephone number. He gave the number to the operator. Then he heard a quiet, clipped voice.

'Van Zordich.'

'Dave Magill, Harry. How are you?'

The voice brightened. 'Dave! I've been expecting you all day. Louise keep you out shopping?'

'She's not with me, Harry. We're divorced.'

There was a pause. 'I hadn't heard.' Another pause. 'Well!

How about lunch tomorrow?'

'Fine. But before that, Harry, I wonder if I could borrow your Jag in the morning.'

Van Zordich laughed. 'Jag? It's a Rolls now, Dave. I'll send it round. Where you staying?'

'Carlos Tower.'

'Would nineish be all right?'

'Perfect. One final thing, Harry. You happen to know a stock-broker named Cavendish? Roswell Cavendish, Throgmorton Street?'

'Can't say I do. Any special reason?'

'No. See you tomorrow, Harry.'

From Jaguar to Rolls Royce. Magill had heard that the diamond business was booming. Van Zordich's success reminded him of his own lack of it. He reread Barney O'Brien's cable. He had better warn Barney not to send any more gloom-agrams. The next one should be enthusiastic, regardless. He glanced at his wristwatch. Just past eight o'clock. It would be near noon in California. He picked up the telephone again and asked the operator to place a call to California. He gave her the number of the radio-telephone unit which he had had installed in Barney's work-trailer. There would be a delay, the operator told him; she was already waiting for an open circuit on a New York City call.

The lobster Cayetana was perfect. The bottle of Blanc de Blancs and the snifter of cognac had been drained. Magill sat with his feet on the coffee table and inhaled his second Pride of Havana. The telephone tinkled shyly. The circuits were still tied up to New York; the long lines department said they would try again in a half hour. Magill scratched his jaw. Damn. He felt like talking to someone. Anyone. The champagne and cognac in his blood-stream called for reinforcement. The American Bar was downstairs.

As Magill left his suite, he noted that the party down the hall was still going strong. He wondered what the occasion was. Who was selling what to whom? A party was almost always somebody promoting a product, or an idea, or simply his own sense of importance. Magill strolled toward the open doorway. He paused amid the clutter of serving carts and peered in. He recognized some of the faces; he had seen them on television and in films. Not stars, but handsome people, all the same, from the studios of Hollywood, New York, Shepperton, and Pinewood. The liquor had taken its toll; men's ties had strayed a bit off-center, women's shoulder straps had slipped askew. Magill found himself staring at a remarkably pretty redhead in a cocktail dress of shimmering silver. She appeared to be trapped in a conversation with a short, bald, much overweight man who waved a cigar in one hand while the other hand slid purposefully down the redhead's back. The girl squirmed uneasily—then she saw Magill watching her. She gestured to him to join the party. Well, why not?

'You a friend of Bill's?' the short fat man challenged.

Magill nodded. 'Isn't everybody?' He turned toward the redhead. But where was she?

'Who you with?' The fat man again.

'Nobody.' Magill was on tiptoes, staring over the circle of heads. No girl.

'I mean, your studio?'

'I'm independent. That girl you were talking to—'

'Miss Chastity? Who cares?'

Magill cared. He saw no one else worth the effort of conversation.

The lobby was deserted except for the hotel staff, and the American Bar was empty except for the glum-faced Italian bartender. Magill ordered a scotch neat, which the Italian poured in morose silence. No chance for conversation there. Magill stared out into the lobby. For a deluxe hotel, the public rooms were surprisingly gloomy. The lobby was small, high-ceilinged and oak-paneled; all that saved it from outright mediocrity was a great sweeping staircase spilling from an open mezzanine. Magill studied the assistant manager, who was standing trancelike behind the registry counter. A very dull fellow. Without imagination; cautious, skeptical, sour. But perhaps a useful tool in the days to come. Magill finished his scotch and sauntered into the lobby. He leaned an elbow on the red marble counter.

'I'll be buying some things around town tomorrow. I'd like you to pay for them when they're delivered.'

The man hesitated. 'Would you have an idea of the amount, sir?'

'Hard to say. I'll be shopping for some gifts.'

'I see. If I might give some figure to our bookkeeper. For his guidance, you understand.'

'Guidance. Uh-huh.' Magill pulled on his left earlobe. 'Maybe this would be easier.' He opened his pad of traveler's checks, picked up the registry pen and signed the bottom line of a hundred-dollar check. He flipped to a second check, then a third, and on until he had signed ten. The eleventh check was five hundred dollars. He signed it and seven succeeding checks, each a five-hundred-dollar denomination. He stacked the checks neatly and pushed them across the counter.

'Five thousand dollars. How much is that in pounds?'

The assistant manager swallowed and cleared his throat. 'Nineteen hundred, sir. If you will excuse me, while I get your receipt . . .'

'No matter. Just put it in my box.' Magill made the words sound airy. Inwardly, he quailed at the number of days in drilling costs which were represented by his grand gesture. As he turned away from the counter, there was a trill of laughter, a woman's laughter. It was the redhead in the silvery dress. The girl from the party upstairs. She descended the staircase with the grace and poise of a woman used to being admired. She was, Magill thought, either society or an actress. No, not society; her bust was too good. But whom was she laughing at or with?

'Mr Magill. You placed a telephone call to California?' It was the assistant manager.

'Yes. Where can I take it?'

'I'm sorry, sir. Operator says your party does not answer.

Should she try later?'

'No. Tell her to cancel it for tonight.'

He turned to look at the girl again. She had reached the lobby and was going toward the street entrance. She was holding onto a man's arm, onto the escort who must have followed her down the staircase while Magill was distracted by the assistant manager. Magill saw only the man's back; but there was something familiar about him. It was his walk. A slight limp, a hesitation, a drag of his left foot. If Magill had not been so keyed up by the champagne and cognac and scotch, he would not have reacted so impulsively. But he *had* consumed enough alcohol, he *had* written five thousand dollars worth of checks, his nervous pitch *was* intense. He hurried after the couple. Just as they reached the double entrance door he came almost abreast of them. Close enough to see the man's unusually large earlobes. Without waiting to confirm the face, Magill called out, 'Ward! Ward!'

Magill thought he saw the man stiffen. Certainly, the man turned and stared. And the resemblance to Ward Farren vanished. This man's hair was black and straight; Ward's had been red and curly. This man wore horned-rim glasses and a guardsman moustache which bushed out beneath a nose that seemed too small for his face. Ward's nose had been large and slightly crooked.

'I'm sorry,' Magill mumbled. 'My mistake.'

The man eyed him coolly. Then, seeing the redhead on his arm inspect Magill with interest, he swung open the glass door and propeled her into the street and into a taxi.

Magill stared at the still-swinging door. A damned fool, a drunken fool, that's what he was. Ward Farren was dead. Killed in that airplane explosion. His name had been in that casualty list in the *Times*. The limp, the big pendulous earlobes, had been a coincidence. Strange how the subconscious could play tricks. Magill had been interested in the redhead—after all, she *had* welcomed him to that party upstairs and then melted away. Somehow he had confused his motivation. He had wanted to speak to the girl and, not having an excuse, he had shifted his attention to the man with her.

Magill went back to his rooms. The exhilaration of the liquor was gone; now there was only a throbbing in his forehead. He was bushed. He walked to the french windows, threw them open, stepped onto the narrow balcony, and breathed in the clean, damp, night air. Damn! If that fellow had only spoken. If Magill could have heard his voice. The vocal chords never change. He lit a cigarette. And those eyes. After four years dorming together, Magill could hardly forget that hawklike glare. Or that characteristic limp, the hesitation and drag of the left foot.

Magill yawned. God, he was tired. He flicked his cigarette over the balcony railing and watched it fall to the glistening pavement below. Across Carlos Square, on the sidewalk a man in a rain slicker stared up at him, then moved into the shadow of a doorway.

3

'I'm afraid my secretary should have explained. Our methods are somewhat different from Americans'. We prefer a letter of introduction before opening an account.'

Mr Cavendish, of J. Roswell Cavendish & Associates, smiled bleakly across his desk at the American innocent who sat in the wing chair with one leg crossed over the other so that he exhibited a hole in the sole of his shoe. His socks slipped down his garterless calves; there was a gravy spot on his wrinkled tie; his shirt was beginning to fray at the collar points. The one presentable item of Dave Magill's attire was his tweed suit, but it could not overcome his general appearance of seediness.

'Letter of introduction, huh? Never occurred to me.' Magill shook his head in bewilderment. He understood the type of man he was dealing with. Physically, Mr Cavendish was short, plump-cheeked, with the face of an aged cherub. Spiritually, he was as exciting as cottage cheese. In brief, he was the perfect subject.

'Letter of introduction,' Magill repeated thoughtfully. 'Well, well! Bax just told me that if I wanted to pick up some stocks over here, I ought to look up your outfit.'

'Bax?'

'I told him I was coming over here for the Petroleum Congress, you see. So I thought—'

'Excuse me. You are in the petroleum business?'

'In a small way. So when Bax gave me your name—'

'Forgive me, please. May I ask Mr Bax's first name?'

'That's it. Bax. You know, Baxter Randall.'

'Baxter Randall?'

'Of Texas.'

'Ah-h-h . . . Yes. Of course.' Mr Cavendish folded his hands across his broad waistcoat and examined the far corner of the ceiling. 'I believe that is the Baxter Randall of petroleum . . . Or is it cattle?'

'Chemicals. Everything else was just dabbling around.' Magill was correct in one respect. Baxter Randall had been his high-school chemistry teacher. 'Say! Maybe I've got you mixed up with somebody else.' Magill started to rise. 'Is there another Cavendish in Throgmorton Street?'

The eyes swept down from the corner of the ceiling. 'No, no. There is no mistake. I was just considering, Mr Magill . . .' The grandfather clock behind Cavendish's desk ticked gravely for all of five seconds, and then the considering was completed. 'Perhaps we should ignore protocol. Let us proceed on the basis that you have been properly introduced, after all.'

'Okay by me.'

'Of course, I should like the name of your bank.'

'It's plural. Banks.'

'Of course. And the names?'

'Oh, they're all in California. But whatever I buy here, my hotel will pay for.'

'Your hotel?'

'Yep. The Carlos Tower.'

'Mmmhmm. The Carlos Tower.' The eyes returned to the far corner of the ceiling. 'And the stocks which you are interested in?'

'Just one. Anglia Petroleum. Thought I might pick up some calls on it.'

'"Options" is our term. And what size position did you have in mind?'

'Oh, say five thousand, to start with.'

The eyes descended again and fixed benevolently on Magill. 'Yes. I'll see if I can get you a quotation.'

Cavendish rose from his desk and churned his short legs toward one of the doors leading from his office. Once alone, Magill got to his feet and strolled to the full-length Queen Anne mirror on the wall in front of the broker's desk. He surveyed his stained tie and the frayed shirt collar, held up his left foot, and grinned at the hole in the shoe. The effect was exactly right. Any businessman who cared so little about his appearance must have his mind on far more important matters. He must be very rich indeed. At that very moment, Magill felt sure, Cavendish was verifying the fact by a telephone call to the Carlos Tower. As for Mr Cavendish himself, Magill already knew about him. Two weeks before, in California, he had run across an advertisement in the *Oil World Journal* which stated:

Certain British investors are available for petroleum partnerships. Details may be forwarded to J. Roswell Cavendish, Throgmorton Street, London.

'I think we have it here, sir.' Cavendish slipped back into his desk chair and studied a slip of paper in his hand. 'The quote is in dollar equivalents. Seventy-two cents per share, one-hundred-share lots. Option expiry ninety days.'

'That would be seventy-two dollars, American, per one hundred shares. Or thirty-six hundred dollars for five thousand shares.'

Cavendish blinked. 'I see you have no need for a calculating machine.'

'I checked the quotes in this morning's *Financial Times*. Okay, buy me options on five thousand.'

The broker nodded happily. If the options were exercised, this American would be obligated to almost one hundred thousand dollars—not including the American interest equalization tax. Yes, it would be a very satisfactory commission. 'I take it, Mr Magill, that you think Anglia is due for a rise?'

Magill shrugged. 'I just like the company.'

'But I don't see—'

'It's my way of reminding myself. I want to salt away a little something, say, about two months from now.'

'The rise will be in two months?'

'Have no idea. It's just to put away something of my own. I've got a little play out in California.'

He watched the broker's eyes glaze in thought. The fuse was lighted. Magill rose and held out his hand. 'You can deliver the options to the Carlos. They'll pay you, as I said.'

'Certainly. If I can be of any further service . . .'

'I'll let you know.'

Cavendish escorted him to the door. 'Would Mrs Magill be with you? That is to say, here in London?'

'I'm not married.'

'I see. Yes. Well, good day.'

The chauffeur opened the door of the Rolls Royce. As Magill bent to step inside, he glanced across Throgmorton Street and upward to the window on the third floor. He saw Mr Cavendish's hand release the draperies. Magill smiled contentedly. He was fairly sure why the broker had asked about his wife. Time would prove it out.

The Rolls threaded its way slowly through the traffic of the City. At one intersection it came to a full stop. It was there that a bank messenger, very properly silk-hatted and frock-coated, saw a man in the rear of a Rolls who was naked to the waist. He seemed to be changing his shirt.

It had been five years since Magill had last seen Hatton Garden. Nothing had changed. The ground floor of the jewelry shop still turned the same musty face to the street. The steel netting over the two small display windows had rusted a bit more. The gilt lettering on the oaken door was a shade more difficult to read. But the lettering was the same.

VAN ZORDICH & COMPANY

LONDON / ANTWERP / PARIS / NEW YORK / JOHANNESBURG

Inside, a white-haired, motherly woman was bending over a display case to arrange some jewelry. That would be Mrs Hellbron, Magill remembered. She was Van Zordich's assistant. She looked up at the sound of the front door and smiled as someone trying to recall a forgotten face. Magill gave her his name. She brightened. It was a great pleasure to see him again. Her right hand reached down the rear of the display case and pressed a hidden button. Magill knew that Harry Van Zordich was being alerted in the inner office; that he would be viewing the visitor through a two-way mirror. Several moments later, Magill heard a door being unlocked, the one at the rear of the display room, and then Van Zordich was standing there, beaming his welcome.

'Come in, Dave! Marvelous to see you!'

Henry Van Zordich was in his mid-forties. Born in the Netherlands, schooled at Eton and Cambridge, his speech, manner, and appearance were as British as the lions in Trafalgar Square. His hair was darker brown than Magill's; in height, he topped Magill's six feet by at least three inches. The face was narrow; the nose, prominent; the eyes, umber, intense, searching.

Magill seated himself in the worn leather armchair which was cater-corner to the big desk. He noted that everything was as before, when Louise and he had visited this same room during their honeymoon. A coal fire burned in the grate; the crystal decanter filled with sherry sat on its Georgian side-table. On the desk, to Van Zordich's right, were the jewel scales, protected in their dust-proof glass case. Alongside the case there was the microscope with the special light-refracting device used for the interior examination of gemstones. Behind the jeweler's desk chair loomed the huge safe where the most valuable stones slumbered in steel-girt security. The atmosphere of the office was one of old-fashioned dignity; a pleasant contrast, Magill reflected, to the flash and show of the New York branch on Fifth Avenue, which was managed by Van Zordich's cousin Marius.

The jeweler leaned back in his chair and smiled quizzically. 'So. A vacation at last.'

'London? No. It's business.'

'The Petroleum Congress?'

'Partly.' Magill shifted uncomfortably. He did not know how to bring up the subject.

'I'm sorry to hear about you and Louise.'

'Yes. I know you liked her.'

'I did. I hope that you are still friendly.'

'She's remarried.'

'Oh.'

'She's better off without me.'

'In what way?'

Magill grimaced. This was the opening. He fished into his waistcoat pocket and brought out a man's ring, a platinum band topped by a five-carat diamond solitaire. He pushed it across the desk.

'Because I've had to do this too many times.'

Van Zordich picked up the ring and stared earnestly at the diamond. 'My father sold this to your father in—in 1948. New York.'

''Forty-nine. It's about all I've got left from him. You think it might be good for two thousand pounds?'

The jeweler frowned; he ran a thumb down his cheek. Then abruptly he opened a desk drawer and took out a box of cigars and slid them across the desk. Magill chose one, bit off the tip, lighted it and inhaled the delicate perfume. The cigar must have aged at least five years in Van Zordich's humidor.

'Three thousand.'

'What?'

'Wholesale, it's worth three thousand pounds.'

Van Zordich rose and went to the big safe, swung wide the door, and pulled out a drawer. He extracted a manila envelope, brought it back to the desk, drew out a package of Bank of England notes from the envelope, and counted out three thousand pounds. He placed the diamond ring on top of the currency and slid both across the desk.

Magill cleared his throat. 'I'll give you my IOU. Payable in thirty days.'

Van Zordich shook his head. 'Between your family and mine, there has never been paper. If you cannot repay, we still shall be in your debt.'

Magill understood the reference. In 1949 Van Zordich's father had suffered a disastrous loss in the New York stock market; Magill's father had lent the jeweler the half-million dollars which forestalled bankruptcy. The elder Magill took repayment of the loan in diamonds for his wife. More than once those jewels had gone to pawn when the elder Magill ran a streak of dry wells. Each lucky discovery had brought them back to brighten Eleanor Magill's throat and wrists, until that final well, the unluckiest of them all.

'I hope you won't mind a question, Dave.' Van Zordich was watching Magill fold the pound notes into his billfold. 'The last time I saw you, you were well on your way to being a millionaire. What happened?'

'Nothing I can't survive. A string of dry holes, a loan to a friend, a divorce settlement in cash—and this.' Magill tossed Barney O'Brien's cablegram across the desk.

Van Zordich read the message. He quoted Barney's concluding words: '"Any luck your end?"—I presume that means money. You're in London to finance another well.'

Magill gave him the whole story, including a detailed account of his visit to J. Roswell Cavendish.

'You spent all that money on stock options, but didn't try to sell him a percentage in the well?'

'No.'

'Why not?'

'Harry, if you had an unusually valuable diamond, how would you sell it to a customer?'

Van Zordich smiled. 'I'd show him everything else in the shop first. Then I'd let him get an accidental look at the stone. But it would not be for sale. I'd be holding it for my most important client.'

'Exactly. Cavendish will line up some mullets, and they'll damn near kill me to get a piece of the action. Understand, I won't be cheating them. I'll give them all the facts. They won't believe the bad part. They'll think I'm holding out. But if the well comes in, they'll make out fine. And I'll still own enough of the play so I'll be okay, too.'

As Magill finished, the lamp on Van Zordich's desk winked on and off, on and off. The jeweler scowled; he rose, stepped to the wall, and peered through the two-way mirror into the front showroom.

'Dave, have you noticed anyone following you?'

'Me? Hardly!'

'Have you flashed any large amount of money around?'

'Hell, no! Wait a minute. Last night, at the hotel. I signed quite a wad of traveler's checks.'

'Who saw you?'

'Why, no one. Harry, what is this?'

'When you left Cavendish, did you notice anyone odd?'

'No.'

Van Zordich beckoned Magill to the two-way mirror. 'Do you recognize him?'

Magill saw a man talking to Mrs Hellbron behind the counter. He was gesturing toward a tray of assorted rings; but his eyes were flicking about the room as if intent on something else. The man was of medium height, very dark-skinned, with a heavy, drooping nose. He wore a crush hat and a rain slicker.

'Never saw him before.'

'Well, he's no one in the trade.'

'Maybe he's a walk-in.'

'We don't have them. He's not buying; he's casing. Mrs Hellbron can smell one before he gets through the door.' The jeweler turned away from the mirror. 'I did promise you lunch, didn't I? We can step out the back way.'

Magill hesitated. 'Mrs Hellbron?'

'She's in no danger. He's no smash-and-grab. And if there *were* trouble, her foot is right alongside a button that will fetch every constable in Hatton Garden.'

Van Zordich opened a door which gave into a broom closet. Once the two men were inside the closet, Van Zordich unlocked a second door. It opened with a dazzle of sunlight, and they stepped out into the alley behind the shop.

They decided they should lunch in style, where the food would be superb. Magill remembered that the morning's *Times* had reported that several committees of the Petroleum Congress were to meet at the Savoy Hotel, and that the presidents of three Standard Oil companies were there in residence.

They chose the River Restaurant where, after an extravagant tip to the maitre d', they were seated at a window which overlooked the Victoria Embankment and the Thames beyond. Magill's eyes roamed the room, enjoying the beauty of London's society girls and models and actresses. The males were of all nationalities—British, American, French, Italian, drab and uninteresting in their conventional sack suits. But there were Nigerians in striped robes, Indians in long-waisted white tunics, Malasians in flowery wraparounds. An Arab, in Western attire except for his white turban, was directing the placing together of four tables to accommodate his own party.

'The police don't understand it. Or, if they do, they don't want to talk about it. Quite simply, the more materialistic our society, the more crime will grow.'—

What on earth was Van Zordich talking about? Then Magill remembered. While they waited for their table, the jeweler had said something about the man they had seen in the shop. How, Magill wondered, could the jeweler be so relaxed about the possibility of robbery? The answer was that he lived with it every day. Crime was everywhere. Van Zordich had developed a philosophy about it, on which he elaborated over their first whiskey.

'How do most men and women spend their lives? In a dull, pointless grind. There is no challenge. The welfare state promises us medicine when we are ill, state farms when we are old and feeble, burial when we are finished. Life is a bore. And what is boredom? It is the belief that there is no mystery, nothing to unfold, no surprises. A man wants to feel alive. How? By putting all on one throw of the dice. When one steals, one risks capture, trial, prison. One is gambling with one's freedom. It tauts the nerves. One feels he is a hero in his own drama.'

Van Zordich's monologue blurred on. Magill's attention wandered, then focused upon a line of haughty Arabic men who were being escorted to the long table in the far corner of the room. The lead Arab was resplendent in white burnoose and flowing robe. His face was dark and as ugly as a camel's; it would have faintly suggested that animal, if a camel could grow a spade beard of dirty gray. The Arabs trailing behind—Magill counted eight—

were younger men, clean-shaven and wearing Western business suits with their burnooses. The eight waited for their chief to seat himself; then they, too, sat down. There was one vacant chair, Magill noted, at the left hand of the leader. After a moment, the maitre d'hotel escorted the final guest, a young woman, to the vacant chair. She was Western, tall, slender, beautifully tailored. The sunlight through the river window glinted off her hair in a blaze of red. Magill felt a jolt in his stomach. The girl of the night before. At the Carlos Tower. The girl who had beckoned him into the party and then melted away.

'Dave!' Van Zordich grunted. 'For God's sake, put your eyes back in your head.'

Magill wrenched his attention away from the redhead. 'Sorry. I recognized that girl.'

'Obviously. She seems to have noticed you, too.'

'I saw her last night at the hotel. She was with a friend of mine who's dead. I mean, I *thought* he was a friend of mine.'

Van Zordich squinted carefully at Magill. 'I think you need another drink to sober up.'

The waiter brought a second round of whiskey, and Magill explained about Ward Farren and his death in the plane explosion and the accidental resemblance of the man at the Carlos Tower. Van Zordich listened coolly, then returned doggedly to his analysis of the attractions of crime. The men ordered their food and consumed it with references to the Mafia, the internationalism of crime, political corruption, and similarity of guilts shared by bank robbers and bank embezzlers. The dessert cart was being wheeled to their table when the maitre d'hotel appeared and bent down to Van Zordich's ear.

'Sir, His Excellency the Sheikh invites you and your friend to sit with him.' The maitre d' nodded in the direction of the Arab table.

'But I'm afraid I don't know His Excellency.'

'He knows you, Mr Van Zordich. Or his aide-de-camp does.'

The jeweler and Magill exchanged glances. What was this all about? Also, what was there to lose? They rose and followed the maitre d'hotel. At the table, chairs already were being crowded together and two extra seats provided. The aide-de-camp, a lean-faced man with a trim moustache, introduced himself as Colonel Mahmoud bin Jarrah, cousin of His Excellency the Sheikh Ali Muhammid el Barin of Khafer. He was sorry that the Sheikh spoke no English, but he would act as an interpreter. He gestured the guests to take the two vacant seats directly opposite the Sheikh. This arrangement placed Magill face to face with the girl with the red hair. She was even prettier than he had remembered and, for the first time, he realized the color of her eyes—electric blue. He gave her his name and heard that she was Sandra Morgan of New York. He waited for her to show some sign of recognition. When she did not, he said, 'I saw you last night at the Carlos Tower.'

'Oh?'

'At the party on my floor. In fact, you invited me to join it.'

'Hospitable, wasn't I?'

'You don't remember?'

'I have a very poor memory. Especially after a few drinks.'

Magill flushed. Was he that forgettable? 'We met again down in the lobby. You were leaving with a man with a big moustache. And a limp.'

'Oh, yes. Tommy.'

'I didn't get his name. He would be Thomas—?'

'Mr Magill, last evening was last evening. I had a very good time. I'm having a good time now.' She paused, then smiled sweetly. 'So let's start with the present.'

Magill could feel the heat in his cheeks. Everyone at the table was watching, which made him even more persistent.

'I take it you are an actress.'

'Like all the girls at the party. That's why I'm in London.'

'Films or television?'

'Stage. I came over with the ANTA Company. The O'Neill Trilogy at the Royal Court.'

'Wonderful! I'd like to see you.'

'Sorry. I quit yesterday.'

Magill accepted his defeat. He glanced around the table. The Arabs were no longer watching. Their eyes were on the Sheikh, who was talking to his aid. Colonel Mahmoud nodded agreement to whatever was being said, then turned to Van Zordich.

'Sir, His Excellency wishes to know if you have anything of interest on your person?'

'Of interest?'

'Jewels.'

'Oh. No, nothing of importance, really.'

'May we see?'

It was Van Zordich's turn to show embarrassment. 'They're only a few small stones. I'm trying to match them up for a brooch. A little costume piece.'

'As a particular favor?'

The jeweler shrugged. He took out his wallet and withdrew a fold of white paper. He handed the paper to the colonel, who unfolded it and stared down at a dozen loose diamonds. The colonel handed the paper to the Sheikh, who grunted and nodded. The colonel turned in his chair and whispered to the waiter standing behind him. The waiter hurried off and returned with a plate on which sat a single chocolate-covered dessert cake. He set it in front of the Sheikh. Slowly, with unsmiling deliberation, the Sheikh plucked the diamonds, one by one, and pressed them into the chocolate top of the cake. Then, with a bow of the head, he placed the cake in front of Sandra Morgan. Her hand went to her throat in a gesture of astonishment. For a moment she seemed hypnotized by the glitter. When she looked up, she avoided Magill's eyes.

Colonel Mahmoud produced a bank check, signed his name and handed it across to Van Zordich. 'Sir, you will fill in whatever you consider proper.'

The jeweler nodded absently. He was almost as dazed as the girl. He took out his pen, wrote a figure on the check and showed it to the colonel, who smiled his agreement. Then, as if the business was concluded, or a treaty signed, the Sheikh and his retinue got to their feet. The girl looked around uncertainly, then decided that there was nothing else to do. She wrapped the cake and the diamonds in a napkin and tucked the whole into her purse. As she rose, Magill tried again.

'Miss Morgan, I hope that you may be free tonight. I'd like very much to—'

'I'm sorry. I'm sure it would be pleasant.' This time she was courteous, almost warm.

'Then perhaps tomorrow night?'

'I'm afraid not. Tomorrow night I'll be on The Night Ferry for Paris. Goodbye.' She took Colonel Mahmoud's arm and the party left the room.

Van Zordich chuckled. 'You've certainly got ego, old boy. Trying to make off with the Sheikh's girl friend!'

'She? Not with that old goat!'

'He didn't give her those diamonds for nothing.'

'Then why was she out with another man last night?'

'Variety, perhaps. That's the reason she was so snotty to you. You were making headlines out of her little escapade.'

'I don't get this whole thing.'

'Nor I. I wanted to ask how they knew my name and that I'm a jeweler.' Van Zordich shook his head. 'But never quarrel with a profit, I say. Now about getting you a girl—'

'I haven't asked for one.'

'You asked for *her*. I'm sure I can find you a reasonable facsimile. Or at least reasonable.'

They compromised on dinner together at the Carlos Tower. After Van Zordich left him, Magill wandered the Savoy lobby in hope of a familiar face from the American oil industry. There was none. He went to the American Bar; the noontime drinkers had gone. He left the hotel and strolled to the Victoria Embankment and watched a freighter glide toward the Pool of London. He realized that he was going to have trouble putting in the afternoon. He could go to a movie, or to the British Museum—but he was not in the mood for either. He could go to Crockford's—but there was something unhealthy about daylight gambling. In the end, he decided on a long roundabout walk back to the hotel.

He swung off down the embankment until he reached Westminster, then turned right onto Birdcage Walk and so into St James's Park. He reached the Mall and trudged through the crowds of St James's Street and along Piccadilly. He turned in at the Burlington Arcade and browsed from window to window. He recognized the antique shop where he and Louise had bought their first English silver. And there was the haberdasher where he had ordered all those silk shirts. He paused at another window and admired a display of jeweled toilet articles that must have been the treasures of some archduchess of the Russian Imperial Court. Magill cupped his hands around his eyes, to reduce the reflections on the window glass. As he did so, he saw another reflection—his own—mirrored in a lovely filagreed looking glass. The glass was held upright on a small jeweled stand, positioned at the exact angle to catch Magill's face. And to mirror someone behind him. A man who stood in the doorway of the opposite shop. He was aiming a mini-camera at Magill.

He whirled, but not quickly enough. The man was off and running through the crowd of shoppers. Magill wished that he had gotten a clear glimpse of his face; it had been obscured by the camera held to his eye. His clothing was another matter. He wore a rain slicker and a crush hat.

Magill thought of the man he had seen in Van Zordich's showroom, and the jeweler's question: '*Have you noticed anyone following you?*' But how many men in slickers and crush hats had Magill seen in his walk from the Savoy? Ten? Twenty? Easily. Perhaps fifty. This man could have been a camera-bug. Perhaps trying for a candid show, a human-interest thing. The American tourist enthralled by the wares of Burlington Arcade. Just as simple as that. Magill knew that he was rationalizing. There was one solid fact which denied all those comforting explanations: the man had run.

Mrs Cavendish and I should take great pleasure in you being our houseguest this weekend. We are giving a party at our place in Kent. A few friends you might find congenial. Hoping to hear from you in the affirmative.

Faithfully
J. Roswell Cavendish

The note was waiting for Magill in his box at the Carlos Tower. He read it through again, then stretched out on the sofa and grinned happily at the tops of his shoes. It had worked beautifully. Cavendish, of course, had asked if his wife was with him in London, in case she should be included in the invitation. Magill wondered how many congenial friends would be assembled; how many he might convert to mullets; and how large a percentage in his well he dared let go. And what cut Mr J. Roswell Cavendish would demand. At least, now he had something encouraging to tell Barney O'Brien. And, damn it, Barney had better send him a cable reeking with enthusiasm. Mullets always went for the up-to-the-minute reports, and a trans-Atlantic cable would be very impressive.

Magill decided that he would place a call to Barney later that evening, after his dinner with Van Zordich. Meanwhile? He yawned and snuggled his head deeper into the sofa pillows.

He was awakened by insistent knocking on the hall door. He raised up and blinked around the room. It was in darkness. The knocking repeated. Magill got to his feet, stiff and irritable. He flicked on a table lamp and shuffled to the door. He opened it and looked into the face of a man with black hair, horn-rimmed glasses, and a guardsman moustache. As he stepped towards Magill, he dragged his left leg.

'You were right, Davey boy. It's me.'

4

Ward Farren closed the door behind him. His eyes circled the sitting-room, taking inventory. 'Not bad! Not bad at all. It looks like money. It smells like money.' He paused and grinned wickedly. 'Or is it just the look of the look and the smell of the smell?'

Magill winced. Farren had seen through it so quickly. 'I think I'm the one to ask the questions, Ward.'

Farren laughed. 'Christ! You sound like a woman. The wronged wife!' He clapped Magill's shoulder. 'It's great to see you again, Davey. But what in hell brings you to this place?'

'The Petroleum Congress.'

'So? Then you really have made it, huh?'

'All right. Quit stalling. Why the dyed hair, the glasses, the moustache? Why did you pretend you didn't know me last night?'

'The girl I was with thinks I'm somebody else.'

'Obviously. She calls you Tommy.'

'That's right.' Farren's face clouded. 'I didn't see you at the party last night.'

'I wasn't. I just stuck my head in.'

'Then how did you—'

'I had lunch with Sandra Morgan.' It was stretching the fact; but it just might catch Farren off base.

'Still a fast worker, huh, Davey?' He frowned, then recovered with a smile. 'I suppose she told you all about me.'

'I want to hear it from you. A man doesn't come up with a new name and a new face just for kicks. Not after he's been reported dead.'

Farren held onto the smile. 'I was supposed to be on that plane. At the last minute, I remembered something I'd left behind. By the time I got to the airfield, the plane had gone. After the crash,

I just decided not to report in, so I let the casualty list stand.' As he talked, Farren sauntered to the bedroom door and peered inside; then he crossed to the french windows, opened them and stepped onto the balcony.

Magill followed him. 'Meaning you were running out on some kind of a mess.'

'The only kind of mess there is.'

'A woman?'

'The sweetest piece of tail a man ever had, even if she was a wog.'

'Where was this?'

'Oh . . . North Africa.'

Magill sensed the lie. 'London is a long way from North Africa. No need for the phony getup here.'

'You don't know Arabs. This wog's got a father and a brother who'd follow me home to Indiana. And the money to do it. I figure it's safer, it's more convenient, to play the dearly departed.'

Magill watched him wander back into the sitting-room and drop down onto the sofa and prop his heels on the coffee table. 'Safe? It's stupid as hell! How do you expect to get another job? You can't give Anglo-Tex as a reference. You've dearly-departed yourself right out of the oil business.' Magill hesitated. 'Is that what you're really after? You want Anglo-Tex to close the book on you?'

Farren's answer was to reach inside his coat and take out a cigar case. He flicked it open, selected a cigar, and offered one to Magill, who refused it. He bit off the tip, lighted it and inhaled deeply. He blew a cloud of smoke and sighed.

'Forty pence a throw, that's what this cost. Almost one buck.'

'You didn't come here to teach me the rate of exchange.'

Farren blew a perfect smoke ring and smiled tightly. 'We're old buddies, aren't we?'

'*Were!*'

'Okay. Then let's say businessmen. We *are* that, I hope.' Another smoke ring. 'Suppose I told you I'm in something big. So big I need help. And from somebody I can trust—'

He was interrupted by the ringing of the telephone. Magill strode to the writing desk and picked up the receiver. He heard a man's voice, heavily accented, ask for a Mr Wilkins. Magill placed his hand over the mouthpiece and turned to Farren.

'Are you going by the name of Wilkins?'

For a moment, Magill thought that he had not heard, then he realized that Farren was strangling on his cigar. He held his chest and made gurgling sounds and finally gasped, 'Not here! Say I'm not here. No! Wait!' He was on his feet, coming toward Magill. 'Tell 'em I *was* here. I just left.'

Magill took his hand off the mouthpiece. The man was talking to the operator, repeating that he wished Mr Wilkins in Mr Magill's room. He cut in.

'I'm sorry. Mr Wilkins just left. Is there a message?'

There was a long pause, then a click. Magill hung up and frowned at Farren. 'Were you expecting somebody to join you here?'

'No, no. Well, in a way.' He coughed again and cleared his throat. 'I gave someone your name and hotel. In case he needed to get me in a hurry.'

'Then why wouldn't you talk?'

'We can go into all that later. Dave, right now, I want to put you into this deal. Now that I know you're interested—'

'I didn't say I was.'

'You will be. Let me go back to my place and line up some papers. We'll go over them at dinner.'

'I've *got* a dinner date.' Magill snapped out the words.

'Break it! This is the chance of a lifetime. For both of us!' Farren was already headed for the door. 'Meet me at Brown's Hotel. Half an hour. I'll be in the lobby.'

Farren opened the door, then paused and dug out his cigar case again. He tossed a cigar to Magill. 'Meanwhile, have one on me. Start getting used to the finer things of life!'

The door closed behind Farren. Magill sniffed the cigar absently, then tucked it into his outer breast pocket. Something was wrong. Everything that Farren had said, from the moment the telephone rang, sounded false. More than false—frightened.

Before the telephone call for Mr Wilkins, Farren had been his old sardonic, strutting self. After it, he was a man anxious to be gone.

As Magill considered it, his uneasiness grew. Farren's dyed hair, eyeglasses and moustache, his false name and his talk of a big deal—all these added up to more than run-of-the-mill dishonesty. And he was trying to involve Magill. Perhaps he was already involved. Farren had given Magill's name and hotel to the telephone caller. That decided it. Magill would have dinner with Farren, after all. He would find out what the deal purported to be. Then he could protect himself.

He went to the telephone again and gave the operator Van Zordich's number. He listened to her repetition of the number, her dialing, the measured buzz at the other end. Almost subconsciously, he sensed another sound. A noise from his own balcony window. A muffled scraping. Of course. The wind. Farren had gone onto the balcony, forgetting to close the windows.

'Van Zordich here.'

'It's Dave, Harry. About our dinner tonight. Something's come up that I—'

What followed from Magill's lips was a soft moan as the butt of the pistol crashed against his skull. For a dreamlike instant, he saw the telephone drop from his hand, he saw the edge of the writing desk coming toward his face. Then darkness.

His forehead felt very cold and wet. He groaned. The back of his head seemed split in two. His eyes wavered open. He could see nothing. Then someone lifted the wet washcloth from his eyes. Magill squinted upward and made out, very hazily, a face staring down at him.

'You're a hard one to bring round.'

It was Van Zordich.

Magill raised his head carefully. 'God, what happened? We were talking on the phone, and then . . . and then—'

'—Then somebody coshed you. I heard it over the phone. Here, take my hand.' Van Zordich pulled Magill up to a sitting position. 'I heard your groan, then some sort of a crash. Somebody hung up the phone. I was going to call the desk and have them look in on you. Then I decided it might be unwise to bring in outsiders.'

'Unwise?' Magill blinked up at Van Zordich's face, which was very solemn.

'All day I've had a feeling about you, Dave. That you're mixed up in something which you aren't prepared to tell me about. Something—not quite right.'

Even in his battered condition, the remark irritated. '*I'm* into something? Christ Almighty, Harry—'

'Then how do you explain *that?*'

Magill's eyes followed Van Zordich's pointing finger. Not more than eight feet away, crumpled on the carpet, was a man's body. His dead eyes stared straight at Magill with an expression of sad surprise, as if somehow Magill had disappointed him.

'Oh, God!'

'Yes. You recognize him?'

Magill felt the stomach juices rising toward his throat. He was going to be sick.

'*Do* you recognize him?'

He gulped back the sourness and steadied his hands on the floor. He breathed deeply for a few moments and then forced himself to look at the body again. There was something familiar about the man's features.

'Well?'

'The man in your shop. You wondered if he was following me.'

'It seems he was.'

'All day, I guess. He photographed me.'

'When?'

Haltingly, Magill told of his walk back from the Savoy, the incident of the camera in the Burlington Arcade, the man fleeing. He concluded with a defiant, 'But I didn't kill him!'

'I'm sure you didn't. Unless you can cosh a man and then smother him to death while you're totally unconscious.'

'Smother?'

'When I came in—your door was unlocked, by the way—I

found him with a bed pillow over his face. That's the pillow there.' Van Zordich indicated a mound of white tossed near the balcony windows. 'I suppose I should have left everything in place, but I was rather curious.'

'You've called the police?'

'Not yet. I thought we should sort things out a bit first.'

Magill struggled to his feet and stared around the room. For the first time, he saw that the drawers of the writing desk had been pulled out and emptied, the pictures on the walls thrown down, the pillows on the sofa slashed and the stuffing strewn on the floor.

Van Zordich nodded. 'Your bedroom, too. And the bath. Every jar opened, your toothpaste squeezed out, pomades spilled. Everything.'

'What the hell were they looking for?'

'You don't know?'

'I do not!'

'How about your billfold? Your passport?'

Magill's hand went to his inside breast pockets. His passport was still there, and his billfold held the right amount of pound notes.

Van Zordich shook his head. 'It doesn't mesh. I've been robbed now and again—that goes with the jewel business—and I've been ransacked and threatened. But never a dead man around. These jobs usually don't involve murder. Here we have the appearance of theft, yet nothing stolen. Very curious.'

'Very. So what do I tell the police?'

'Let's give ourselves some more background first, such as our dead friend's identity. Shall I, or you?'

Magill nodded that he would do the search. He knelt and stared at the face. He swallowed and rubbed his sweating palms on his trousers. He had never touched a corpse. He took out his pocket handkerchief and wrapped it around his right hand and felt inside the man's coat. Yes, there was a billfold. And a passport. He opened it.

'Huh! This is issued by Lebanon.'

'So! A Levantine, just as I guessed.'

'Name, Ahmid Barakati. Occupation, merchant. Born, 1937. April. He arrived England, according to the entry stamp. Heathrow Airport. The date is . . . hmm, just four days ago.'

He put the passport back in the man's pocket. He examined the billfold. There were slightly over two hundred British pounds. He replaced the billfold and glanced up at Van Zordich.

'He wasn't robbed, either. But why does a merchant break in on me? Why does he slug me, and why does he get killed? Did he ransack my things, or was it done by someone else?'

Van Zordich looked steadily at Magill. 'There is a more important question. Was there some sort of an interruption? Something that interfered with or postponed your own murder.'

It was out in the open, at last. All the while Magill had been examining the passport and the billfold, one part of his mind had been dwelling on the possibility. His nausea, his sweating, had not been entirely because of another man's death.

Van Zordich nodded, as if Magill had made answer. He crossed to the writing desk and picked up the telephone. 'Operator, put me through to CID, London Central. I wish Superintendent of Detectives Bromley.'

5

Van Zordich and Superintendent of Detectives Bromley had known each other almost half of their lives. They had met when Bromley began as a constable assigned to Hatton Garden. The acquaintance grew into friendship and trust when Bromley was transferred to Scotland Yard and called on Van Zordich for professional advice in various jewel robberies. Now Bromley was with the CID, in charge of an entire district.

All this Van Zordich had explained to Magill before the arrival of the superintendent. Magill was impressed and encouraged, until he met the man. Somehow, he seemed inanimate, not human; more like an atmosphere. Stale boiled cabbage in a musty bedsitter. His hair was gray, his eyes were gray, his skin was gray; even his voice was gray. When he spoke, the words trailed off as if in another moment he would melt into a gray mist. Yet he was thorough. While the police photographer recorded the position of the body and the fingerprint detail dusted surfaces, Bromley dictated, in his dreamlike voice, a complete inventory of the murder room, down to the ashtrays and the number of burnt matches. He went through the murdered man's clothing and described every item and in which pocket it was found. When he had finished, he directed the detective inspector to read all the notes back to him. Then, finally, he turned his attention to Magill and Van Zordich. He beckoned them into the bedroom, and his assistant. He sat on the bed and propped the two slashed pillows behind his back. He blinked lazily at Magill and Van Zordich, who stood at the foot of the bed, then nodded to his junior to take down 'the gentleman's preliminary statement'.

Magill told his story, including what Van Zordich was to hear for the first time—the visit of Ward Farren. Bromley listened in silence, seemingly almost without interest. When Magill finished, Bromley leaned back in the bed, folded his hands, palms outward, in front of his eyes, and belched. Then, after he had savored it to the full, he said, 'A question, Mr Magill. Do you believe in God?'

'What?'

'Do you believe in God?'

'I suppose so. I haven't given it much thought.'

'If not God, perhaps some sort of hereafter? A totting up of rights and wrongs, of injustices and so forth?'

Magill threw a bewildered look at Van Zordich, who came to his rescue. 'The superintendent means that punishment may have to be left to another authority. The CID, the Yard, the police anywhere are helpless sometimes. Crimes are solved because someone talks. An informer, someone with a grudge against the criminal.'

Bromley belched again in organlike agreement. 'Mr Magill, the odds are always with the wrongdoer. You have given me a number of clues. But where do they lead? What can you make of them?'

'Well, nothing, so far.'

'Yet you know more about this crime than we can ever hope to. *You* were the victim. It happened in *your* life, to *you*.'

Magill snorted. 'You mean, I'm to just chalk up tonight as an interesting experience? There's nothing you can do?'

'There are many things we can and will do. But time is our best ally, time to allow someone to talk, to act in revenge or fear or greed.'

'And time for somebody to kill me! That's the lead you're waiting for.'

Bromley's gray cheeks began to tinge pink with irritation. 'Let's go over the events again. Perhaps there is something important you've forgotten.'

'There's nothing!'

'Tell me, say, from the moment that this Mr Farren, alias Wilkins, knocked on your door.'

Magill repeated it all, underlining every word with sarcasm. When he ended, the superintendent folded his hands over his eyes again.

'Has it occurred to you, sir, that Mr Farren might not wish you to reveal that he is still alive? That he might wish to silence you?'

'It has.'

'Do you believe it?'

'No.'

'Why not?'

'He wants me in this deal of his.'

'You believe that?'

'Yes.'

'Why do you believe it?'

'Because he didn't have to look me up. He didn't have to prove that he was alive.'

'Unless he had intended to kill you.'

'He could have done that the moment he walked into the room. No, he's into something, and he wants my help because he's afraid.'

'Very well. Now tell me what happened *before* Mr Farren knocked. What you did during the day.'

What Magill had done during the day seemed, as he recounted it, to belong to another year. There was the visit to the broker Cavendish; calling on Van Zordich; the Lebanese in the jeweler's showroom; lunch at the Savoy; the invitation to sit at the Sheikh's table; the Arab's gift of diamonds to the American girl; Magill's walk through London after lunch; the Lebanese taking his photograph in the Burlington Arcade.

'Curious, very curious,' Bromley mused. 'Since Barakati was following you, he did not need your photo for himself. He wanted it for someone else. Mmhmm. I think, Mr Magill, that you are very important to this someone.'

'But who? Why?'

'That is the key to everything.' The superintendent dropped his hands from his eyes and went back to scratching his stomach. 'It might be fruitful for us to contact the Interpol man in Beirut.

He may have a file on this sod Barakati.' More stomach scratching. Then he reached for the telephone on the nightstand. He asked the operator to give him Brown's Hotel. A moment later he was talking to the registry clerk. Was Mr Ward Farren a guest? How about Mr Thomas Wilkins? The inspector hung up with a shrug. 'It was too much to hope for. Mr Magill, I'd like a description of Mr Farren, alias Wilkins, as you last saw him, and also as he might look without disguise.'

'You're still trying to tie him in to this?'

'Not necessarily. But Passport Control is always interested in persons who enter the country with assumed names and altered credentials.'

When Magill finished the description, the superintendent clambered off the bed and shook hands. 'You have been very co-operative, sir. You realize, of course, that you should hold yourself available for further questioning.'

'Certainly. But if you don't mind, I think I'll switch hotels.'

'A wise precaution.'

Van Zordich interrupted, 'Better yet, Dave—move to my place. If somebody's after you, he won't like my burglar alarms.'

Magill seized the idea. He would be packed in ten minutes. Bromley added a final thought:

'When you check out downstairs, there may be some newspaper chaps hanging about. Tell them nothing.'

Magill smiled. 'I'm sure the hotel will go for that. No publicity.'

'Also my people. One word in the press, and the killer will be jinking about like a hare in the corn stooks.'

For the first time in many hours, Magill laughed.

Van Zordich's quarters were directly above his showroom. By the time Magill had carried his bags to the guestroom and returned to the living-room, the jeweler had opened a bottle of champagne and poured two glasses.

'I have one unfailing rule,' he announced, 'when all the world has gone smash, and it's women and children to the lifeboats:

Steady on, and knock back a few!'

After the champagne, they went to the kitchen and assembled a dinner of sorts, accompanied by stiff jolts of scotch. With each succeeding glass, the events of the evening seemed more bearable, less threatening. To Van Zordich, Superintendent Bromley was an excellent man. Brilliant, even. A bit of the self-dramatist, of course. His stretching out on the bed and scratching himself was a device; it was to put Magill at his ease, to demonstrate that authority could be human.

'How about me? I'm human, too! Damn it to hell, Harry, you haven't the faintest idea the jam I'm in!' Magill's self-restraint snapped; his gratitude for Van Zordich's help was forgotten. 'Out in California I've got a crew kicking a hole in the ground a mile deep and expecting me to come up with the cash to keep going! Just when I think I've got it, got Cavendish and his mullets ready to bite, I get messed up in a lousy murder! Something I can't explain to myself or to that bastard Bromley!' Magill folded his hands over his eyes in imitation. '"Tell me, Mr Magill, do you believe in God? A totting up of rights and wrongs?" Of all the crummy, dead-ass luck!' Magill dropped his hands and fumbled in his pockets. 'You got a cigarette?'

'Sorry. I'm pipes and cigars. But downstairs—'

'Never mind.' Magill remembered the cigar which Ward Farren had tossed to him. It was still in his breast pocket. He bit off the tip and flicked his lighter. 'How the hell,' he went on, 'am I going to hole up here like some scared-shit coyote, and the same time go down to Kent and make a deal with Cavendish?'

'Well, if the fellow is really anxious to be let in, I'm sure we can get him here on some excuse.'

'What about his friends? I've got to talk to the whole gang! It won't work. And if I start stalling Cavendish, he's the sort of bastard that can smell trouble six blocks away!' Magill was sucking noisily on the cigar, which had gone out. He struck his lighter again and the flame curled around the dead tip. 'If a single line of this gets into the papers, I won't have a prayer! With Cavendish or anyone else! Money runs scared, and anything—oh, hell!' He plucked the cigar, still unlit, from his mouth and glared at it as if it personified the whole of his misfortune. 'I might know Farren would hand out dud cigars.'

Van Zordich was suddenly alert, tense. 'Farren gave you that cigar?'

'Sure. Damned thing must have a leak in the wrapper.'

'No, no! Don't try to light it. Let me have it.'

Magill watched curiously as the jeweler—completely sober now—took a loupe from his pocket, fixed the optical under one eyebrow, and carefully examined the cigar. 'I may be wrong, but I doubt it. It's one of the oldest tricks in the book, and a good one. Mmhmm. Yes.' He handed the cigar and the jeweler's loupe to Magill. 'Look at the binder, there in the middle.'

Magill squinted through the loupe. 'Huh! There's a little dot, a piece of tobacco different in color.'

'Not tobacco. Paraffin. Brown paraffin. It's a plug to cover the part hollowed out inside. I've seen some very fine gems smuggled this way. That wouldn't be Farren's line, would it?'

'God knows what his line is! But sure as hell, he wouldn't make me a present of a diamond.'

Magill took out his penknife with the intention of cutting open the cigar. Van Zordich restrained him. It would be better, he said, to go downstairs to the office, where he had the proper instruments and lighting.

It was the same office that Magill had visited that morning. Only ten hours ago. Once more he was seated in the worn leather chair across the desk from Van Zordich. This time the jeweler wore a visor and a pair of magnifying spectacles as he hunched over the cigar and guided a pair of gem-tweezers around the paraffin plug. In a moment it was out. Van Zordich twisted the cigar a half turn and shook. A tiny black pellet dropped onto the white blotter. Again the gem-tweezers. The pellet began to unravel.

Van Zordich nodded. 'Microfilm.'

Magill stared. 'Why would Farren carry around something like that?'

'Spies do all the time.'

'Farren? Never!'

'Not a spy?'

'He wouldn't have the guts. Besides, maybe he didn't know there was anything inside the cigar.' Magill sank back in the chair. He frowned. 'No, that won't wash, either. He made a point of giving it to me.'

'Which means one thing. He wanted the cigar off his person. He was afraid of being searched.'

Magill pondered. 'Suppose he suspected that someone was following him when he came to my room. Suppose that phone call asking for Wilkins was from the man trailing him.'

Van Zordich snapped his fingers. 'Dave! You said the voice on the phone had an accent. Perhaps the Lebanese—'

'Yes! Barakati! But why did he slug me, instead of following Farren?'

The two men puzzled for a moment, then Van Zordich smiled. 'Barakati thought you and Farren were working together. He assumed that you were Farren's contact, that he had passed the microfilm to you.'

'Uh-huh. So he ransacked the place. But overlooked the cigar.'

'He would have found it eventually. Somebody killed him too soon.'

Magill bit his lower lip. 'We're still going in circles. We don't know this somebody. We don't know if he was following Barakati or Farren. Or even me.'

'Perhaps this will tell us.' Van Zordich tapped the roll of microfilm with his tweezers. Then he rose and went to a wall cabinet and brought out a desk film projector. He used it, he explained, to show jewelry designs to his clients. He slid one end of the microfilm between two glass slides, then inserted the sandwich into the projector. He went back to the cabinet for a collapsible screen, which he set up a few feet in front of the projector. He switched on the machine.

At first, there was nothing but a blur. Then, as the jeweler adjusted the lens, an image began to take shape. It appeared to be nothing more than a pattern. Against a white background, long black lines curved and arced. At random intervals there was a small dot or a circle. Figures were penciled alongside the dots. 3,400, 2,750, 4,800.

Van Zordich smiled. 'So your friend is not a spy?'

Magill sighed. 'Not in the usual sense.'

'Then what?'

'Up in the right-hand corner of that shot, you see the figure one?'

'Yes.'

'Move the film along and see if the next shot is numbered two.'

Van Zordich withdrew the glass slides and repositioned the film strip. But the next shot was numbered three. Again there were waving lines and dots and circles and penciled figures. Magill asked for the film to be advanced one more frame. This time the number was five.

'Well, Dave?'

Magill lit a cigarette. He could feel beads of sweat forming on his forehead. He wished he were ten thousand miles away from this room.

Van Zordich scowled. 'It seems to mean something to you. What? Military fortifications? A road system?'

Magill shook his head gloomily. 'It's worse, from my standpoint. It's a geophysical.'

Van Zordich gave a long, low whistle. 'So?'

'Yes. A survey map. Before an oil company drills an area, they send out crews to make test borings. That's why those figures. They drop a load of dynamite down a hole, then measure the shock waves. Seismographic. If the shock waves bounce off a salt dome, it may indicate an oil pool underneath. The dome can be measured and mapped. A good geophysical can cost hundreds of thousands, and it can make hundreds of millions.'

'Then if a survey were stolen or copied it would be worth a bit of money.'

'To a competing oil company, plenty! It can save months, years, of exploration.' Magill stared grimly at the projection screen. 'So that's Farren's big deal! Stolen oil maps. And London, during the International Petroleum Congress, is the place to sell them. Christ, has Bromley ever got me by the balls!'

'The truth is your best defense, Dave.'

'Who'd believe me? Don't you see—this is my motive to kill Barakati. We were going to peddle the microfilm to some oil company. We had a fight over our split. I murdered him. I faked a ransack of my hotel rooms. As for Ward Farren, *he* died in that plane explosion. It's a matter of public record. I brought him back to life to make him the suspect. What more does Bromley need?'

'Proof.'

'Hah!'

'I know. It *looks* as if you are in the sticky, but it still takes proof.'

'For me, the look is all that matters. When this gets out—goodbye, Cavendish, goodbye mullets. Goodbye, career! My name will be so tainted all through the industry—'

He broke off, aware of his self-pity, his morbid insistence on defeat. He got up from the chair and began to pace the room. After a while, he nodded to himself. 'The only way I can clear myself is to get this film back to the company that made the geophysical. Harry, crank up the projector again.'

It was past midnight when the last frame of film had been projected. Nowhere was the name of the oil company indicated. There were no markings of rivers, mountains, lakes; no landmark to reveal the region which had been mapped. Nothing but those interminable wavey lines, dots and circles and figures. The frames were labeled with odd numbers, from one to thirty-nine. That meant, Magill decided, the film was incomplete. There must be a second film, numbered from two to forty which would match up with the first and give a complete map of the geophysical.

'It's the way Farren's mind would work. He wouldn't show a prospect the whole thing until he had the money. He's got the second film stashed somewhere. Probably with an overlay marked with latitude and longitude.'

Van Zordich sighed and looked dejected. 'There is just no starting place. You don't know the oil company, you don't know the area of this survey. It might be the British Channel, Africa, the Near East, South America, Australia, anywhere!'

'Yep. The only way I can find out anything is to corner Farren.'

'That's Bromley's job.'

'No. Farren has to come to me. He's got to get those microfilms back.'

'And when he does, he'll leave you with a knife between your shoulder blades.'

Magill shrugged. He had had enough for one evening. His eyes were bloodshot from staring at the projection screen; his head throbbed from the blow behind the ear. He was falling-down-tired. Van Zordich locked the microfilm in the big safe and the two men went upstairs.

Magill frowned at the ceiling of the guest room. He had to get to sleep, he told himself. But he could not. Something was nagging him. A feeling. Almost a far-off whisper that he could not quite distinguish. It would not go away. Somehow, somewhere, there was a point that he had overlooked. Too much had happened too fast. But there was something he had ignored. What was it?

6

It was almost noon when he opened his eyes and saw, through the lotus-shaped window, the dome of St Paul and the great shaft of Britannic House. He felt truly refreshed. The swelling behind his ear had subsided, although it was still sore to the touch. He told himself that he ought to be up and doing; and in the next instant asked himself why. The doing must come after the thinking, and Magill always thought more clearly in bed. He began to review the happenings of the day before. Everything seemed a jumble of coincidences. That was life. Everything was chance. And since that was so, it was up to him to exploit chance, to make it work for him. If he were playing seven-card stud, he would analyze his opponents' probable cards; if he guessed correctly and held a good hand, he could win. Even with a poor hand, he might win—if he bluffed with the right degree of daring. It would be a gamble, and Dave Magill was a gambler. That was the prerequisite of the wildcat oilman. But gamblers and wildcatters, the good men, never based their plays on whim. A wildcatter would study the showings, the cores of rock and sand delivered up from the depths of the earth. These showings could tell a story; rock and sand could point the way toward oil, if the proper deductions were made. So it was that Magill studied the showings of the past twenty-four hours and drew a conclusion.

Sandra Morgan. She was the factor he had overlooked. The redhead who had been with Ward Farren on Magill's first night in London. The girl who had lunched with the Arab party the next day and who had rebuffed Magill's questions about Farren. She might—just might—know where Farren was hiding. She might somehow lead Magill to him.

He rose, showered and shaved. As he came out of the bathroom, he found Van Zordich waiting with the bedroom telephone in one hand. He gave the receiver to Magill.

'Progress, Mr Magill.' The flat voice on the line could belong only to Superintendent Bromley. 'Interpol report from Beirut on our dead man. The so-called Ahmid Barakati.'

'You say, "so-called"?'

'Beirut has no record of such a person. False name, false passport. Criminal type, undoubtedly.'

'And that's progress?'

'It is. We know who he is *not*. Next thing is to fly a set of his fingerprints East. If Beirut identifies, we can start looking for the clot who hired him. Now about your friend, Mr Ward Farren—' The inspector paused; Magill could hear the rustle of papers. 'Yes. Went by the alias of Wilkins, wasn't it?'

'That's right.'

'How about another alias. Colin W. Ramsay of Brisbane, Australia?'

'How would I know?'

'Never heard the name?'

'Never. I doubt Ward would try to pass himself off as an Australian.'

'Could be done. You Americans aren't all that different. Heathrow says a chap of that name, fitting your description, took BEA last night. Flight to Amsterdam.'

'Then can't the Dutch help?'

'We've asked. Too soon to hear. Doubt they could hold him, anyway. No basis for charging.' The superintendent hesitated, as if waiting for Magill's reaction. 'You have an idea for us, sir?'

'About what?'

'Amsterdam. Any reason your friend would go there?'

'None I can think of.'

'Too bad. Well, I'll keep in touch.'

As Magill hung up, he saw Van Zordich frowning at him. 'Dave, we've got to tell Bromley about the microfilm.'

'Why?'

'Good God, Dave! We can't withhold information from the

police. Those oil maps are the motive. Bromley will have something to work with.'

Magill shook his head. 'Bromley will work, all right. On me! The first thing he will do is check me out with every oilman in London. He'll raise a question in their minds: "What's with this Dave Magill?"'

'All right, let them wonder!'

'Oh? You think that's all? Bromley knows I went to Cavendish. He will, too. Cavendish will tell him I bought options on Anglia Petroleum. A hundred thousand dollars' worth. And where am I getting that hundred thousand? By selling stolen oil maps. That's the way it will add up.'

Van Zordich scowled. 'Dave, *I* have to live here. I have decent relations with the police. They are going to stay that way.'

The two men eyed each other coldly. The break had come. Magill was the first to speak.

'I'd like the microfilm, please.'

'What are you going to do with it?'

'That's my affair. It was planted on me. It will stay with me until I'm ready to turn it over.'

'It's better off in my safe.' Van Zordich saw the danger come into Magill's eyes. He sighed. So be it.

Magill made a pot of coffee and fried a plateful of eggs. Van Zordich came into the kitchen with the roll of microfilm and the hollowed-out cigar. He laid them on the kitchen counter and walked out. Magill inserted the film into the cigar and thrust it into his breast pocket. He poured himself a second cup of coffee and drank it moodily. The hell with Van Zordich. Magill had to think about himself. He had to think out his next move. Until proved to the contrary, he must assume that Ward Farren had indeed fled England. But could he sell the oil maps in an incomplete form? He needed the microfilm that he had left with Magill. In that case, perhaps Farren was relying on Magill's discovery of the contents of the cigar, and relying on Magill to find Farren. That would mean Farren hoped to lure him out of England. He would be, in effect, a courier carrying the microfilm to the thief.

Magill was rinsing out his coffee cup when he heard the footsteps behind him. It was Van Zordich. With him was Superintendent Bromley, unsmiling, stern-eyed.

'Mr Magill, I asked you last night if there was anything you might have forgotten to mention. It seems there was.'

The preamble was curiously worded. It had to be a trap. 'I forgot?'

'You told me about the American girl. You said her name was Miss Sandra Morgan.'

'That's right.'

'You did *not* tell me she was an actress.'

Magill glanced at Van Zordich; his expression revealed nothing. 'I didn't suppose it mattered.'

'Everything matters. If you had told me, if you had said "actress", I should have placed her at once. The theater is my hobby. I see everything that is good and most of the things that are bad.'

Magill's tension began to turn to anger. He thought, Go ahead, you British bastard—drop the other shoe!

'Sandra Morgan is playing at the Royal Court. O'Neill's *Mourning Becomes Electra*. Very talented, very attractive. She has what you Americans call a flair for publicity.'

'Inspector, I enjoy theatrical reviews in their proper place. The newspapers.'

Bromley's face softened. 'Background information, sir. To indicate to you that I should have recognized the girl immediately, if you had said actress. As it was, I learned that only now, from my sergeant, when he checked out the names you gave us. She did quite a dust-up.' He paused dramatically, as if waiting for his audience to beg for the revelation. 'Three or four days back—I shall have to verify the date—the young lady visited the office of the deputy commissioner. She demanded an investigation of the death of her brother. He had been killed in the explosion of an aircraft. An oil company aircraft.'

Magill stared. 'Belonging to Anglo-Tex Petroleum?'

'The one. The commissioner advised the lady that the matter

was beyond the jurisdiction of the department. She left in something of a temper. There were newsmen in the hallway, to whom she unburdened herself of opinions not flattering to our people. She alleged that her brother had been murdered and that she had proof. The tabloids played it out very big.'

Magill thought rapidly. Ward Farren's evening with the girl had not been a coincidence, after all. He had seen the news stories, he had looked her up to find out what she knew about the plane explosion. But why should it matter to him?

The superintendent paralleled Magill's thoughts. 'The girl is definitely a link to your friend Farren. But there is something that does not please me. If Miss Morgan had evidence about her brother's alleged murder, it seems an odd thing that she should spend an evening with a man who supposedly died in the same aircraft explosion.'

'They certainly had a common interest. They may have talked over this proof she had of her brother's murder.'

Bromley shook his head. 'It does not wash. She knew Farren under the alias of Wilkins, a name not in the plane's casualty list. Whatever the link between the two of them, we have still to find it.'

Van Zordich broke in. 'I take it you haven't talked to the girl yet.'

'No. My sergeant is at the theater now. As soon as he gets her address, I shall talk to her.' The superintendent turned back to Magill. 'Meanwhile, sir, I think we should go over what you told me last evening.'

'Again?'

'Again. This time, omit nothing. No matter how trivial.'

Since there were no chairs in the kitchen, they went downstairs to the comfort of Van Zordich's office. Magill had barely launched into his recital, when the telephone rang. It was a call for the superintendent. When he hung up, he gave Magill another of his gray smiles.

'Our Miss Morgan signed out of her hotel this morning. No forwarding address.' The superintendent clenched his left hand and scowled at the knuckles. 'I believe I shall drop by the

American Embassy and ask what they have on the lady.' He shook Magill's hand.

Van Zordich escorted the officer to the outer showroom. When he came back, Magill greeted him with an affectionate smile.

'Thanks, Harry. For a moment, at the beginning, I thought you had told him.' He was referring to the microfilm.

The jeweler shrugged, as if it were nothing. 'There was something *you* might have told him. That the girl is leaving for Paris.'

'Damn! I forgot. She did say that.'

'Yes. I heard her.'

'Huh! She said she was taking a channel ferry. But she didn't say which port—'

'It would be Dover. And she *didn't* say a channel ferry. She said The Night Ferry, which happens to be the name of a train.'

'From London to Paris, by train?'

'Certainly. A very posh affair. Sleeping cars. Leaves Victoria Station every night at ten. Loads aboard a ferry at Dover.'

Magill felt a surge of excitement. 'Then she's still in London! If I can find her, if I can talk to her, get a lead on Farren—'

'That's Bromley's job.'

'I can help him, can't I? If I just had an idea where to look for her. She could be killing time shopping, at a movie, or jawing with a friend.'

'Or working under the Sheikh.'

'You're really hung on that idea, aren't you?'

'My dear chap, the Arabs are notorious lechers for our women. When the Sheikh sprinkled my diamonds over her plate, it was more than a charming gesture. I said that at the time.'

Magill was already reaching for the telephone on the desk. 'What's the number of the Savoy?'

Van Zordich waved him away. 'Let me handle it. I've got the perfect excuse.'

Magill listened tensely as the jeweler talked to the Savoy operator; then to someone who answered in the Sheikh's suite; then to the first secretary; then to the aide, Colonel Mahmoud bin Jarrah. Van Zordich was very smooth. He was certain that Miss

Morgan would like to have those unset diamonds displayed in a proper mounting. The next time the colonel saw her, if he would—

He paused in mid-sentence. But surely the colonel remembered? Just yesterday, at lunch. Miss Sandra Morgan. The American actress. A paper of unset diamonds. Of course it happened! Van Zordich had the colonel's signed check in payment . . . Magill heard the click over the telephone. Van Zordich hung up and stared at the desk top.

'There were no diamonds. There was no Sandra Morgan. You and I never sat at His Excellency's table.'

'Hmm. Then she *is* important. Maybe in a different way than we thought.'

'Quite possibly. I'd say she's gone to ground right in the Sheikh's own quarters.'

'Then it won't do any good to tell Bromley. She's got sanctuary.'

'I'm afraid so. As a foreign ruler, the Sheikh and his people are beyond the police.'

'Then it's up to me.'

'You?'

'Not at the Savoy. No busting in on the Sheikh. But if she takes that train to Paris—'

'No. She's changed her plans.'

'We don't know that. Look, Harry, we agreed there is some kind of a tie between her and Farren. And he's in Amsterdam. The girl goes to Paris, then cuts up to Holland. If I can follow her, she'll lead me to Farren.'

Van Zordich frowned. 'I can't stop you, Dave. But it's wrong. This is Bromley's job.'

'And how will he do it? He can't get into the Sheikh's rooms. So he waits and tries to get some answers from her in the railroad waiting room. She's already proved what she thinks of the London police, and how much she would cooperate. With me, she might not have her guard up. Not if I play it right.'

'What will I tell Bromley? I'm responsible for you, you know.'

'Hell! I'm a businessman. I had to make a meeting in Paris. I'll be back in twenty-four hours.'

Van Zordich sighed heavily. 'Be a love, and do that.'

The arrangements were made by the jeweler. He sent Mrs Hellbron to buy Magill's railroad ticket. The two debated what should be done with the microfilm. Magill insisted that he should take it with him; it would be a bargaining point with Farren. If they met. But how to carry it? Van Zordich proposed, and then discarded, the idea of secreting it in Magill's rectum. 'The classic method; but devilishly uncomfortable. And if you should get the tourist trots . . .'

They decided to wrap the film in a fold of tissue paper, which was then sewn inside one lapel of Magill's coat. Later, when he packed his suitcase, he discovered Van Zordich's final precaution. Nestling in one pocket of the case was an automatic pistol. The serial numbers had been freshly filed away.

A few minutes before eight P.M., Van Zordich's Rolls Royce pulled to the loading ramp at Victoria Station. Magill got out, carrying his case and topcoat, and made his way into the station. His eyes searched the milling heads in the waiting room. Most of the people were boarding locals. He prayed that he had made the right guess. But was it? After all the argument, all the preparations, his confidence was already failing him.

At the far end of the waiting room, he located the turnstile with the sign overhead:

THE NIGHT FERRY
DOVER—DUNKIRK—PARIS

As Magill pushed toward it, he saw a young woman hand her ticket to the train agent. She was dressed in a cream-colored suit with matching boots. A checked jockey cap perched atop her red hair.

7

The train twisted like a giant steel snake through the conglomerate of south London. It began to lurch and bang as it went into the great bend of the rails which would now aim directly toward Dover. Magill scratched his message on a pad of telegraph blanks.

> I hope you are as thirsty as I am. Let's remedy the situation in the bar car.
>
> David Magill.

He folded the paper twice and handed it to the car steward, along with a pound note.

'Miss Sandra Morgan. She's wearing a light-colored suit. And boots. She has very red hair.'

The steward smiled understandingly. 'No one like that in this car, sir. But I'm sure I'll find her.'

Magill followed the steward out of the compartment and paused in the passageway to light a cigarette. He had already walked the length of the train without discovering the girl. Obviously, she had closed her compartment door. The steward, of course, would describe her to each car attendant. All Magill had to do was follow at a discreet distance.

The first car forward produced no result, nor did the second, nor the third. Then, as Magill came through the vestibule door of the fourth car, he saw the steward knock at a compartment door at the far end. The door opened, then closed. Magill hurried forward.

The note was still in her hand as she opened the compartment door again. Her intense blue eyes widened, then narrowed.

'You certainly don't waste time.'

He tried his most ingratiating smile. 'I thought I ought to let you see who David Magill is. In case you don't remember our lunch at the Savoy.'

'I remember.' Her face clouded. 'Are you following me?'

'I wouldn't blame you for thinking that. I was boarding the train and happened to see you. I've always been lucky, you know. You *do* believe in luck, I hope.'

She came close to a smile. 'Of course. It was pure luck that I happened to tell you I was taking The Night Ferry to Paris.'

'You did? Well! There's another coincidence. Now about that drink?'

She hesitated; the door inched wider. Then she shook her head; the door started to close. At that moment a voice echoed along the corridor.

'Mr David Magill! Telegram for Mr David Magill!'

'Here, boy!'

The surprise made him forget the girl. He stared at the telegram which the train courier handed to him. He tore it open.

BON VOYAGE EXCLAMATION
POINT YOUR DEAREST.

Who in hell was Dearest? The telegram must have been meant for someone else. No. There was his own name, and addressed, 'On Board The Night Ferry, London/Paris.' Of course. Van Zordich. He was the only one who knew. But what was the meaning?

Magill looked up from the telegram. Sandra Morgan, the door still ajar, watched him with amused eyes.

'Someone telling you that *she's* thirsty, too, Mr Magill?'

Before he could think of a rejoinder, and before Sandra Morgan could close the door, his face was splashed with liquor.

'Oh, God, I'm sorry! What a clumsy fool!'

Someone was simultaneously brushing Magill's soggy coat-sleeve and waving a flask. Magill blinked through the haze of gin and saw a big, thickly built man whose child-like face was larded with jowls and a double chin.

'Ma'am, could you give me a towel?' He was appealing to the girl. 'Something to sop up your friend?'

Magill seized on it. 'Yes! A towel, please!'

In another moment he was inside the compartment. But the blundering stranger was right at his side.

'My old lady would kill me if she saw what I've done!' The flask was still waving about.

Magill took the towel which Sandra had found and wiped his face and dabbed at his sleeve and assured the man that accidents would happen.

'Very kind of you, sir. But no excuse. I just wasn't looking. Least I can do is make it up to you. Oh, steward!' He craned his neck out into the hall. 'A bottle of champagne for this compartment! Set-ups for three!'

Protests. A flurry of *no's, please don't's* from Magill and the girl. He waved them off. 'My pleasure! I owe it to you folks. Name is Carter. Sam Carter. Sales rep Acme Supplies, USA. Surgical goods.'

He deposited himself on one of the two seats and motioned Magill and Sandra to sit opposite him. The girl gave Magill a glance of defeat and sat. Magill pretended the same despair; secretly, he welcomed the intruder. Even a three-way conversation was better than Sandra closing him out of her compartment.

'This your first trip to Paris, miss?'

'Is it that obvious?'

'No, but I figured you too young to be an old Paris-hand. Now you, sir, I'd say you've been before.'

Magill nodded, and watched with relief as Carter finally screwed the top onto his flask and slipped it into a pocket.

'Yes, sir. I can peg people for who they are, what they're doing, or about to do. That's a salesman's job, knowing about people. You, sir, you're on vacation, doing the whole continent or most of it. Right?'

'Right.'

The champagne arrived and the steward uncorked the bottle and poured the three glasses. Carter lifted his.

'To a very happy trip for all of us. May we all find what we're after!'

Sandra's cheeks colored. From Carter's insinuating tone, he obviously took it that Magill and the girl were rendezvousing in Paris. As if to confirm it, he added, 'You know, this sort of reminds me of the first time I was ever on a train, first time I ever struck up with a girl. My sixteenth birthday, it was, and I was running away. Had just enough money for the train to Chicago. She was sitting across the aisle from me. Christ, she was a looker! She wore city clothes and a cute little hat. A red hat . . .'

How am I going to get rid of this bore? He'll talk her to sleep before I can get anything out of her.

Magill glanced carefully at Sandra. She was far from asleep. She seemed amused by Carter's monologue. Magill noted something else: that she was wearing less makeup than she had in London. There was a sprinkle of freckles on both cheeks and across the bridge of her nose. He liked girls with freckles.

'She did the talking,' Carter went on. 'I was so damned shy I couldn't spit, let alone string words together. She was going to Chicago, too, she said. She lived there. Then she asks me what I did for a living. How about that? Asking a sixteen-year-old what he does for a living! I came out with some lie about going to a job in Chicago, and she says, Wonderful! Maybe her father can help get me something better. Here, miss. Let me top that off for you.' Carter poured fresh champagne into Sandra's glass. 'So then she says her father is a world-famous architect. He's built some of the biggest buildings in America. His name is McMurdo, she says, and because he's so important, they always put his initials in the cornerstone of each of his buildings. And a Roman numeral after his initials, a serial number to show which of his buildings this one was. She says I must have seen at least one of her old man's buildings, and when I thought about it, I said I had. The courthouse at the county seat. I remembered the cornerstone. It had those Roman numerals. They read MCMXII "That's it," she says. "McMurdo Number Twelve." McMurdo's twelfth building.'

Carter paused, waiting for the laugh. When it came from both his listeners, he stood up. 'Well, now you know about my first train trip, and my first run-in with a girl. Enjoy the champagne, folks.' He touched a finger to his forehead in a mock salute and stepped smartly out into the passageway. 'See you in the morning!'

'Not if I can help it,' Magill muttered.

Sandra laughed. 'Oh, he wasn't that bad. He meant well.'

Magill saw that Carter and the champagne had smoothed the way for him. Sandra was no longer holding him at arm's length. At least, not yet.

'You know,' he began, 'I was glad to hear this is your first trip to Paris.'

'Why?'

'Because I'd like to show you some of my favorite spots. If I may. And if you aren't meeting some Arab Sheikh who insists on pouring diamonds over your dessert.'

She laughed comfortably. 'Wasn't that the craziest? I took those stones around to a jeweler afterwards. He said they were worth two thousand pounds. That's over five thousand dollars!' She shook her head in wonder. 'I suppose it was all deductible. A sort of above-the-line cost.'

'Are you an actress or an accountant?'

She smiled. 'He *is* a movie producer, you know.'

'The Sheikh?'

'Yes. He's made some sort of a Near East thriller. They wanted some pre-release publicity. I guess the diamonds were my bonus.'

'You guess? You don't know for sure?' He remembered Van Zordich's insistence that the girl was the Sheikh's mistress of the moment. Magill felt like correcting that to Mistress of the Non Sequitur.

'Oh, who knows anything with Arabs? They're crazy people. Do you know, the Sheikh took over one whole floor at the Savoy? He brought his own doctor, his own cook, his own coffee-maker, his own bed-maker. They say his whole suite was redecorated. Gold fixtures put in the bathrooms and—'

Magill cut through her rambling. 'You say you did publicity

work for him?'

She hesitated. 'Well, I suppose there's no harm in telling now. They made me swear I wouldn't. But I won't be seeing them again. I was doing the O'Neill thing at the Royal Court. After one of the matinees, this Arab came backstage to see me. The Sheikh's aide, the one you saw at the Savoy—'

'Colonel Mahmoud?'

'Mmhmm. He gave me the usual stuff. How much he enjoyed my playing, I was a great emotional actress, all that. He said he wanted to hire me to do some publicity for a movie. He'd pay me a thousand pounds for ten minutes' work.'

She raised her glass and drained the last of the champagne. Magill studied her intently. It was coming too easily.

'The colonel laid it out for me. There was this movie about the Near East and an American oilman for the hero. That's a switch, right there. Anyway, the picture is going into release, and they want a newspaper story that will tie in with the picture. So, I'm to go to Scotland Yard and tell them I'm the sister of an American oil scientist who's just got himself blown up in a plane. And I'm to say that I know it's murder, and I have the proof.' She paused and smiled at Magill's expression. 'I know! Sounds like a pot-dream, doesn't it?'

He nodded. So far, she was confirming what Superintendent Bromley had said. 'So you went to Scotland Yard, they brushed you off, then the reporters picked up your story and gave it the works.'

'Ah, you read it!' She tossed her head and laughed. 'Those pictures of me were pretty awful, weren't they? But the money was pretty, period!'

'That wasn't the end, though, was it?'

'No. The colonel came to the theater again. It was the night performance after I had been to the police. He said there would be a bonus for me if I would do one thing more. If some man telephoned me at the theater, or my hotel, and if he asked me out, I was to say yes. But just for one date.'

'Uh-huh. And you got the phone call. From the man I saw you with that night at the Carlos Tower.'

'Tommy Wilkins. He said he was an old friend of my brother. He'd read the story in the papers, and he thought maybe he could help me. I almost broke up while he was talking.'

'Why?'

'Because I don't have a brother! Oh, I caught on, all right. This was his way of getting a date.' She grinned at the memory. 'Come to think of it, maybe those pictures of me weren't too bad, after all.'

She couldn't be that naïve, Magill thought. Her face was far too intelligent.

'So this man, this Wilkins, took you to the party at the Carlos.'

'That was my idea. The cast was having a thing, and I didn't want to miss it.'

'And during the evening, Wilkins asked you what sort of proof you had that your brother was murdered. Who killed him, or how the plane had exploded.'

She crossed her legs and kicked one booted foot uneasily. 'You seem to know a great deal about this. You're asking an awful lot of questions.'

'Because I'm interested.'

'So interested that you follow me onto this train just to hear the story.'

'I didn't ask for it. You volunteered.'

She thought that over. 'You've been very careful not to tell me anything about yourself.'

'I'm in the oil business.'

'Oh? Another friend of my brother?'

Magill laughed, but the chill had set in. She uncrossed her legs and stood up.

'It's late, Mr Magill. I'm very tired.'

He rose. 'I'm sorry. Perhaps we can have breakfast together, before the train gets in.' She ignored it. 'Oh, one thing you forgot. Something important.'

'Yes?'

'Did you tell this Mr Wilkins that you had no brother? That it was all movie publicity?'

'Goodnight, Mr Magill.'

The compartment door closed with a bang and the lock snapped on.

The train swung into a sharp curve at high speed. As Magill lurched back toward his own car, he passed a compartment with an open door. Inside, a man was hunched up on the seat, viewing the corridor. It was Sam Carter. He made an elaborate face at Magill, as if sympathizing with Magill's poor luck with the girl. He raised a bottle of scotch from his lap.

'How about a night cap?'

'No thanks. I'm turning in.'

'Come here.' He crooked a finger toward Magill, as if he had a secret to impart.

Magill stepped through the doorway. 'You going to be in Paris awhile?'

'It depends.'

'Uh-huh. Well, I know a couple of girls. Oh, not the class of your young lady, but good enough for the purpose. We could have some fun. I could give you a call at your hotel.'

'I don't know where I'll be staying.'

'Then I know just the place. It's central and cheap, and—'

'We can talk about it in the morning.' Magill was already edging out the doorway.

'Think about it!' Carter called. 'We could sure have some fun!'

Sleep did not come easily. Magill lay in his berth and stared upward into the darkness. He had made progress this evening. Almost too much. Sandra Morgan had talked too freely, and she knew it. Now her guard was up. Some of her story was true, but how much? Superintendent Bromley had described her as having a flair for publicity. He had chosen the right phrase. But why had the Arab Sheikh hired the girl? He was not a motion picture producer, Magill was positive of that. The Sheikh, through his aide Colonel Mahmoud, had wanted to lure Ward Farren from hiding. It had worked. But what was the purpose? Another question. Was Barakati working for the Sheikh? And why was he interested in Magill? The train wheels clacked on. Then Sandra

Morgan's words came back to him. 'The Sheikh took over one whole floor at the Savoy. He brought his own doctor, his own cook, his own coffee-maker, his own bed-maker.' Yet the Sheikh had *not* dined in his quarters. He had chosen the River Restaurant. He and his party came in after Van Zordich and Magill. Good God! Of course. That explained why Magill and Van Zordich had been invited to join the Sheikh's table. Someone had reported that Magill was in the restaurant. The Sheikh appeared, with Sandra Morgan to *identify* Magill. She would recognize him as the man who had spoken to Ward Farren in the lobby of the Carlos Tower. And Magill had confirmed it in so many words in the Sheikh's presence.

Sandra Morgan was more of an enigma than ever. She was a link to Ward Farren, and something else as well. She was an agent of the Sheikh Ali Muhammid, for reasons still unknown. Magill was convinced on one point. He had been right in following her. In Paris, he would be her Siamese twin.

'Well, good morning!'

'Welcome to France!'

Sandra Morgan and Sam Carter smiled up at Magill from their breakfast table in the diner. There were two vacant chairs at the table. Magill chose the one opposite Sandra, where he could best observe the girl of the mercurial moods. Only a few hours before, she had pushed him out of her compartment and slammed the door in his face; now she was cheery and pleased to see him. He gave his breakfast order to the steward who stood beside him, then stared out at the French countryside which was slipping past at eighty miles an hour.

'Any idea if we're on time?' he asked.

'Ahead, Mr Carter says. We'll be in the Gare du Nord before you've had your second cup of coffee.' Sandra was as knowing and nonchalant as if she made the trip every day.

Carter wiped his mouth with the napkin and beamed at Magill like a kindly old uncle. 'I was just telling the young lady here, Paris is my second home. Like to show her around a bit, and you, too. I was here with the Signal Corps during the war. I got myself separated over here. Stayed a while and really got to know the place.'

The steward set the orange juice in front of Magill. He downed it, then noticed that Carter seemed to be waiting for something from him.

'I've been to Paris several times, Mr Carter. I think I can find my way around.'

'Well, if you change your mind, and want a guide . . .' He rose from the table. 'I'll be staying at the Lotti, so if you want to give me a jingle some time—'

Sandra beamed up at him. 'I just may take you up on that, Mr Carter.'

'Good, good!' He clapped Magill on the shoulder and made his way out of the diner.

Magill saw that Sandra was about to rise also. 'I'm sorry if I offended you last night.'

'You did, but I'm the one who was at fault. I never stopped to think about it, until I was telling you the whole thing, just how bad it sounded. How foolish I was to get involved.'

'You mean, with the Sheikh's publicity?'

'Yes. I knew it was wrong. Secretly, I knew. I just wouldn't face it. I was greedy.'

'A thousand pounds is a lot of money.'

'To me. More than I'd ever seen at one time in my life. I told myself all I could do with it. A chance to see Paris, to have a real fling spend money like an heiress. Even if it was all gone in a week.'

Magill smiled vacantly. It made sense. It was plausible. It was, also, a perfect excuse for her to rendezvous with Ward Farren.

She got up from the table. She said she had to hurry back and lock her suitcases.

'Sandra, I want to see you in Paris.'

She looked down at him thoughtfully. Then she grinned. 'I hoped you'd say that. After all, a lone girl in a strange city—'

'You wouldn't be alone very long. Look, when we get off, let's share the taxi to the hotel.'

'Well, I'm going to the Ritz. Would that be out of your way?'
'No. It's perfect.'
'Good! *A bientôt!*'

He saw a flash of her red hair among the crowd milling along the dank platform in the Gare du Nord. He called out her name and waved, but she neither heard nor saw. Or she chose not to. The crowd closed around her, and she was gone. Magill swore in frustration and pushed his way to the Customs desk set up in front of the entrance to the main waiting room. He cleared inspection and then a blue-smocked porter had his case under his arm and they ran toward the street and the taxi rank.

All the taxis had been taken. It was necessary to wait for one to cruise past. Magill cursed. The thing which he had determined would not happen *had* happened. He had lost the girl. But at least he knew where she was staying. The Ritz. He would check in at the same hotel.

He heard a voice at his elbow. 'Say, I got an idea for tonight.' It was Carter. 'It's a private club, but I can get us in. The members come dressed up like the animals they wish they were.'

'Taxi! Taxi!' Magill and the porter were both waving.

'Last time I was there, I saw something in monkey fur going at something else in eagle feathers. You can join in, if you want. They stock a whole zoo of costumes.'

'Some other time, Carter.'

Magill had the taxi door open. The porter threw in his bag.

'You may change your mind. Tell me where you're staying and I'll call you—'

'I haven't the faintest idea. Goodbye.'

Before Magill could close the door, Carter had propelled himself into the taxi, slammed the door, and was pushing money at the driver. It was an American hundred-dollar bill.

'*A l'Orly! Vite!*'

'Oui, m'sieur! *Plus vite!*'

Magill shouted a countermand, but the driver ignored it. The taxi shot out into the traffic. Magill reached for the door on his side.

Carter grinned at him. 'It will be awful messy.'

Magill sank back into the seat and glared. Carter's whole personality was suddenly different. He was in charge. To underline the fact, his right hand was tucked inside his coat and there was an ominous bulge pointing at Magill's chest.

'What the hell do you think you're doing?'

'Kidnapping you.'

Magill stared. The man meant it.

'Who in Christ's name are you?'

'Your Dearest.'

Magill choked. Now he knew who had sent him the telegram on the train.

8

The man was mad. Sane people did not do such things, Magill told himself. If only he had Van Zordich's pistol—but it was packed away in his luggage. It was useless to appeal to the taxi driver. He was already bought off. If he tried to shout out the window, to catch the attention of an *agent de police*—no, the officer would think it was just another crazy *Américain* . . .

The taxi vibrated alarmingly; such speed was never intended for the old Citroën. The Paris city limits were long past. Ahead, in the sky, Magill could see jets lowering along the glide path into Orly. He glanced sideways at Carter. He had not changed position nor expression. For once, his chatter was stilled. There was no longer need for him to talk, to camouflage, to deceive.

The taxi swung through the airport entrance and sped toward the terminal building. Magill would have to make his break the moment the taxi slowed enough for him to jump. But just as he steeled himself, Carter gave another order to the driver, and the taxi swerved off onto a service road and speeded up again. They were not going to the terminal. Buildings blurred past, service hangars, parking lots, fuel trucks, then straight out onto the landing field. They cut in front of a taxiing Caravelle and on straight across the field. Finally, the Citroën screeched into a tight semicircle and pulled alongside a parked passenger plane. Magill noted that it was a twin-engined executive-sized jet. He stared at the license number painted on the soaring tail. Not an American plane, nor British, nor a serial number that he could identify from any European country. The boarding steps were already lowered; alongside stood a man in a flight steward's uniform. Would he help Magill? No. He swung open the taxi door and saluted.

'Good morning, Mr Buck.'

'Morning, Jim. Take Mr Magill's bag aboard, please.'

'Yes, sir.'

Buck? So that was his real name. Magill hunched forward on the seat, gauging if he could leap past the steward. But where could he go? The plane was parked too far away from hangars and service people. If he tried to dash across the field, they could run him down in seconds. Magill meekly got out of the car and, with his captor grasping his arm, he climbed the stairs into the plane.

It was several moments before his eyes adjusted to the subdued lighting of the interior. He was in a cabin which was arranged like a club room. Half a dozen easy chairs, upholstered in light blue leather, were placed about a cocktail table which bore a small bronze bust. Even in the poor light, Magill recognized in the metallic features the aged baby-face of his host. Up forward there was a bar with a mirror behind it. At the aft end, a closed door blocked off view of the other compartments. Alongside the closed door hung a large oil painting. It was a portrait of Mr Buck, wearing a khaki shirt and a sombrero.

'How about a drink?'

Magill shook his head.

'Well, I'm going to.' Buck strode toward the bar. 'I always like to talk business with a glass in my hand.'

'Or a gun.'

Buck threw back his head and snorted. 'What gun? Who's got a gun? You mean, *this?*' He shoved his right hand inside his coat and then withdrew it; one finger pointed at Magill in imitation of a gun. 'You see, boy, what an imagination can do to you?'

Instead of sagging with relief, Magill turned coldly furious. He had been had, tricked, intimidated. Well, he wouldn't give the bastard the satisfaction.

'Your plane, I take it?'

'My flying office. I can go anywhere in the world and take care of my business. No fuss over tickets, no waiting in Customs line, no reporters bothering me.'

'Yet you took the train last night.'

'To meet you, boy. To meet you.' Buck came forward, drink in hand, and patted Magill's shoulder. 'I can see you still don't know who I am: Preston Buck of Calgary. Former American citizen, former Okie, now Canadian. Past, present, and future number-one boy of Buck Oil and Gas Corp.'

He was probably telling the truth. Magill remembered reading somewhere of such a company.

'Think I'll take that drink after all.'

'Good boy!'

Magill selected a glass, chose a bottle of Black Label and poured himself three fingers. He heard the cabin door open behind him, and then a woman's voice.

'Good morning, Preston.'

Magill turned and saw a gray-haired woman in a pink negligee with maribou scuffies on her bare feet. Her face was without makeup; the skin was blotched with tiny broken veins; the eyes watery and bloodshot.

'May I?' She held out her hand for Magill's glass.

'My wife, Mr Magill.' Buck's eyes were hard with displeasure. 'Hadn't you better get dressed, honey?'

She ignored him. She took a long gulp of the whiskey, then handed the glass back to Magill and smiled her thanks. 'Have you ever been aboard anything like this, Mr Magill?'

'No. I haven't.'

'I wish I could say that. I spend most of my life on landing fields.'

'Honey!'

'Yes, dear?'

'Later.'

Mrs Buck took Magill's drink from his hand again. After a swallow, she smiled. 'I want you to be nice to my husband. Don't disappoint him.'

'In what way, Mrs Buck?'

She shrugged. 'Preston doesn't explain his ideas to me. But I'm sure you know. You see, disappointments just . . . they just *bother* him.' She halted, smiled vaguely and held out her hand to Magill.

Both men watched her make her unsteady way out of the cabin. The door closed behind her and opened again and a dark-haired young woman peered in.

Buck glowered at her reflection in the mirror behind the bar. 'All right, Miss Wilson. Haul your snatch in here!'

Miss Wilson went to a chair in the corner. She put on black-rimmed glasses and took a notepad from her dress pocket.

Buck's attention returned to Magill. 'You know, boy, I just might be interested in that little play you got going out in California.'

Magill blinked. His jaw sagged.

'So you've been investigating.'

'Always do. Last forty-eight hours Miss Wilson here has run a check on you from the cradle up. Phone calls to New York, San Francisco, Los Angeles, Colorado Springs, Houston. You got yourself a pretty good name as a wildcatter.'

'Why the interest?'

'Coming to that. Only one or two things bother me. You're digging for the deep stuff. It's going to take a bigger kitty than I figure you got.'

'That's why I went to London.'

'On the chance of finding mullet money?'

'Why not? The International Oil Congress means plenty of people thinking about oil.'

'Uh-huh.' Buck swung around from the bar. The face was still bland and schoolboyish. But the voice was sharp, commanding. 'Tell me about you and Cavendish.'

Magill stiffened. This man was unnerving. No wonder his wife had taken to the bottle. He would allow no mysteries, no secrets, no privacy.

'Cavendish,' Buck repeated. 'The broker. Throgmorton Street. What's your deal? Who got you together?'

'No one. I saw an ad of his in the *Oil World Journal*. It said he represented some English investors.'

'Just that innocent, huh? Maybe so. Maybe.' He pursed his lips in thought. 'Couple of days ago, in London, your friend Cavendish phoned me at the airport. We had a line strung out to the plane here. I happened to be in town with Miss Wilson at the time, so my wife took the call. Cavendish tells her he has an important matter to discuss with me, and he invites us down to Kent for the weekend. Were you going to say something?'

'No. Go on.'

'Well, Mrs Buck is sick of hanging around landing strips, so she accepts. And when I get back, I can't shake her loose from going. Now while I'm busy giving her excuses why I can't go, in comes another call from Cavendish. He says he's so delighted we're coming, and tells me how to find his place in Kent, and then, just by the way do I happen to know of an American oilman. A David Magill, from California? I tell him no.'

Magill smiled to himself. Cavendish had done his part too well. Magill had expected him to round up mullets, not a blue-fin shark.

'"Well now," I said to myself, "Mr C. has got himself some sort of a pudding, and he's setting himself up to cut a piece of it. And the pudding is this Mr David Magill. Now, if he's a good pudding, I'm not sharing with Mr C. I want all of it. So where do I find this guy Magill?"'

'You checked with the American Embassy.'

'Miss Wilson did. Only you hadn't signed in.'

'So you went over the register at the Oil Congress.'

'Miss Wilson did. And you hadn't signed in there, either.'

'Then you tried the hotels.'

'Miss Wilson did. Finally, she hit you at the Carlos Tower. So, after dinner that night, I take a taxi to the hotel. When I ask the desk clerk, he says you just checked out, but to hold on a minute. He disappears, comes back with somebody from Scotland Yard or the CID. And *he* starts in on me. What do I know about Mr David Magill? Where is he?'

So Bromley had been checking. The superintendent had not been as trusting as he had appeared.

Buck paused to watch his listener's reaction. There was none; Magill was careful about that. Buck went on, speaking slowly now, and smiling like an undertaker at a millionaire's main event.

'I've never been a fan of the police, so I just ducked the questions, the same as he ducked mine about why he was asking. I walked out of the hotel and around the block. Then I came back and saw the cop gone. I hunted up the telephone operator, I laid a hundred-pound note in her lap and said I'd like a list of all the numbers you had called.'

'Good God!'

'You've never done that? That's why you're still scrounging, and why I'm here.' Buck swept his hand around, indicating the airplane. 'Anyway, she got out the records, and I had my list. There were some uncompleted calls to California and three London calls. Two of them were to one particular number.'

'To Henry Van Zordich.' There was no use for Magill to hold it back. He could see every link in the chain now.

'Uh-huh. The fancy jeweler. Of course, I didn't know who it was until Miss Wilson gave the phone number to the detective she hired and he had traced it out for us. It didn't take much figuring that you holed up with Van Zordich. A jeweler's place would be wired and guarded good.'

'So you had the place watched.'

'Right. When you finally broke cover, went to Victoria Station, you were followed. My man phoned me, and I just had time to get there, write out the bon voyage telegram, and climb aboard. When the telegram was delivered, it homed me right in on you.'

He was so damned proud of it all, Magill thought. So vain about his ingenuity. That was his weakness. Egotism. That would be the weapon to use against him, if Magill had to.

'I admire your ingenuity, Mr Buck. And your energy. But it would have been so much easier to go directly to me while I was staying with Van Zordich.'

Buck shook his head. 'I was still investigating you. When the law is on a man's tail, I don't go barging in until I've got the picture. My man was shadowing the jeweler. Maybe the law was doing ditto. I wouldn't want them connecting me up until I was sure about you.'

'And now you're sure.'

'Just about last midnight, I was.'

Midnight. Magill thought back. 'Dover. You got off the train and telephoned Miss Wilson.'

Buck chuckled. 'I like the way you follow through, boy. That's when I ordered the plane to fly over and be waiting here at Orly. So now we're right up to date. I know about you, you know about me, and so how much is it going to cost me for half your play out in California?'

Magill inhaled deeply and looked away. He could feel the tension in Buck, the electric current passing between the two men. He had come one-third of the distance around the world to raise money for that cursed hole in the ground; the money was being offered right now, yet he dared not take it. At least, not yet.

'Well, boy?'

'Half of my play. At best, it's going to be a small operation. I doubt it would be worth your time.'

'It isn't.'

'Well, then?'

'The pudding. Fifty percent of the *real* pudding.'

'You think I've got something besides that well?'

'I damned well know you have! Something that high-tailed you out of England. You're not the kind of boy who'd run out on the police. It's got to be awful important.'

He was guessing. It was up to Magill to kick dust in his eyes. 'You're right. You've got it pegged.'

'You bet I have!'

'I've gotten involved with someone.'

'Yes?'

'Well, you know how it is when you're traveling alone and you meet a girl.'

Buck's cheeks began to redden. 'The girl on the train? Sandra Morgan?'

'Let's not go in for names.'

'Boy, don't give me *that!* I haven't got toe-jam for brains! Every time you went out of your hotel in London, there was tail for the asking. You didn't walk out on Cavendish and mullet money just because you wanted to fuck some broad! Feed me crap like that, and I'll shove it right back up your chocolate speedway!'

Magill glanced at Miss Wilson, expecting to see her blush or pretend a sudden attack of deafness. Instead, she was leaning forward in her chair, her eyes bright with interest. Dirty talk? She loved it.

'The pudding, boy. Fifty percent of the pudding.' Buck's voice was soft now, cooing, coaxing. He *had* to win. Or at least, to *know*. The irony of it, Magill thought, was that Buck was only feet away from the pudding—the microfilm which nestled inside the lining of his coat lapel.

Buck's voice dropped to a whisper. 'Come on, boy! The pudding! How much?'

Magill sighed. 'I'll have to think about it. I always sleep on a proposition.'

Buck regarded him sadly. 'You're shopping, huh? Think you can get more than I can pay. Just because I'm not from Texas, don't think I can't deal as big as they do. Maybe bigger!'

'I haven't said anything about Texas.'

'And don't! Let me tell you something. Out in Calgary, we got fifty thousand American oilmen. Lot of them taken up Canadian citizenship, like me. We can spend millions just as easy as those Texas big mouths. They make me puke! They think their shit smells sweeter than anybody else's!'

Magill smiled at his fury. 'Okay. I'll think about it. I'll sleep on it.'

'You do that. And tomorrow, you call me. Miss Wilson!'

'Yes, sir?'

'Phone the terminal. Tell them to send a taxi out for Mr Magill.'

The interview—or audience—was over.

Buck followed Magill down the steps from the plane and waited with him until the taxi swung alongside. As Magill opened the door, Buck laid a hand on his arm.

'One other thing. When you see Sandra Morgan—'

'*If* I see her.'

'*When* you see her, tell her I'm sorry about her brother. He worked for me at one time. Out in Calgary. Damned good geologist. Tell her if she needs anything, any help at all—just get in touch with Preston Buck.'

9

The room director at the Ritz Hotel beamed across the front desk at Magill. All single rooms were booked; but, *quelle chance!* there was one suite available. Magill nodded; he would take it. He signed the registry and gave the room director his passport. The man puzzled at his name, then brightened. He turned to the concierge at the next desk. '*Le lettre pour Monsieur David Magill, s'il vous plaît.*'

Magill waited until after the room director and the porter had installed him in his suite on the third floor. When the hall door closed behind them, he opened the envelope.

Dave—
Have gone shopping. Back by five. If you happen to be free, we could have cocktails. Either way, leave a note.
Sandy

Magill scowled. Shopping. He hoped so. At that very moment she could be making contact with Ward Farren, or running an errand for Sheikh Ali Muhammid. That bastard, Preston Buck. His interference had wrecked Magill's surveillance of the girl.

He opened the tall windows in the sitting-room and stepped out onto the shallow balcony. He gazed at the Place Vendôme and the great gray column topped by the hulking figure of Napoleon. 'If you happen to be free, we could have cocktails.' At least, she was giving him an opening. He would have to exploit it for all he was worth. He went back into the sitting-room and wrote his reply.

Will be waiting for you in the American Bar. Six o'clock. Let's make an evening of it.

In light of what Sandra and Preston Buck had told him, he decided to telephone Henry Van Zordich in London. But he would not call from the Ritz. Instead, he chose to walk to the Grand Hotel, on Rue Scribe. He arranged with the hotel operator to take the call on one of the lobby telephones.

Van Zordich greeted Magill's voice with a mixture of relief and concern. 'God, I was hoping you'd check in, Dave,' he began. 'I wanted to warn you . . .'

'About what?'

'Last night, while I was driving you to the railroad station, someone broke into my apartment.'

'Oh, Christ!'

'At least, I didn't get coshed. They'd done their work by the time I got back. They went through everything. Even the kitchen and bathroom.'

'God, Harry, I'm sorry I got you into this. Have you reported it to the police?'

'Don't intend to. Your hotel room ransacked, now my place. Bromley would really get the wind up. How about you and the girl?'

Magill sketched his talk with Sandra, on the train, and Preston Buck's interest in the girl. When he described Buck's kidnapping and the weird interview aboard the private plane, Van Zordich reacted with concern.

'Dave, the man sounds dangerous to me.'

'He could be. That's why I'm calling. See what you can find out about him at the Canadian Embassy.'

'Will do.'

'One more thing. Go around to the Carlos Tower and talk to the telephone operator. See if anyone besides Buck paid her to hand over a list of my telephone calls. That's how Buck traced me to your place.'

'Good God! Of course! If the operator gives me a name, we'll know who ransacked last night.'

'Exactly.'

'I'll ring you up as soon as I've got something. Where can I get hold of you?'

'Don't. I'll call you. I don't want any more telephone operators keeping books.'

'But in an emergency? If there's a real crunch—'

'The Ritz Hotel.'

As Magill stepped out into Rue Scribe, there was a tremendous concussion. He lurched against the side of the building as if he had been drilled by a .45 Magnum. Then he realized what it was; the sonic boom from some far-off aircraft. He stared around sheepishly. No, thank God, no one had noticed his reaction. No one had seen his hand clutch at his lapel, instinctively guarding the pellet of microfilm. He dropped his hand and wiped his sweating palm against his trousers. So he was nervous. Okay. He would walk it off. That decided, he set off briskly toward the Champs Elysées. He reached it at the Rond Point and stalked toward the Arc. He came to one of the sidewalk cafés and seated himself at a table under a red and white striped umbrella. He ordered a cheese sandwich and a bottle of Strasbourg beer. As he waited for his order, he watched the passing parade. Girls from the nearby perfume bars were gabbling in their high-pitched voices; an old man's tiny poodle was walking on its hind legs, for the coins of the lunch crowd; blowsy American women in print dresses complained about their feet to red-necked husbands who struggled with their cameras and pretended that they were not aiming at the French girls.

Why shouldn't he be jittery? He had left London, but not his problem. Whoever had ransacked Van Zordich's apartment knew about the microfilm. He had traced Magill from the Carlos Tower to Van Zordich's. Just as Preston Buck had traced him. But *who?* Perhaps even someone hired by the peculiar Mr Buck.

The waiter brought a cup of coffee and a dish of sugar cubes. Almost without thinking, Magill chose two cubes and, with his pen, inked the sides and made dice. He rolled. His number was nine . . . Or the ransack might have been done by a partner of

Barakati, the murdered Lebanese. Or somebody working for the Arab Sheikh. Perhaps someone Sandra Morgan could tell him about. Nine, a second time . . . Whoever it was, he had likely seen Van Zordich drive Magill off to the railroad station. He knew he could enter the jeweler's without challenge. Strange, though, that the burglar system had not sounded the alarm. He must have tampered with the wiring . . . Nine again . . . Having failed to find the microfilm, what would be his next step? Would he follow Magill? Would he be in Paris at this moment? Perhaps sitting at another table behind him? . . . Nine . . . There was one consolation, one truth to which he must cling: The only safety is to know that there is none.

'M'sieur is very, very lucky!'

The waiter was grinning at the cubes of sugar.

'Five parfait rolls! M'sieur is what we call *l'homme formidable!*'

Magill grinned back. All at once, he felt better.

He strolled into the American Bar a few minutes before six and went directly to his reserved table in the far corner. He ordered a martini. He sipped the drink slowly while he gazed around the room and noted the changes since his last visit. Georges was no longer smiling and nodding to his favorite customers. Henri was gone, too. The new bartenders seemed pleasant enough; but they were not the old faces. The room had been redecorated and softened. But the customers were the same. American businessmen, French café society, Argentine cattle money. Magill closed his eyes and listened to the hum of voices. It was a game he played whenever he was in the Ritz Bar. The volume of sound was just right for six o'clock. Half an hour earlier, it would have been only a light buzz. At six-thirty, it would be just comfortably loud. At seven, a shouting contest. At eight, silent as death. As he listened, Magill sensed a muting of the voices. He opened his eyes and discovered the reason.

Sandra walked toward him, threading her way among the

tables, where eyes stared, appraised, approved, or criticized—depending on the sex of the viewer. Other women in the room were more beautiful, but she was outstanding. A stole of white fox billowed around her shoulders. The dress beneath was white silk jersey. Her legs flashed in boots of silvered leather. She wore no earrings, no bracelets, no rings. Youth was her jewelry.

Magill rose and she seated herself across from him. She tugged the fox stole tightly around her as if she needed its protection. 'Quick!' she whispered, 'Order me anything!'

'Something wrong?'

'Entrances! God, how I hate them!' She was actually blushing.

Magill grinned. 'If there's any hating to be done, the women here are taking care of that.'

Sandra hurried through her first martini. It seemed to give her courage. She threw back the fur stole and revealed bare arms, graceful and very white. The top of the dress was a series of artful folds, tucked and drawn to outline and emphasize each breast. As for the back—where was it? She was naked to the lower waist.

She smiled guiltily. 'Pretty bitchy, isn't it?'

'Uh-huh. Pretty.'

'I just *had* to have it. And then the fur to hide under. I'll probably spend the evening sweltering or freezing.'

With the second martini, she grew more relaxed. Magill noted a subtle change in the girl. It was not the dress. Nor the hairdo—bangs and swirls of glittering red caught up in back. Nor the perfume. It was her voice. It was pitched lower, with a slight husky quality. Unconsciously, she was on stage. She was not so much talking as reciting. She listed her visits to a dozen boutiques, the excitement of meeting Cardin, her first sauna bath, the hours at Alexandre's, where the master had 'created' her hair.

Magill was relieved. He knew from his married days how many hours could be consumed on a new hairdo alone. Sandra's day had been too full for her to contact Farren. If Farren was in Paris. She could, of course, telephone him somewhere, or pick up a message. Damn it, he liked the girl. He wanted to trust her—if he had never seen her with Ward Farren. If she had not lunched with the Sheikh. If Preston Buck had not shown interest in her. If Van Zordich's place had not been ransacked. A wall of *ifs* separated them.

'But that's enough about me,' she concluded. 'Tell me about your day.'

'Oh, I just wandered around. Paris is a great city for walking. Don't set yourself a goal, don't follow a time schedule. That's the secret. You bump into old friends you'd never suspect. Matter of fact, I ran into one this afternoon. Preston Buck. The Canadian oilman.'

No reaction. No recognition. Test One completed.

Magill signaled the waiter for the check, then turned back to Sandra.

'I'm not going to be in Paris as long as I thought. Probably only a day or two.'

'Oh-h-h!' Her disappointment was genuine.

'So, tonight we're going to concentrate on the right things. No tourist traps, no Lido, no Crazy Horse, no discotheques. You can find carbon copies of them in any big city. Tonight, your first night in Paris, I want you to have special memories.'

Magill chose a restaurant which he remembered from his honeymoon. It was on the Left Bank, hidden away in a musty alley. The entrance was no more than a doorway with a lighted number overhead. Inside, it was a different matter. A staircase curved downward into a room of marble walls, crystal chandeliers and red velvet banquettes. There was a tiny dance floor. In an alcove, a jazz quintet played.

Magill ordered Belon oysters and a bottle of Chablis Grand Cru. By the time the waiter returned, Magill had steered the conversation around to Sandra's background. She had grown up, she said, in a small Ohio town. Her father was an attorney, her mother the head of the local PTA. An older sister was married, with two babies. Sandra loved her family, but thought their lives stale, unimaginative. Since she wanted more for herself, she ignored college in favor of an acting school in New York.

After the oysters, Magill ordered roast pheasant and Chambertin. Then he guided Sandra to the dance floor. The band was playing a slow bossa nova.

'So the theater is all you want in life?'

'For now.'

'What about marriage?'

'Someday.' She smiled. 'It would have helped, I'm sure.'

'In what way?'

'If I had hitched my wagon to a star, not to just another wagon. Or even a very public affair with some producer. That's what gets a girl ahead in show business.'

'In all business. For men, too.'

'You really think so?'

'Ben Franklin said it. "Early to bed, early to rise."'

She laughed delightedly, then snuggled closer into his arms.

They went back to their table. The waiter served the pheasant and poured the Chambertin. Sandra ate and drank with growing astonishment. After the salad and coffee, there was cognac in great crystal snifters. Magill found himself talking about his own past. About his first years, when he worked for his father; then being on his own, the ups and downs, the dry holes, the good ones. Finally he interrupted himself.

'How about some champagne?'

'After cognac?'

'I don't mean here. To take with us.'

Without waiting for her answer, he gestured the waiter to him and ordered two champagne glasses and a chilled magnum of Blanc de Blanc.

Sandra clapped her hands like a pleased child. A wonderful stroke. The grand gesture for her first night in Paris.

Magill grinned. 'You know what Napoleon said about champagne?'

She struck her forehead in mock anguish.

'Not another quotation!'

Perhaps he was sounding pompous. No matter. 'Napoleon said, and I quote: "Champagne is made to show etiquette to the door."'

Sandra gave him a sharp look, then arched an eyebrow. 'How about *two* bottles?'

Outside, it was raining. The evening had started warm and muggy, but neither of them had thought of rain. They splashed along the alley, arm in arm; Magill carried the magnum, Sandra, the glasses. Somewhere there had to be a taxi. As for waiting back at the restaurant for one to be summoned, Sandra had dismissed the idea as 'chicken'.

'So I get soggy hair! It'll dry. And so will the fur. Besides, this is my first Paris rain!'

Magill finally hailed down a taxi on Quai Malaquais. He ordered the driver to take them along the bank of the Seine to the Tour Eiffel. The driver grumbled and then, at the sight of franc notes, fell into the spirit of the thing.

They peered through the streaming taxi windows at the Tour and sampled the first of the magnum. Then off to circle the Arc de Triomphe. After that, down the Champs Elysées, past the Louvre, across the Pont d'Arcole, to gaze up at the dark mass of Notre Dame and to toast its continued good health. For Sandra, it was like a child's first visit to the circus. The places which she had read about, the backgrounds which she had seen in the films—they were there in solid stone and marble.

The rain stopped. Magill remembered that they were on the Ile de la Cité and he knew a very special spot. He ordered the driver to the Parc du Vert Galant, the little patch of greenery at the tip of the Ile which jutted out into the Seine.

Magill paid the driver and they walked out to the point. Yes, the bench was there. Very wet, but still there. They sat down, ignoring the seep through skirt and trousers. Magill filled the glasses. They drank in silence—Sandra with her curls straggling, Magill with his hair matted; she with her limp and discouraged fur, he with his soggy shoulders. They stared up at the moon which peered through the clouds and down at its reflection in the water. They watched a barge with its tug swim slowly past. They counted the lights on the houseboats anchored to their left, and wished each one goodnight as it winked out. At some time Magill turned her face up to his and kissed her. She accepted the kiss tentatively, then her arms circled his neck. Her fur slipped away from her bare back as she pressed herself to him.

There was a clatter, a smash of glass. They pulled apart and stared down at their feet. The rest of the champagne was spreading across the ground. They laughed, then looked solemnly at each other. Magill spoke first.

'Which side of the hotel does your room face?'

'The wrong side. The Rue Something.'

'Rue Cambon.'

'That's it.'

'Mine, onto the Place Vendôme.'

'With Napoleon up on that pedestal?'

'Yes.'

'It must be a lovely view.'

'It could be.'

10

'I'll always have a warm memory of Napoleon,' she murmured. 'He's watched us make love and hasn't frowned once.'

Magill raised up on one elbow and gazed across her body to the window and the bronze figure beyond in the moonlight. 'He hasn't frowned because he's looking the other way.'

'He is? How discreet!' She stared upward at the chandelier, which was a cascade of crystal. 'What perfect stage lighting.'

It was true. With the switches off, the bedroom still glowed with reflections. The moon, low in the west, gleamed from every window on the eastern side of the Place, reflected back into the bedroom and glinted downward from a hundred crystal drops and gave form and flattery to their nakedness.

Sandra turned her head and looked thoughtfully at Magill. 'How old are you?'

'I wondered when you'd ask.'

'Thirty?'

'Thirty-four. And you?'

'Twenty-one.' Then she laughed. 'Oh, what the hell, twenty-three.'

'I'm a little old for you.'

'You don't act it.'

'Thank you.'

'Besides, I like older men.'

'Even in bed?'

'Especially.'

'Why?'

'They've had enough women. They're not so struck with the wonder of the plumbing. And they know the right buttons to press.'

Magill smiled. Was this the same girl on the train, the aloof one who had slammed the compartment door in his face? He bent down and brushed his lips across her breasts. He took a nipple into his mouth. His tongue curled around the eager peak.

'Bite!' she whispered. 'Hard!'

He did. With each chew, she gasped her pleasure. Then, abruptly, she pulled away. Almost in one movement, she rolled him flat on his back and swung astride him. She grinned down impishly and crowed, 'Ride a cock horse!'

She lowered her head onto the pillow and drew deeply on the cigarette. It glowed bright and cast a momentary light over her face. The eyes were wide and brooding.

'Tell me why you followed me on the train.'

He had been waiting for this. 'Because I wanted you. Here. Like this.'

'That's *a* reason. Not the main one.'

'All right. What do you think it is?'

'I don't know. I've been waiting all evening for you to tell me. People are supposed to tell everything in bed. Don't be different.'

'Okay. I wanted to know about your brother.'

'You're kidding.'

'I'm not. How do you know he was murdered?'

'I don't have a brother! I told you! It was a publicity stunt!'

'Paid for by the Sheikh, for some phony movie production?'

'Yes!'

He would try another tack. 'Okay. I was jealous. I wanted to check on the other man.'

'There isn't! Haven't I proved that?'

'I didn't know. I thought you were coming to Paris to meet Farren.'

'Who?'

'Ward Farren. The man I saw you with in London. The Carlos Tower.'

'Oh—Tommy. Tommy Wilkins.'

'That's what he called himself. I hope that you told him the bit about your brother being murdered was a publicity stunt. And that he believed it.'

'Why shouldn't he?'

'He'd better.'

'You keep talking in circles.'

'Look. There *was* a plane explosion. The real thing. A lot of men were killed.' He paused for her reaction. There was none. 'If Farren was involved in that explosion, maybe caused it, he wouldn't let you hang around to point a finger.'

She took the cigarette from her lips and dropped it into the champagne glass on the night stand. The cigarette hissed and drowned. 'If you're trying to frighten me . . .'

'I am.'

'You sure got a lousy sense of timing.'

'I don't want anything to happen to you.'

'You mean that?'

'I do.'

'Hmm. Then I guess I ought to be grateful. Thanks.'

Magill reached for the telephone.

'Now what?'

'Ringing down for more champagne.'

'On the theory that what's in sober will come out drunk?'

'No. That what's in sober will come out wanton.'

She laughed. The tension was gone. 'I don't need champagne.' She pulled the pillow from under her head and positioned it under her hips. She raised her arms to Magill.

She stood at the open french windows and stared out into the night.

'It's raining again.'

He sighed. 'Rain? Or God sweating?'

She came back to the bed and sat beside him.

'So bitter, about me?'

'About you. But not bitter.'

'Then what?'

'I'm still trying to figure you out.'

'Me, too.' She threw back her shoulders and stretched. 'If God *is* sweating, it's not over this little girl. I'm not worth it.'

'Now who sounds bitter?'

She shook her head. 'I never thought I could be like this. Maybe it's the actress in me. Opening Night in Paris, the Big Role, the Fallen Woman.'

'Thanks for the compliment.'

'I didn't mean it that way. I'm sorry. I just never felt so—well—crazy. A sort of don't-give-a-damn, everything goes. Like—' She broke off.

'Yes?'

'Well, remember when we were out there on the bench, with the river all around?'

'When we were kissing?'

'Uh-huh. I wanted you to take me right there. I wanted to throw up my skirt and wiggle my bare ass at the moon and the Seine and the barges and the tugboats—and you. I wanted to wink my hole at the entire city of Paris.'

'Jesus, you're graphic!'

'Shocked? Darling, I said I'm an actress. I didn't say I was a lady.' She yawned and lay back with her head on Magill's chest. One hand reached down to fondle him. 'Dave, I wish I could tell you whatever it is you want to know. I just haven't got anything.'

'I'm glad you haven't.' He thought ahead, arranging the words carefully in his mind. They had to sound casual, if there was to be any surprise. 'I was just thinking about Sam Carter.'

'Who's Sam Carter? Oh, yes. The man on the train.'

'Sorry. I meant Preston Buck.'

'And who is Preston Buck?'

'I told you. The oilman I met today.'

'God, I'm really slipping! Still in sight and already out of mind!'

'Buck asked me to give you a message. He said your brother used to work for him. He's sorry about his death.'

He felt her hand tighten, then relax. She raised herself and stared down at him. 'You're making this up.'

'No. He said that if you want help, just ask him.'

He waited. Then suddenly she was laughing and punching his stomach. 'Oh, you idiot! He bit on it, too! He got it from the newspapers! Don't you see?'

'No, I don't. If it was all phony publicity, why does Buck act like he believes it? Why does he want to see you?'

She shrugged. 'He's your friend. You explain him.'

'I can't.'

'Then why expect me to?'

'Because I think you know. You're not Little Miss Innocent.'

She frowned. 'You're not so damned antiseptic yourself.'

'Don't toss the ball back to me. I want to know why you were working for the Sheikh.'

'I told you.'

'Why did you suddenly appear in the Savoy Restaurant with a whole tribe of Arabs?'

She looked away. 'You were brought there to check me out, weren't you?'

He pulled her face back to him. 'You were there to finger me. That's it, isn't it?'

'Yes! Yes! Yes!'

'All right. Why?'

She sighed hopelessly. 'I can't tell you. Oh, I knew there was something fishy. They told me I was doing a publicity stunt, and I believed it because I *wanted* to believe it. They said the big Arab boy was a movie producer, and I *wanted* to believe that, too.'

'For the money they were paying you?'

'The money! I was tired of being broke! Have you ever gone hungry? Do you know what it's like? Have you ever gone to the automat and bought a bun and poured chili over it because that's all you could pay for dinner? Or sneaked a cup from the next table and hoped it had some cold coffee in it and not just cigarette butts?'

'Sandy, you were working. You had a job. You were acting—'

'In London, yes! In New York—you want to know what it was like in New York? I waited counters! Drugstores, dimestores, cafeterias, moving to a new job—when I could find one—every time some greasy straw boss ran his hand up my skirt. Always hoping that the next casting call would include me. Too God-damned proud to go back home and let my family and my friends know I flunked Broadway. And then I *did* get a part. And it was no better. Every penny had to go on clothes, so I could look successful. So I could eat where producers and directors could see me and think I had something big on the burner. I was still broke. And you ask me why I worked for the Sheikh! Why I grabbed the thousand pounds!'

Magill sighed. 'I understand. At least, that part.'

'No! You just think you do. If I hadn't taken the money, some other girl would have. I was just lucky to be asked first. That thousand pounds was the first real money I'd ever seen. It meant a chance for me. A chance for memories. Without it, I wouldn't be here in Paris. I wouldn't be staying at the Ritz. I wouldn't have met you. I wouldn't have had tonight. I'd never know what it was like to have maids and waiters and dress designers bowing and smiling at me. Now I know. And it's good! It's lovely!'

'And after this? When the money's gone?'

It was a while before she spoke. Her voice was husky, resigned. 'Maybe nothing. Maybe just God's karate chop.'

She sank back in the bed and turned her face away. Magill heard a strangled sob. He bent over her and ran his fingers soothingly through her red hair. She was no longer the gay sophisticate; she was a naked child afraid of the dark. He kissed her softly on the cheek. She sniffed and straightened her head and looked up at him almost timidly.

'What's going to happen, Dave?'

'I don't know.'

The telephone was ringing. So was Magill's head. He rolled over and groaned. His eyelids wavered open. It was daylight. He closed his eyes. The telephone stopped ringing. He reached out for her and touched—nothing. His eyes opened again. She was gone. No. He could hear water splashing in the shower. He inhaled deeply. Her perfume, the scent of her, clung to the pillows and sheets. He smiled contentedly. This was what life was all about. The telephone rang again. All right, all right. He reached for the offending instrument. A woman's voice twittered into his ear. 'A call from London, m'sieur.' Magill pulled himself upright, sighing and scowling at this other reality.

'Dave? . . . Are you there, Dave?' It was Van Zordich.

'Yes. What's up?' He remembered that Van Zordich was not to telephone the hotel unless it was urgent.

'Inspector Bromley just rang me up. Has a flash from Interpol about your man.'

'The Amsterdam gentleman?'

'Yes. He flew into Beirut last night.'

'Beirut?'

'Lebanon. Positive identification.'

'Just a minute.'

Magill clapped a hand over the mouthpiece. The bathroom door had opened. Sandra, naked and dripping, was sidling toward him, dragging the big bath towel along the floor behind her. She smiled wickedly. 'Who is she?'

Magill shook his head and scowled. He kept his hand over the mouthpiece and strained to follow Van Zordich's words.

'. . . landed at Beirut using the same alias as in Amsterdam. Interpol says he cleared Immigration, then seems to have gone to ground.'

'Just a second, Harry!' Magill managed a quick off-and-on with his hand. She was beside him, grinding and bumping into his face.

'Sandy, for Christ's sake! Get dressed and out of here!'

She stuck out her tongue. She was not leaving. Magill slid around her and strode to the bathroom with the telephone. It had a long cord which he was able to slip under the door and close himself in. He spoke quietly into the mouthpiece.

'What could you find out about Sandra Morgan?'

'Probably not a fraction what you have. I take it, she's the interruption.'

'Yes. What is there about sex that makes women so damned energetic afterwards?'

Van Zordich chuckled. 'Wouldn't have it any other way, old

boy. She seems to be clean. No record, no bad associates, beyond those you know about. Now about coming back to London—'

'Beirut first.'

'*What!*'

'Beirut. Today.'

'Don't! Whatever you do, *don't!*'

'I have to, Harry. The man we found in my hotel room was from Beirut. The plane exploded on a flight from Cairo to Beirut—'

'I know. And the Sheikh at the Savoy has some important connections there. I found out that much about him. But, Dave, the Middle East is not like London and Paris. One mistake, and you can get your heart—'

The bathroom door opened and Sandra's head appeared. She puckered her lips into a kiss and then whispered: 'Tonight!'

The door closed again. Van Zordich was spelling a name.

'P-a-s-s-a-c-o-u-g-l-i. Alex Passacougli. Importer, exporter.'

'In Beirut?'

'Where else? Dave, will you pay attention!'

'I am. What about him?'

'I said, look him up! *If* you insist on going.'

'Can I trust him?'

'Absolutely! We've done business for years. But Dave, how am I going to explain this to Bromley? I had to tell him you're in Paris. He expects you back today.'

'You'll think of something.'

Van Zordich grunted. 'Well, let me know your airline and time of arrival, so I can alert Passacougli.'

'Will do.'

After Magill had hung up, he realized that he had forgotten one of the most important points. He had forgotten to ask about Preston Buck.

Magill ate a light breakfast in his rooms. It helped the queasiness in his stomach, but had no effect on the pounding in his temples. He doubted that Sandra felt much better, in spite of her gaiety.

That thought brought him around to a tally of the night before. The lovely redhead had been exuberantly generous in bed; she had given him one of the memorable nights of his life. Yet how much, really, had she shared with him? Her body had withheld no secrets, but what about her brain? She was a smart girl, an ambitious girl; and, by her own admission, greedy. She had told him nothing new, she had given him no leads on Farren. Perhaps she could not. Farren was in Beirut.

Magill was struck with the enigma of his own behavior. Here he was, proposing to dash clear across Europe and the eastern Mediterranean, as if it were no more than going across Paris. And once in Beirut, what made him think he could find Farren? Beirut was the capital of Lebanon, a country sandwiched between warring Arabs and Israelis. Everything would be confusion where a man might easily disappear permanently. There was another possibility. Beirut might be only a way-station to India or Hong Kong. Then what? Magill thought of the microfilm sewn into his lapel. It would be so easy to tear it out and burn it. Simply stuff the whole crazy thing and go home to California. Easy, but too late. He had to go on simply because he could not turn back.

He taxied to the Lebanese Embassy and secured his visa. A second taxi took him to the ticket office of Pakistan Airways, which he decided would be the least likely to be watched either in Paris or Beirut. Then he sent a cable to London, giving Van Zordich his flight number and time of arrival.

He returned to the Ritz and wrote two notes on the hotel stationery.

Sweet Sandy—
Forgive me, but tonight is impossible. I am flying to Munich.
Enjoy Paris as I know it will enjoy you. Luck.

Dave

The second note he addressed to Preston Buck, Orly Airport.

Dear Mr Buck:
Business requires me to leave for Beirut immediately. Will contact you on my return which will be three days at the latest. Regards.

David Magill

He took Sandra's note to the room clerk and asked that it be placed in her box. Then he went to the concierge, where he asked that the note to Preston Buck be sent to Orly, by special messenger, to be hand-delivered to Mr Buck aboard his private plane.

He checked out of the Ritz immediately afterward. He whiled away the day on the Left Bank, where he was certain he would not run into Sandra, and, at four-thirty P.M. he taxied to Orly.

The great Boeing trundled out onto the runway. It lumbered past hangars and service buildings, then swung around for takeoff. The whine of the jets increased to a full-throated roar. The plane surged forward. Magill pressed his face against the window and searched for a glimpse of Preston Buck's private plane. It was gone.

At Rome, Magill's flight was scheduled for a thirty-five-minute stop before onto Athens, Beirut, Kabul and Karachi. Time enough for him to leave the plane and sprint into the Terminal Building and place a telephone call to Munich Airdrome. He made the call person-to-person. He listened tensely to the Italian and German operators gabbling to each other, then the Airdrome operator and, almost immediately, a man's voice helloing at the other end. There was no mistaking that voice. Magill hung up.

Now he knew. His note to Preston Buck had said Beirut. His note to Sandra had said Munich. The wily Mr Buck had rejected the truth in favor of the lie—relayed to him by Sandra Morgan.

II

The jet shuddered and banged from the sudden drop of air speed. Magill looked at his wristwatch; it was past midnight. He peered out the window and saw the splash of lights that was Beirut rushing upward toward the plane. The moonlight emphasized the high bluffs arcing the bay and picked out the dark forms of freighters at anchor in the roadstead. Off to the south, there was a small cluster of lights which was Sidon; and, to the north, a smaller cluster, which was Byblos. To the east, the mountains of Lebanon hulked like a great black camel kneeling in sleep.

As Magill went down the steps from the plane, the heat, after the cool of the air-conditioned cabin, felt solid, three-dimensional. It was like walking through very warm, invisible cotton. He followed the other passengers who had de-planed into the cool of the terminal building. The immigration officer leafed through his passport and stamped his visa. The customs man ran his hand through his case and chalked his inspection mark. Magill was on his own. He picked up his case and pushed through the swinging glass doors into the waiting room. Considering the hour, he thought, the terminal was remarkably alive. The passengers who had preceded him, all male, were being embraced and kissed by other males. Groups of women stood shyly to one side. Porters and taxi drivers and fruit vendors shouted for customers. And everywhere, Magill noted, there were armed guards and soldiers with rifles slung over their shoulders.

Magill's eyes circled the room. Somewhere there must be a public telephone. Before going to a hotel, he had decided, he should contact Alexander Passacougli, assuming that the man was listed in the directory. Then, just as he spied the telephone, someone collided with him. A pair of arms flew around his neck and a woman's face pressed against his.

'*Ahala washala! Ahala washala!*'

He pulled back to survey the surprise. She was young, black-haired, dark-eyed. Her European street suit was pale lemon, her tarboosh, also pale lemon, tilted rakishly over one brow.

She clutched him again. He was conscious of a heavy, musky perfume.

'*Humdillah be-majeek bis-salami!*' Then her voice dropped to a whisper. 'We are cousins. Keep your voice down.'

She jerked his arm. 'Sssh! They may be watching! Take my arm and walk with me.'

Magill stiffened. 'Who are *they*?'

'I'll tell you in the car. Come! And smile! You are glad to see me.'

He took her arm, then dropped it. He did not like this. He remembered being shanghaied at another airport.

'I'm not going anywhere. I don't know you.'

'Very good! Why don't you shout it?' she hissed. 'I am a friend of Mr Passacougli. Mr Van Zordich telephoned him.'

'When?'

'Today!'

He relaxed. 'I'm sorry.' He took her arm and they walked smilingly out of the terminal. They pushed through a crowd of boys who were hawking soft drinks and postcards, and went toward the parking area where she said she had left her car.

'How did you recognize me?'

'The immigration officer. When he cleared you, he took off his hat and scratched his head.'

'I didn't notice.'

'I did. I made that arrangement. Chantal Larrigues.'

'Pardon?'

'My name. Chantal Larrigues.'

Then it happened. The boys they had passed came yelling after the pair. One charged, head down at Magill. Another leaped for Chantal's handbag. Others circled, butted, struck, and kicked. 'Run!' Chantal cried. 'Get away!' Instead, Magill let fly with one foot and caught a boy in the chest: his knee connected with another's groin. As he swung around to protect Chantal, he saw her bring the heel of her shoe down on a head and follow it up with a vicious kidney punch. Another boy went flat beneath the hurtling weight of a huge black Great Dane. Moments later the gang had fled into the night.

'Your passport,' Chantal panted. 'It is gone?'

Magill felt inside his breast pocket. 'No. It's okay.'

'Good!' She slipped her pump back onto her foot. 'They did not want my handbag. That was pretend.'

'Just my passport?'

'Or your money. They knew you were a *faranji*. An American. You would have many dollars.'

Magill checked his coat again. 'Nothing missing.' He eyed the Great Dane, which appeared ready to take on Magill. 'Yours, I hope.'

She nodded. 'Saladin is my private army. But he was supposed to guard the auto.'

The auto was a bright red Maserati sportster. Chantal snapped her fingers and the Great Dane jumped over the back of the seat into a compartment that had been designed for him. Magill eased himself into his bucket seat and gamely tried to ignore the hot breath at his ear.

She swung the Maserati onto the airport road and then the expressway toward Beirut. She drove with a heavy foot, with the assurance of a racing driver. Someone else was driving fast, Magill noted. A black Cadillac limousine whined past them, then pulled in front.

The girl saw Magill's frown. 'Mr Passacougli thought we should have an escort.'

'We could have used them in the parking lot.'

'They were there. But Saladin was enough.' She nodded toward the rear-view mirror. 'Also Mr Passacougli's.'

Magill ducked his head around the grinning Saladin and saw a second black Cadillac following a hundred yards behind.

'Because of the *they* you mentioned?'

'Three men. Mr Passacougli got word they have been waiting

for someone since yesterday morning.'

'But I didn't decide to come here until today.'

'Then perhaps they are interested in someone else. But one must not risk. That is why Mr Passacougli did not come himself. He would attract the eyes.'

'I'd say you would, too.'

She acknowledged the compliment with a shrug.

'They are used to me. I fly in and out very often.'

This Mr Passacougli, Magill decided, was a man with the means to command. Cadillacs, bodyguards, and Miss Chantal Larrigues. He looked at her carefully. When she had intercepted him, in the terminal, he had been so taken off guard that he had not properly appreciated her. The cheekbones were high, the lips full and sensual without being coarse. In the flash of oncoming headlights, he noted a small mole just below the flare of her right nostril. He compared her mentally with the girl he had left in Paris. Sandy was pretty, but this one was a genuine beauty of great class. He stared at the wrists which grasped the steering wheel. They were slender but strong and gleamed with gold bracelets set with diamonds and fire opals. 'A friend of Mr Passacougli.' A very close friend, indeed.

She gave him a sidewise smile, as if reading his thoughts. 'Yes, I like Beirut. I've been here almost one year. And I met Mr Passacougli on the Riviera. Cap d'Antibes.'

Magill chuckled. 'People are always asking you?'

She nodded. 'Also, my father was French, my mother Turkish.'

'You speak excellent English.'

'A Swiss school. I was a roommate with an American girl and an English. I visited them at home. London and San Francisco.'

'I'm from San Francisco.'

'Yes. You talk with the hard *r*.'

'A good ear!'

The Maserati swept along the Corniche and then slowed at the approach to St George's Bay. They were passing through the *quartier* known as Ain-Mreisse. The yachts in the harbour, the sprawl of beachside hotels and apartments, all looking like upended dominoes, reminded Magill of Miami Beach and Cannes. He read the names of the hotels: the Phoenicia, the St George, the Palm Beach, the Alcazar, the Excelsior—and wondered aloud at which he should stay.

'It is arranged,' the girl said. 'You are Mr Passacougli's guest.'

'Oh, I don't want to impose.'

'And you do not want to insult. Mr Passacougli does not invite often.'

'In that case, I'd like to know something about my host.'

'Yes?'

'Van Zordich said something about him being in the import and export business.'

'True.'

'What's his line?'

She frowned. 'Line?' It was a word outside her experience.

'What does he deal in?'

'Everything.'

'That covers a lot of ground.'

'It was meant to.'

The economy of her answers was frustrating. Perhaps if he turned the conversation to himself . . .

'I guess you'd like to know something about me.'

'I do.'

'Oh?'

'Mr Passacougli explained.'

'I see.' And there it ended.

The city was all around them now. Magill felt the old tingle of excitement which came with his first view of any new city. Contrasts were everywhere. One moment, in the *quartier* Bab Edriss, he was admiring the marble facades of banks whose home offices were in London, Paris, New York and Moscow; the next moment, he was looking at a donkey and its turbaned owner both asleep in a garbage-strewn doorway. New office buildings of ugly poured concrete were flank to flank with Turkish mosques and minarets. Neon signs flashed in French and scroll-like Arabic. At almost every intersection there was either a police car or a pair of military sentries with rifles and fixed bayonets. Beirut was

Magill thought, a city under siege.

The Maserati and the two Cadillacs circled the Place des Canons with its Riviera-like park and fountain and towering date palms. Then on up an alley where sagging balconies almost touched overhead, where the names of girls were spelled out in flashing light bulbs and neons, and where dark figures leaned over the balconies and called down their prices and special talents. Finally, the cars came out of the city proper and began to climb a massive hill. When they reached the crest, they swung to the right and flashed past a series of walled villas. This was Sursock, the preserve of Beirut's great families. The front Cadillac slowed and came to a stop in front of a pair of high iron gates. The gates swung wide—radio-controlled, Magill guessed—and the three cars went up a driveway lined by tall date palms. Ahead, on a rise, was a huge stone house whose architecture reminded Magill of the mansions of Bel Air and Palm Beach. Every room on all three floors appeared to be lighted; windows glowed red, green, blue and yellow.

The driveway divided. The two Cadillacs branched off and disappeared around the side of the house. The Maserati continued on and glided under a columned portico. The Great Dane leaped from the car and barked thunderously at the front door, a towering affair of cedar studded with brass bosses. The door opened and there was an outrush of cool air. A Negro—tall, turbaned, robed and slippered—bowed his welcome. Chantal, with the dog padding beside her, led Magill along an entry hall which was lined by stone pillars that rose into pointed Arabic arches. Room after room led from each side. Magill had an impression of high ceilings, varicolored glass and brass chandeliers, Persian rugs and gilt furniture.

Finally, they reached what appeared to be the central room. It was a big rectangle, opened to the third floor, and bordered on three sides by arcades. A green marble staircase curved upward at the far end. The furniture was a clutter of divans and gilt chairs, taborets of teak and circular brass coffee tables. Persian rugs were on the floor, and a Gobelin tapestry hung from the second floor. In the farthest corner of this astounding room

Magill saw a bald man seated behind a refectory table. He was talking into a telephone which had a bulky square mouthpiece designed so that none could overhear. The man waved a hand in greeting, gestured Magill to one of the divans, and went on with his conversation. Chantal tinkled a hand-bell and, almost immediately, the Negro appeared who had let them into the house. He bore a tray on which there were tiny coffee cups, a miniature silver samovar, and dishes stacked with sweet cakes. Chantal filled the cups, handed one to Magill and carried another to Alexander Passacougli. She returned and seated herself on the divan and watched Magill take his first swallow of the coffee. It was more than strong, more than candy-sweet; it was so thick that Magill felt he should not drink it, he should chew it. Chantal smiled at his expression and fed a sweet cake to the Great Dane. 'You will get used to it,' she said. She crossed her knees and her skirt rode up her thighs. Magill noted that the legs were superb, and that she did not adjust her skirt when she saw his eyes on her. He glanced quickly toward Passacougli. He appeared to be in his early fifties. His face was round and with his baldness gave the impression of Ho Tai, the Chinese god of good luck. The face was never at rest; it was a parade ground of expressions. Quick smiles, dark frowns, grins and scowls; cheeks sucked in and puffed out; lips chewed and puckered and pouted.

Finally, Passacougli put down the telephone and Chantal crossed to his desk and began speaking in rapid guttural Arabic. Whatever she was saying Passacougli took in with a series of grunts and frowns. When she had finished, he bounded to his feet and came toward Magill with arms outstretched.

'My dear friend! So good! So good!'

He pumped Magill's hand and clapped his shoulder and repeated the 'so good's'. His accent was a curious blend; perhaps Greek out of Armenian by Italian. He was short, Magill realized; not even as tall as Chantal. Passacougli turned to her and said, 'Thank you, my dear. Goodnight.' She was being dismissed. She held out her hand to Magill, then snapped her fingers for Saladin. As she went up the marble staircase, Magill thought again, Really fantastic legs!

'And now, my friend, we have much to tell each other.' Passacougli slipped his hand around Magill's arm and guided him to a chair beside the big desk. Magill started to speak, but Passacougli put a finger to his lips. 'Wait!' He pressed a series of buttons on the desk and immediately the room was a confusion of sounds. From a hidden speaker in one wall issued organ music; from another, a man chanting the Koran; from another, a piano concerto; from still another, the surging roar of a racetrack. Magill smiled to himself. So the man was afraid that his servants would eavesdrop or that his house might be bugged—but this was really too much.

Passacougli leaned forward so that his words could be heard. 'Our friend Van Zordich, he has asked me to protect you.'

'Protect?'

'That was his word. Would you like to say help?'

'Yes. It's not so dramatic.'

Passacougli grunted. 'I think it is dramatic to find a man murdered in one's hotel room.'

'Van Zordich told you?'

He nodded. 'Ahmid Barakati was not his true name. I have made a small investigation. He was not Lebanese. He was Afghan.'

'And not a businessman in the usual sense of the word.'

'No. But a man of many talents. Smuggling, stealing, spying, killing. Whatever one paid him to do, he did.'

'Any idea who was paying him in London?'

'No idea. But he was not one to work alone. He had friends. It is my opinion—' Passacougli paused and pursed his lips, as if trying to decide which series of expressions he should next run through. He settled on a solemn smile. 'It is my opinion that these friends were waiting for you at the airport. Yes, for two days.'

Magill shook his head. 'That's what Miss Larrigues told me. But I decided on Beirut only today. Hardly more than twelve hours ago, Paris time.'

Passacougli's smile grew arch. 'So? Perhaps you turn around the cause and the effect. It is possible these men wished you in

Beirut. They *willed* you here. They *caused* you to come. You, then, are the effect.'

Magill hesitated. 'No, I thought it up myself. I came here to find a man.'

'Van Zordich said.'

'Did he tell you his name?'

'Ramsay. Colin Ramsay, of Brisbane, Australia.'

'He also called himself Thomas Wilkins. His real name is Ward Farren. An oil geologist. He was supposed to be aboard that Anglo-Tex plane—'

Passacougli cut him off. 'Van Zordich told me everything.'

Magill frowned. 'How do you know it was everything?'

Passacougli slapped the desk in delight. 'You are right. Your brain works very Lebanese. Yes. I will enjoy our time together.' Then he was solemn again. 'Why does this Farren come to Beirut?'

'He's looking for a buyer for the microfilm. If Van Zordich told you about that.'

'Of course. But why Beirut?'

'Because the Arab States deposit their royalties in your banks. And all the oil companies. The money is in secret accounts, like Switzerland. Easy to collect, easy to move out.'

Passacougli nodded understanding. 'There is one point I must be clear about. I understand that you found only part of the microfilm. Perhaps one-half . . .'

'Right.'

'You bring that half with you?'

'No.'

'You swear it?'

'I swear.'

Magill lied without consciously deciding to do so. It was automatic, instinctive; as if his father were alive and standing beside him and repeating his favorite maxim: 'Never undress until you are ready to go to bed.'

Passacougli considered for a moment. He clucked his tongue and hummed to himself. Then he leaned close to Magill. 'This is how we proceed. Tonight I shall telephone our newspapers. I shall give them a story about you, that you are my house-guest.'

'Well, let's not advertise it.'

'But yes! You are in danger.'

'That's what I mean.'

'So Beirut must know that you are my dear friend. Then you will not be touched.'

'Just like that?'

'I assure you. This story will also say that you are an important oil man. This will be most provocative. Beirut will read this and Beirut will say: "Aha! Passacougli is going into oil. He and this Mr Magill are doing a deal." You see, for us, the Lebanese, the deal is everything. An arrangement, very involved, very complicated, with much artistry—that is what we admire. It is the spice of life.'

Magill gloomed to himself. The hell with Passacougli's spice of life. He could get his jollies some other way.

'No. It won't work.'

'Ah?'

'It won't get what I'm after. Farren. The microfilm.'

Passacougli threw out his arms. 'Forgive me! I forget that you do not know Beirut. It is eyes and ears and tongues. Everyone will want to be a part of our mysterious deal. Men will call me. "*Passacougli, my dear friend. Why am I not included in this arrangement with the American? What is your price?" And I shall answer: "I want a man. A Mr Ward Farren. Deliver him to me. That is the price.*"'

Magill took a deep breath. 'Okay. I guess there's nothing to lose. Now if you don't mind—'

'Of course. No more talk. Now we drink.'

'Not for me. Just sleep.'

They rose from the desk, then Passacougli placed a finger on Magill's arm. 'Forgive me again. Chantal made report of the trouble at the airport, the boys who attacked you.'

So that was what she was telling him in Arabic. Magill shrugged. 'It was just one of those things.'

'Perhaps. What did they steal from you?'

'Nothing.'

'Very well, then what did they *give* you?'

'Look, the kids were probably just anti-American.'

'Please go through your pockets. As a favor to me, sir.'

Magill felt ridiculous. Passacougli simply would not knock off the melodramatics. He ran his hand through both outside coat pockets. Only his cigarette lighter. His inside coat pockets. A pack of cigarettes, his billfold, passport, pen and pencil. His left trouser pocket. A handkerchief. His right trouser pocket. A few small coins. His right hip pocket. He felt something small, about the size of an almond. There was a sudden emptiness in his stomach.

'You find nothing?'

'Nothing.'

He closed the guestroom door and listened to Passacougli's footsteps fade down the marble hallway outside. Why, Magill wondered, had he lied to the man? Not once, but twice. Surely, he could trust Passacougli. Van Zordich had vouched for him. And yet . . .

Magill glanced around the room. More Persian carpets, more crystal chandeliers, a huge bed with the satin coverlet turned down. Overhead, a ceiling fan, relic of the days before air conditioning. He walked to the tall french windows and opened them. In the distance, below Sursock Hill, he could see minarets fingering the night. A few scattered lights still glowed from the hotels around St George's Bay. From somewhere up the Bay, to his right, he heard the growl of invisible speedboats bringing gamblers home from the Casino du Liban. Magill sighed. California and that oil-less oil well seemed light-years away.

Then he remembered the object in his hip pocket. He dug it out and carried it over to the bedside lamp. It was paper, tightly balled. He picked at it carefully until he had it smoothed out. It was India paper, printed on both sides in English. He held it up to the light. It was a page torn from a Bible. Verses from the Book of Ezekiel. Beneath certain of the words there were tiny pinpricks.

12

An air-raid siren? The shriek of jet motors? Some monster in its death throes? Magill yanked himself upright in bed, although he was still half-asleep, and swiveled his head to learn the direction of the ungodly sound. The first gray of dawn lighted the room. The yelping, shrieking, wailing, was human. It was mechanical, too. A public-address system. Not one, but dozens, all over Beirut. Magill relaxed. Of course. The call of the muezzin. 'God is most great! There is no God but Allah and Muhammed is his prophet! Come to prayer and to security!'

There was knocking on the bedroom door, then it opened. A white turban and robe bowed to him.

'Good morning, effendi. I am Yussef.'

Magill recognized the face—black and long and thin, elongated in the style of an El Greco. It was the porter who had admitted him to the house the night before. Magill pulled himself upright and surveyed the brass tray which Yussef was placing beside the bed. A half melon, orange-fleshed and sweet-smelling, toast in a silver rack, the promise of bacon and eggs steaming under a covered dish. Yussef's face broke into a smile at Magill's reaction. He bowed and was gone.

Magill poured himself a second cup of coffee. In spite of its syrupy sweetness, he was learning to tolerate it. Life was definitely looking up. Then he thought of the page from the Bible. His hand darted under his pillow and retrieved it. He held the paper to the light and considered the words which had been pin-pricked.

> . . . the top of a rock . . . a place to spread nets upon . . . with silver . . . they traded . . . and all the pilots of the sea, shall

come down from their ships, they shall stand upon the land

Magill lit a cigarette. What did the message mean? Who had ordered it placed in Magill's pocket? Someone who knew last night that Magill was going to arrive at Beirut Airport.

At least, he told himself, something was happening. He was not pursuing a mirage. The message was real, and it gave reality to Magill himself. Someone recognized his existence and his purpose. He lit a second cigarette, forgetting that he already had one. Last night he should have been straightforward with Passacougli. He should have handed over the pellet of paper and let Passacougli get to work on it. Instead Magill had let precious hours slip by.

'I asked you if the street-boys gave you something. You said they did not. You were very clear about it.'

They were again at the desk in the living-room. Passacougli was quietly furious. Magill had not trusted him.

'I was wrong. I thought I had checked every pocket,' Magill lied. 'The question is, do we take this seriously?'

'We take it, yes.' Passacougli pressed the series of buttons on the desk and the speakers began to bray again their confusion of sounds. He squinted at the wrinkled paper in his hand. 'Every Lebanese knows by heart this book of Ezekiel. It is our history, our prophecy. The glories of Tyre and Sidon and the calamities which Ezekiel called down upon them.'

'Then whoever sent this page was Lebanese?'

'Perhaps. He hints that he wishes to trade with silver.'

'My silver or his silver?'

Passacougli shrugged. 'Perhaps he has something of value. Information.' Passacougli returned to the page from Ezekiel. '"The top of a rock . . . a place to spread nets"—yes, that is the place of rendezvous. But our coast is all rocks and places to spread nets.' He chewed his lips and pressed his tongue against his cheek. '"All the pilots of the sea shall come down from their ships, they shall stand upon the land." That is clear. You are to go to this place by boat.'

'That's no help. Unless I know where.'

Passacougli scowled at the paper again. 'Another mystery. These pinpricks under the numbers of the verses: 2, 9, 26.'

'I can't figure those, either. They don't tie into anything. No meaning at all.'

'There is. There must be. Two, nine, six . . .'

'Maybe a date? Like in a memo or letter. Two, nine, twenty-six. That would be February 9—' Magill broke off. 'No. Hardly the year 1926.' He puzzled a moment more, then snapped his fingers. 'Isn't this September 25?'

'Yes.'

'Okay. Ninth month, twenty-sixth day. That's tomorrow! And the two—that could mean two o'clock. Either A.M. or P.M.'

Passacougli grunted. 'What fool would rendezvous in daylight? No. It is two, tomorrow morning.' He eyed Magill carefully. 'Would you go to such an appointment?'

'Certainly.'

'It might not be safe.'

'I haven't been safe since the day I reached London. But that's beside the point. Where in Christ's name am I to go?'

'There will be a second message, I think. This is to prepare you, to give you time.'

'And meanwhile?'

'I shall consider various possibilities. I shall take precautions.' Passacougli saw Magill's expression. He smiled. 'Not to worry, my friend. Your task is simple: to enjoy the company of Chantal I will ask her to prepare a divertissement.'

The red Maserati was waiting under the *porte cochère*. Chantal, dressed in cool lime and barefoot sandals, was already behind the wheel. Magill slid into the bucket seat beside her, and Saladin, appearing from nowhere, leaped into the car and rested his great jaw on Magill's shoulder. Chantal gunned the motor, and they shot down the winding drive and joined the two waiting Cadillacs.

They wove through the congestion of the Bourj Centrale, then onto the main road leading toward the sea. There, they swung onto the waterfront expressway and headed south. Magill asked where they were going. To Saida, Chantal replied, the ancient Phoenician port known as Sidon, the furthest north that Christ had preached. It would be a good place, she said, to make a picnic.

The waves of the Mediterranean curled toward them on the right, date palms and orange groves whipped past on the left. At intervals they met camels and oxen plodding under great burdens of timber and brick. Around the neck of each beast was a rope with a bell and a blue bead to ward off the evil eye. The drovers trudged alongside, sometimes a lone man—pantalooned, booted, turbaned—sometimes whole families.

They overtook a convoy of trucks carrying soldiers and passed several tanks lumbering south.

'This morning,' Chantal said, 'there was report of new fighting on the border.'

'Palestinian guerrillas?'

'And Israelis. Thirty miles south of Sidon.'

'Almost close enough to drop in on our picnic.'

'Not today. But soon.'

They drove on in silence, and then abruptly Chantal asked: 'You are married?'

'No.'

'But you have been.'

'Does it show?'

'A woman always leaves her mark.'

Magill smiled to himself. The female's primary interest. Always the other woman, not the man himself.

'How about you?' he asked.

She ignored the question. 'Down there,' she nodded, 'that is Sidon.'

It was a jumble of buildings, cream and ochre, a tumble of reddish tiled roofs stabbed here and there by white minarets. It was the remains of the great Phoenician port which had sent its ships to trade with Rome and Gaul and the island called Anglia. It was now, as Magill looked down on it, nothing more than a quiet fishing village.

The Maserati and the Cadillacs wound down into the town and passed through dark sultry alleys. They came out onto the harborfront and Magill saw a quay with tiers of houses climbing behind and a breakwater with a rusting navigation beacon. Farther along, there was a stone causeway which thrust seaward and connected with a crumbling ruin of stone. This, Chantal said, was *Qalaat el Bahr*—the Castle of the Sea. It had been built by the French Crusaders over seven hundred years before.

'It is a good ruin,' she added, 'because it does not make one feel small. It is better than Baalbeck, which is very big, or Byblos, which is full of religious fools.'

'You mean, a monastery?'

She shook her head. 'Tourists. They go there because the word Bible comes from the name *Byblos*. It is said that the papyrus—'

'Christ Almighty!'

She stared at Magill. His face was flushed with excitement.

'I've got to talk to Passacougli!'

'It is not possible.'

'It's important! Turn around. Let's get back to Beirut.'

She gave him a patient smile. 'Mr Passacougli is not available. Your importance will have to wait.'

Magill sighed. At least, now he knew where he must be at two A.M., September 26.

The three cars pulled to a stop at the foot of the stone causeway. Chantal slid from behind the wheel and Saladin vaulted after her. As Magill joined them he saw a man in a striped robe approach from one of the Cadillacs. It was Yussef. He bowed to Chantal and held out two small packets wrapped in yellow silk. She took one and handed the other to Magill.

'Your bathing trunks,' she said.

They started out along the causeway. After several hundred yards, they came to a wall of great stone blocks, the outer defense of the fortress. They went through a high arched portal and came out into what must have once been a courtyard. Beyond, Magill saw the massive tower of gray and golden stone which was the seaward limit of the castle. Chantal nodded toward a crumbling archway in the great tower: she would go there to change.

Magill watched her go, with Saladin at her side. He stared around resentfully. The castle was a melancholy place and steamingly hot. What a lousy waste of time. He wanted to see Passacougli. He wanted to get on the trail of Ward Farren. Byblos and Farren were linked together somehow, he was sure of it. Otherwise, why the message?

He lit a cigarette and wandered toward a series of stone steps which went down to the water. Below him he saw, among the slimy stones, a tidal pool in which a starfish swayed languidly. Then a pebble bounced off his shoulder. He turned.

Chantal stood, hands on hips, and enjoyed Magill's startled expression. He had never seen such a minimal bikini, nor a body which so deserved the proud display. The hips were narrow, yet full in the buttocks; the waist, slender, almost fragile, emphasizing breasts of surprising fullness.

'So? You will not swim?'

Magill grinned. The idea seemed suddenly attractive.

They swam side by side for a while, reveling in the warm water which foamed around their bodies. They floated on their backs and watched the contrails of invisible aircraft. White traceries circled and darted and spun as if unseen spiders were weaving gigantic webs across the sky. In reality, it was a dogfight.

They swam back to the landing, toweled, and sat down cross-legged on the Persian rug which Yussef had spread over the stones. They watched him unpack the picnic hamper. There were slices of lambs' tongues and cooked prawns, bunches of purple grapes and dishes of boiled wheat and tomatoes, exotic looking foods which Chantal called *tabbouli* and *hummos bi tehini*. There were even crystal shot glasses into which Yussef poured smoky white *araq* from a thermos. A second thermos contained water, which he poured into a dish for Saladin. That done, he retreated a discreet distance and squatted on the stones.

They ate with enthusiasm and drank shot after shot of the *araq* and enjoyed the sweet, hot sensation as it raced from mouth to stomach. Between liquor and heat, Magill began to feel dizzy. He stared up at the sky. The contrails had disappeared. He heard Chantal say, 'No. I shall never marry.'

He glanced down at her. She had settled back on her elbows.

'Why not?'

'One must be careful of the years one owns. They are precious.' She arched her back and straightened her shoulders. The effect was not lost on Magill. Her breasts were magnificent. 'Life is short,' she added. 'And youth is more short.' She looked at him steadily, then her dark eyes glittered slowly over his body, taking obvious inventory.

Magill stirred restlessly. He felt the old familiar tension in his loins.

'Tell me about Byblos.'

She frowned. She reached for a prawn and tossed it to Saladin. 'It interests?'

'There must be something there besides religious fools.'

They heard steps behind them and then an apologetic cough. It was Yussef. He bowed and said something in his singsong Arabic. Chantal nodded and turned to Magill.

'It is the auto telephone. Mr Passacougli wishes to see you. At once.'

The instructions from Passacougli were that Magill was to return to Beirut in one of the Cadillacs. It would be less conspicuous than the red Maserati. Yussef was to accompany him and take him to the meeting place.

It turned out to be a huge brick warehouse. Yussef led Magill into the dark interior and along first one passage-way and then another. The place was furiously hot and smelled of rat dung. They came out into a large open space, at the end of which there was a long trestle table. A bare lightbulb dangled from a rafter directly over the head of the man at the table. It was Passacougli talking into a telephone. It was almost a duplicate, Magill thought, of the scene when he had first met the man the night before. This time, Passacougli wore no coat; his shirt was open to the waist, his sleeves were rolled above the elbows. He glanced up and motioned Magill forward. Yussef turned and disappeared.

Again like the night before, Magill waited and surveyed his surroundings. On one side, there was a line of grand pianos; on the opposite, stacks of American air-conditioning units; directly behind Passacougli, a jumble of Italian refrigerators, Japanese television sets and motorcycles, and even a pile of elephant tusks.

Passacougli put down the telephone and beamed across the table.

'My small change, Mr Magill. The matters of value are elsewhere. If you wish a race horse, I would take you to my stables at the track. A beautiful woman, then to my cabaret. Gold bullion or diamonds, to my vault at the bank.'

'All this on your own, or with partners?'

'My own. I was a very poor boy, Mr Magill.' He raised his eyebrows as if he expected the fact to be challenged. 'I decided to be rich. But how does one begin? One must possess capital. So I began as most do in this world. By stealing.' He paused to enjoy the effect on Magill. 'One little package of heroin. That was my capital. After that, I bought. I imported heroin from Turkey and exported it to France.'

'At least you're honest about it.'

'Should I be ashamed? As St Paul did not say, but as Passacougli discovered, the love of evil is the root of all money.' He chuckled. 'Now I have a great deal of the root. I am the reformed thief. I can afford to be.'

Somehow Magill was relieved. A reformed thief might be trusted more than the honest man who has not yet met his temptation. It was time to get down to business.

'What did you want to see me about?'

Passacougli glanced over both shoulders, as if he expected eavesdroppers. He picked up a pencil and wrote something on a scratch pad. He pushed the pad across to Magill. There was only one word: BYBLOS.

Magill started. 'That's what I wanted to tell you.'

'Ah? You deciphered the meaning?'

'The page was from a Bible.'

Passacougli beamed. 'Splendid! It is as if you are my own son!'

'How long have you known?'

'From the beginning. I did not tell you because I wished you to make a holiday, to be relaxed, refreshed.' He paused and eyed Magill. 'The picnic was pleasant?'

'Very pleasant.'

'Chantal is good at entertainments, would you say?'

'Very good.' Magill squirmed mentally. The questions were as uncomfortable as the sweat trickling from his armpits.

'You know, of course, that you cannot go to this place alone.'

'I have to. I think that's the way they want it.'

Passacougli held up his hand for silence. He reached across the table to a tiny radio. He tuned it to a talk program and turned up the volume. Then he returned to Magill.

'This message you received, it speaks of trading with silver. Someone, I think, wishes to sell you information about your man Farren.'

'I'm hoping that.'

'The message requires you to approach by sea, does it not?'

'Yes.'

'So I have made arrangements. Tonight, you and I and Chantal, we go to the Casino du Liban. It will appear that we intend an evening of gaming. But we shall go in my own speedboat. From the casino, my boat will be at Byblos in fifteen minutes.'

Magill shook his head. 'No boat. That's what they expect. I want to come up from their rear. By land.'

Passacougli tapped his nose slyly. 'Again, it is as if we have one brain! The speedboat will go without you. It will be a decoy.'

'Then how do I get from the casino to Byblos?'

'It is arranged. Now, I must know if you possess a gun.'

Magill hesitated. 'I hope it's not going to be that kind of a night.'

'Do you possess a gun?'

'Yes.'

'You will carry it tonight. Also—' Passacougli opened a drawer and took out the smallest revolver Magill had ever seen. It was hardly more than four short barrels welded together. An assassin's weapon, Passacougli said, made in Turkey. The calibre was only twenty-five millimeters, but very effective at close range. Passacougli produced a toy-sized holster, to which were attached two straps. It was a crotch holster, he explained, to be worn in the groin, where it would not be found in a routine search. If Magill should lose his own gun, or it was taken from him, he would have a second chance.

'All I do is unzip my fly for a leak, and bang-bang?'

'That is so.'

Magill snorted. 'I'd call it a piss-poor chance.'

When he got back to the big house on Sursock Hill, he found a pair of dress trousers and a white dinner jacket laid out on the bed. Magill tried on the jacket. It was a good fit. Passacougli certainly thought of everything. And so must Magill. He turned the jacket inside out and made a slit in the shoulder padding with his penknife. Then he opened the shoulder of his own coat and transferred the microfilm to the dinner jacket.

At ten o'clock that evening, Passacougli, Chantal and Magill arrived at the Yacht Club below the St George Hotel. Passacougli's speedboat, its twin engines mumbling, waited alongside the loading float. They stepped down into the boat, the young Lebanese at the wheel opened the throttle, and the craft shot northward into the night.

Magill sank back into the soft leather seat in the stern and watched the lights of Beirut fade and slip down into the sea. He stared up at the moon, which was just past the full. He wished that there were clouds. Whoever was waiting at Byblos must be rubbing his hands with satisfaction. The speedboat would be as visible in its approach as if it were high noon. It was a warm, humid night, but Magill shivered.

Passacougli was forward, hunched alongside the youth at the

wheel, when Chantal slipped into the seat beside Magill. She wore a rain slicker over her evening gown, and her jet hair was covered with a gold silk scarf. She took out a cigarette and leaned toward Magill's lighter. 'Mr Passacougli told me,' she whispered. She moved still closer and opened the evening bag on her lap. She nodded down at it. Magill saw, nestled inside, a small silver-handled revolver. She nodded again. He was to take the gun. He shook his head. He was tempted to tell her that two guns were enough. She closed her purse and glanced forward at Passacougli. Then she caught Magill's hand and drew it inside her rain slicker, inside the plunge of her gown, and pressed his palm against the warm globe of her breast. The gesture startled him, almost as much as the fact that Chantal carried a gun.

13

'You should have seen our casino before all this foolishness with the Israelis. Every night was a gala.'

Passacougli, his arms linked to Magill and Chantal, escorted them through the great entry hall of marble and gilt and shimmering crystal. Functionaries and housemen in livery bowed to Passacougli and murmured of the honor he was doing them.

'War. The whole world sickens of this disease,' Passacougli went on as they stood in the entrance to Les Ambassadeurs, the theater restaurant. Inside, the band was loud with Cole Porter while blonde showgirls paraded the stage in plumed headdresses and rhinestoned G-strings.

'The most naked high-class revue in the world—and no audience!' Passacougli mourned.

They went on to the main gaming room. Passacougli bought a supply of chips for Chantal and escorted her to a roulette table. He excused himself and took Magill by the arm and led him along a corridor until they came to a series of glass doors. They pushed through and went out into what Passacougli called the Sea Garden. It was a maze of hedges clipped in the English manner.

They lit cigarettes and Passacougli looked around to see that they were alone.

'All is arranged,' he said. 'At thirty minutes past one you will go to the parking area. You will see a black Cadillac and a chauffeur wiping the windshield. He will light a cigarette and walk away.'

'That's the car I drive?'

'Yes. You will go to the highway. It is one kilometer from here. There you wait for a second car. It will join you. There will be two men, armed. They understand what they are to do.'

'Okay. How far to Byblos?'

'Fifteen minutes. You will see a road sign in Arabic and French. It will say Jebeil—' Passacougli paused to spell the name, which was the modern name for Byblos. 'You will turn to the left. The village is on the beach. You will see many ruins. It is the oldest inhabited town on earth. Over fifty centuries—'

Magill cut in. 'Am I likely to meet anybody? Police or soldiers?'

'No one. There is a restaurant along the water, but it will have closed for the night. Now, I have ordered my speedboat to show itself off in the harbor, but not to enter. It will halt two hundred yards out. Your people will be watching it. And you will come up at their backs. That is our plan, is it not?'

'It is. And after that?'

Passacougli cleared his throat. 'After that, I wish you very fine luck.'

At midnight, Passacougli and Chantal were still winning at roulette. Magill stood across the table from them and watched their plays. Chantal gestured again for him to join them. Again he smiled his refusal. Byblos was gamble enough for one night. But suppose there was nobody waiting there for him. Suppose he and Passacougli had misinterpreted the message, that it was *not* Byblos. Or that they *were* right. Who would be waiting? Magill lit a cigarette and thought about the two bodyguards who were to accompany him, about Van Zordich's pistol in his breast pocket and the assassin's revolver at his groin. Pray God, all of it would be unnccessary. Think of something else. Like the warmth of Chantal's breast, the pressure of her nipple against his hand. He glanced across at her again. Her eyes were bright with the excitement of winning. The same look she must have in bed. That was something else he shouldn't think about. He turned away. He stubbed out his cigarette and shook out a fresh one.

A lighter flamed toward his unlit cigarette. 'Trying to make lung cancer all in one night?'

It was Preston Buck.

For an instant Magill thought he was going to strangle on his cigarette smoke. Then he recovered his poise.

'How did you find Munich?'

'Very German.' Buck grinned ruefully. 'When the son of a bitch tells me he's going to Beirut, do I believe him? Munich, hell! I should have figured you were just getting rid of that red-head.'

'You mean Sandra Morgan?'

'I mean! You must have a hell of a big wart on the end of your prick.'

'What?'

'I never saw a broad in such a sweat to get hold of a guy. Asked me to phone her from Munich and tell her where you were staying.'

This was enlightening. So Sandra had not been working with Preston Buck, after all. The thought pleased Magill. He looked at Buck with new confidence.

'Naturally, it's just a coincidence that you dropped by the casino tonight. Just luck.'

Buck grinned. 'What some people call luck, I call created opportunity. I saw that story in the Beirut papers about you staying with Alexander Passacougli, so I hired me a detective.'

The implication was clear. The detective must have made an arrangement with someone at Passacougli's villa who knew about tonight's trip to the casino. That was not good, not good at all.

Buck broke in on Magill's thoughts. 'How long you known Passacougli?'

'Oh, some time.'

'I hear he's just about Number One around Beirut. You two got a deal going?'

Magill shot him a hard look. 'Let's talk about you. Now that you've found me, what do you want?'

Buck rocked on his heels a moment. 'As I see it, boy, we all want different things at different times.'

'Very profound.'

'When I was your age, all I wanted was to hook up with a nymphomaniac who owned a liquor store. Later on, all I cared about was if she owned the store.'

'And now?'

'We'll talk about it when the time comes.' Buck turned and walked away.

Magill watched him disappear among the gamblers. Damn him. Buck's sense of timing was as uncanny as ever. After all, he'd arrived on the very night, within the hour, when Magill was to set out for Byblos.

Passacougli agreed with Magill's change of schedule. It would be best if he left the casino whenever Preston Buck's attention was elsewhere. Passacougli would contrive to get him to the roulette table. So it was that at twenty minutes past one, Buck pushed his first stack of chips onto Number Seven, and Magill, highball in hand, sauntered casually out of the gaming room. At exactly one-thirty, he reached the parking area. He heard the clump of a car door. He saw a lone chauffeur wiping night dew from the windshield. It was a black Cadillac. Magill hesitated. He needed one more piece of identification. The man was supposed to light a cigarette and walk away. Yes, there was the flare of a match. Moments later, Magill slipped behind the steering wheel.

The exit from the parking area was the same as the entry, which meant driving directly past the main doors of the casino. As Magill swung the Cadillac toward the casino, he saw Passacougli push through the doors and stare in his direction. Then a second man came through the doors. It was Preston Buck, of course.

It was too late to back up. Magill gunned the engine and flashed past. He stared into the rear-view mirror. Their backs were to him. Passacougli was directing Buck's gaze toward the parking area, and Magill thought, Thank you, Mr P.

At the junction of the casino road and the Beirut–Tripoli highway, Passacougli's second Cadillac, with the two bodyguards, caught up with him. When he saw their headlights behind him, he turned onto the highway and sped northward. Clouds, heavy and rain-laden, drifted across the moon. The sea below him on his left faded from silver to dirty lead.

He shifted his legs: the Turkish gun in the crotch holster was digging into his groin. He glanced into the mirror. The following headlights were a comforting sight. A bit like an old Humphrey Bogart movie, but still comforting. His eyes went to the instrument panel. Over seventy. The next moment, the interior of the car, the road ahead, the countryside around, merged into a single blinding glare of yellow orange.

The roar of the explosion hit his eardrums; an instant later the car rocked and skidded from the blow of the shock wave. Magill tramped on the brakes. In the rear-view mirror he could see the flames. He ran the Cadillac out onto the soft shoulder and swung the car into a U-turn. He stopped a distance from the wreckage, then approached on foot as near as the heat would permit. He knew it was hopeless, but he had to see. Then he wished that he had not, for the round object in the middle of the road was a man's head.

Magill stumbled back to his car. He wiped the vomit from his chin. He could not go on, he told himself. Whoever had done this intended to cut Magill off from all help. Or perhaps it was the other way around. Someone wanted to keep him from the rendezvous at Byblos. If the bombing was intended to scare him off . . . Magill got no further with his debate. In the distance, from the direction of the casino, he saw two pinpoints of light. He put the Cadillac into gear, swung it around, its tires screeching, and raced north again.

He watched the rear-view mirror until he saw the car stop by the wreckage. Possibly someone was coming to view his handiwork or to complete his assignment. If the latter, Magill was going to make him work for it. He had no choice. He wiped the sweat from his forehead. He must forget the horror behind him. If he were to function tonight, he must block it totally out of mind, as though it never happened. The struggle was not easy, but as minute followed minute, Magill's determination won out. The healthy mind rejects what it must.

The car crested the hill and started down. He had turned off the Tripoli highway onto the dirt road which curled its way toward Byblos. There it was below him, half a mile ahead. The moon had come out from behind the clouds, as if to instruct him in the topography. He could see the cluster of stone buildings along the old harbor and a low promontory reaching out into the sea. There was the periodic flash of a marine beacon somewhere on the other side of the promontory. Magill flicked off his headlights and braked his speed.

He was at the edge of the village. He could see in the moonlight a high stone rampart to one side. The remains of the old crusaders' fortress. There were shadowy columns from Roman days, and obelisks erected by three-thousand-years'-dead Phoenicians. Magill shifted into neutral and coasted past tile-roofed stone houses. At first, the buildings were scattered along the road; then they were closer together, until finally they sat side by side, wall against wall.

He grew uneasy. He had not expected so large a village. Still, among the buildings, getting lost would be no problem. Now the road split into two dirt alleys. He chose the one going toward the left, down a steep grade. It ought to, by logic, bring him to the harbor.

It did. Abruptly the houses gave place to the beach front, a sort of promenade area of hard-packed earth and stone-paved walks. Beyond was a crumbling seawall and a rocky beach onto which were drawn dozens of fishing caïques. Magill allowed the Cadillac to glide along the seawall until it came to a noiseless stop. He checked the dashboard clock. Two minutes to spare. He got out, pocketed the ignition keys, and closed the car door with an almost inaudible clump. He walked around the car to assure himself that it was screened from view. The seawall was protection against watchers on the seaward promontory, and, at the same time, it cloaked the car in deep shadow on the landward side. It would do.

Magill looked at the sky. Clouds were moving across the moon again. Thick clouds, heavy with rain. The air was growing even more humid. He could use a thunderstorm. It would be perfect for his purpose. He swept his eyes along the harbor front, trying to orient himself, to mark in his memory locations which might become important in the minutes ahead. Looking forward from the Cadillac, he saw a low cliff running northward. To his left, on the south, he recognized the promontory which he had seen from the highway. He counted along the spine of the promontory four stone houses, all single-storied. A fifth house, far out on the promontory, was two-storied. It was flanked on each side by date palms which towered above the roof. Directly below this house was the jetty which Passacougli had described—a low stone wall thrusting out into the tiny bay. At its tip was the flashing navigation beacon.

It was two A.M. Time. Magill surveyed the harbor front. No lights, no sounds, no movements. He moved away from the Cadillac, keeping within the shadow of the seawall until it ended and gave place to open beach were some caïques were pulled up on the rocks. He listened to the sighing of the water on the shore, the lapping against the hulls, the creak of the boats' timbers. Then he was aware of another sound. The low thrumming of engines. Passacougli's speedboat. Magill clambered across the rocks and pressed himself against the bulwark of one of the caïques. He heard the engines stop. He peered over the bulwark. He saw a flash of light from the dark sea. Then a second. Then a third. Magill's eyes hurried around the harbor, searching for an answer.

There it was. Out on the jetty. The quick on-and-off of a flashlight, from directly beneath the marine beacon. Whoever it was had cleverly stationed himself directly under the beacon so that his body seemed part of the silhouette of the beacon itself. One flash. Two. Three.

He was right, after all. Someone *was* waiting for him. Magill felt a surge of heat throughout his body—adrenalin. Sweat poured from his face, his hands, his armpits. It was a moment of triumph and aloneness.

He thought rapidly. The man beneath the beacon would expect the speedboat to enter the harbor and swing alongside the jetty. He would not dare go aboard for the meeting, because the speedboat could make off with him almost instantly. The meeting place must be planned for somewhere ashore. Magill's eyes traveled from the jetty up the low hill behind it. The house with the two date palms would be the nearest, the most practical.

He saw the speedboat flash three more lights and receive three answers. He ran, half-crouching, behind the row of beached caïques. Then out into the open and a scramble up a flight of stone steps. He was on the promontory, midway along the row of four houses. He scuttled past one house, then reached the shadow of another. It had no closed door, no closed window; it simply had openings in the wall. Somewhere inside, snoring echoed.

There was a shattering screech behind him. He whirled and drew the automatic. Another screech. Alley cats, fighting or mating. Magill sighed. He saw three more flashes from the man on the jetty. Magill was impatient. What was the hold up? Come on in!

Magill was sure of the house now. It had to be the one. He measured the distance he would have to cover. At least two hundred feet. He could see two windows facing him and another two facing the jetty. They were all open. He could see no doorway; it must be on the other side. He noted, also, that the house was not a true two-storied building; rather, it was built on two levels, stepping up the hillside. If it was to be the rendezvous point, Magill wanted to be there first, to reconnoitre, to see if someone else might be already inside.

Two hundred feet. He would be in plain sight the whole way. Wearing that damned white dinner jacket. If he took it off, he would still have a white shirt. Without his shirt—no, he dared not strip. He had to stay with his jacket because of the microfilm.

He took a deep breath, gripped the automatic, and scuttled. Christ, he thought, it must be half a mile. Then, heart pounding, lungs gasping, he reached the house and flung himself flat against the wall. His face and hands felt the sea-sweat of the stones. He edged along the wall toward the nearest window. When he came to it, he eased his head around the window frame and stared into the interior blackness. He could see nothing. He could hear nothing. Then he did: the soft sound of a body sliding down from the roof above him and his own surprised grunt as he was smashed to earth.

14

Struggle was out of the question. Magill could feel the nose of the gun, his own automatic, pressing into the nape of his neck. Whoever held the gun pulled him to his feet and pushed him forward along the wall of the house, then around the corner to a doorway and into the dark house. He heard the door close behind him and someone's footsteps on the stone flooring, off to his right. So there were two of them. A match flared, and he saw a hand transfer the flame to a brass lantern hanging on the wall. The man who lit it went quickly from window to window, closing the interior shutters. He was, Magill noted, an Arab of about thirty, heavyset and totally bald. A scar wavered over one eye. His boots and soiled trousers suggested the garb of a farmer or sailor.

Magill felt the pressure of the automatic leave his neck. Then the gun appeared in front of his eyes. The man who held it was also an Arab. His beaklike nose had been broken and badly set. A villainous pair of plug-uglies, Magill thought; long on muscle, short on brain. Broken Nose retreated across the room, automatic still aimed, and took up a position alongside the bald one. They stared at Magill expectantly, as if awaiting his apology for intruding. He had no intention of speaking; his first concern was to define his surroundings. The room was unfurnished, except for a low brass table and a silk pillow behind it. There was a doorway to Magill's left, which led into another room or perhaps a hall. To his right, in the far corner, several oars were stacked against the wall. Beside them was a heap of fish net which reeked wetly of the sea, indicating that a fisherman's house had been taken over for this meeting.

There was nothing more to see, so Magill concentrated on sounds. He could hear the clang of a buoy somewhere in the harbor and, farther away, the drumming of engines. The speedboat. It was going away, at full throttle. Then silence. And a new sound. Footsteps which came from the direction of the doorway on his left. He peered intently into the gloom and saw a figure cloaked in a rain slicker, which meant that he had arrived by boat. Magill could not make out his features until he had moved into the room and seated himself cross-legged on the pillow. Then he recognized the lean, moustachioed face of Colonel Mahmoud bin Jarrah.

The colonel gazed at Magill as though he were trying to classify a new biological species. Magill returned the look with a calmness which he did not feel. Finally, the colonel seemed satisfied with his inspection. A hand swept out of his rain slicker and gestured Magill to be seated. That meant the floor. Magill sank down and crossed his hands in front of his knees. He could feel the damp of the stones through the seat of his trousers.

When the colonel spoke—after the prolonged silence—his voice was as startling as a clap of thunder.

'I regret, Mr Magill, that we cannot offer the luxuries of the Hotel Savoy. Tonight, no pretty girl to dine with us, no diamonds to be bought from your friend Mr Van Zordich. I cannot offer you even a cup of coffee, for that gesture, among my people, is reserved for one's friends.' The colonel smiled to himself. 'But since neither are we enemies—' His hand went inside his slicker and came out with a long Egyptian cigarette with a gold tip. He tossed it across to Magill's lap. The bald Arab stepped forward and lighted the cigarette for Magill. He inhaled gratefully, then exploded into coughing. God, what tobacco! When he regained his breath, he saw that they had been joined by still another Arab, a boy in his late teens, barefoot and carrying a flashlight. Of course. He had been out on the jetty; it was he who had flashed the signals to the speedboat.

The colonel cleared his throat. 'I compliment you, Mr Magill, on your discretion. We invited you to come by the sea, so you chose the land. Your decision did, however, cost two lives.'

Magill felt a chill in his bowels. The colonel was taking credit for the bomb in the Cadillac.

'I compliment you, also, on your deciphering of our message. Your mind is subtle. You are a master of intricacies.'

'Thanks.'

The colonel frowned, as though, by speaking, Magill had infringed some rule of deportment.

'I hope that I may be able to compliment you still further. Particularly on your acceptance of the realities of the situation.'

Magill drew on the miserable Egyptian cigarette. He stifled another cough. 'The situation, I take it, is that you want to make some kind of a deal. That's why I'm here.'

Colonel Mahmoud glared. 'You are here because you make common cause with the enemies of His Excellency the Sheikh Ali Muhammid. You are here because you killed my man Barakati.'

'I didn't kill him.'

The colonel hesitated. 'Prove it.'

'I wish I could. So does Superintendent Bromley of the CID.'

'Assuming that you speak the truth.'

'I am.'

'Then it is clear who was the true murderer.'

'Not to me.'

'An Israeli agent.'

Magill felt the astonishment spread across his face. 'An Israeli?'

The colonel exploded. 'Do not play the innocent turtledove with me, sir! Barakati wanted your microfilm, the Israeli wanted your microfilm, *I* want it! And I shall have it!'

Magill licked his lips. The microfilm hidden in his shoulder padding seemed to balloon in bulk, the weight at least ten pounds, and totally visible to Colonel Mahmoud. But how in God's name had he connected Magill with it? There was no escape. Magill's bodyguards were dead. He was a man outnumbered, alone, with a pygmy gun in his crotch that he could not use.

The colonel leaned forward impatiently. 'Well?'

'First, a question.'

'Yes?'

'Why would an Israeli want the microfilm?'

This time it was Colonel Mahmoud who registered astonishment. 'You are an oilman, yet you cannot read a geophysical?'

'Certainly. But why do you care if the Israelis find oil in their own country?' Magill had jumped to the only conclusion possible.

'We are at war! They fight us with planes and tanks and oil and gasoline. *But it must not be Israeli oil!*' The colonel shouted the words and pounded his fist on the brass table in front of him. 'They must buy their oil! We will make them pay with every dollar and pound and franc and lira they can borrow! We will bleed them to death!'

Magill's chest tightened. His pulse pounded in his ears. He was, he realized, enmeshed in something far more serious than stolen property. The microfilm was a weapon of war, as important as guns and tanks and planes.

Mahmoud eyed him coldly. 'You have asked your question. I have answered it. Now, your microfilm.'

Magill forced a small laugh. 'You certainly don't think I was fool enough to bring it with me. It's my guarantee of staying alive.'

'It is in Beirut?'

'Yes.'

'Then you will bring it to me.'

'Now?'

'No. I shall arrange a new meeting place. I will send you word.'

He gestured for Magill to rise. Then he said, 'Before you go, let me show you something of interest.'

He turned to the man with the broken nose and spoke a command. The man nodded and left the room. A moment later, Magill heard soft scuffling noises from the direction of the dark doorway. Broken Nose reappeared, dragging a man behind him. The man was gagged, his hands were tied. One eye was puffed almost closed. His bare chest was crisscrossed with purple welts. For a moment, Magill did not recognize Ward Farren.

Magill stared incredulously. The long, long hunt was ended. At last, after so much hell, the bastard was *there*. Within choking distance. Farren saw Magill's expression and understood it. He answered with a tired smile. All his old bravado had been beaten out of him.

'Your friend thought that he could escape us,' the colonel said. 'Do not make that same mistake. Until we meet again you shall be watched most carefully.'

'I get the point.'

'Then see that you do not forget it.'

'What happens to Farren?'

'We shall kill him. Tonight.'

Magill pursed his lips. 'You fill me with confidence. You kill Farren, then me.'

Colonel Mahmoud held up his hand; but it was not in reply to Magill. It was a warning to his men. He hissed something and the men froze, listening. Magill heard it, too. Footsteps outside, stumbling in the gravel. The Arab with Magill's automatic darted for the entrance. The bald one dashed after him, leaving only the barefoot boy. He barked an order, and the boy trained the revolver alternately on Magill and Farren.

Now, if ever, was Magill's chance. He turned to the colonel, still seated on the pillow. 'Okay if I hit the floor? In case some bullets—'

The colonel nodded. He needed Magill alive.

As Magill crouched, his right hand slid to his waistband. The next time the boy aimed his gun at Farren, he unzipped his fly. The revolver swung back at him, then returned to Farren. This time, Magill's hand closed on the tiny gun and whipped it out. The colonel shouted to the boy. It was too late. Magill was aiming at the colonel's heart.

'Tell him to drop the gun.'

The colonel did. The revolver clattered to the floor.

Magill sprang and seized it. Now he had two guns trained on the colonel. Magill ordered him to have the boy untie Farren. When it was accomplished, Farren whispered to Magill, 'My microfilm. The colonel's got it.'

'Then grab it!'

Farren jerked the colonel to his feet and rummaged through his pockets. He withdrew a gold pillbox. He opened the lid.

'Got it!'

'Put it in my pocket.'

Farren hesitated. He eyed Magill's two guns. Discretion won out.

Footsteps were running toward the house. Magill moved closer to the colonel and pressed one gun to each temple. The two Arabs burst into the room. They took in the scene and wilted. Magill slipped the tiny assassin's gun into his pocket and reached out for his own automatic, which still dangled from the hand of Broken Nose. Then he turned to the colonel. 'Tell your men not to follow us. I've got friends outside.'

Broken Nose spat, 'There is no one! Only a pig eating fish-heads!'

The Cadillac, tires singing, swept up the hill south of Byblos. Ward Farren was at the wheel. Magill, beside him, aimed his automatic at Farren's belly. It was the only arrangement possible. If Magill drove, he could not keep his eyes on Farren, who might decide to throw himself out of the car. True, Magill could tie him up, but Magill had no rope. True, also, he could knock him unconscious, and so dispose of the problem. But this would have canceled Magill's overriding purpose—to let Farren talk. And talk he did. A flood of words, as if he must compensate for the enforced silence of the gag in his mouth.

'They meant it, Dave. They were going to kill me. The slow way. I've seen it done. They bust a guy's ribs, one by one, then his legs and his arms and his fingers. If he passes out, they bring him to. They kick his kidneys until they hemorrhage. If he begs for a quick bullet, they just tear out his tongue. I tell you, Dave, seeing you was the most beautiful moment of my life!'

'I can imagine. What bothers me is why did they let us go so easy?'

'Because they know they can find us again, unless we move damned fast.'

'We're going to. How did they get hold of you, in the first place?'

'Right at Beirut Airport. I was waiting for you to come in.'

'You knew I was coming?'

Farren focused his one good eye on Magill and the automatic. 'Sooner or later, yes. I didn't try to cover my tracks. I wanted you to find me. So we could go partners with the microfilm.'

'Only because I had half of it.'

'Sure! We *are* partners, aren't we, Dave?'

Farren was incredible. He cared nothing about the significance of the microfilm. It was simply merchandise to peddle. Magill decided to lull him along; there were many things still to learn.

'Let's have some background. How did this start with Colonel Mahmoud?'

'About a year ago. I was heading up the geophysical for Anglo-Tex. I was in Beirut on r. and r., and Mahmoud comes to me. How about being on his payroll? he says. In case my geo turns up oil for the Jews, I'm to slip him the report first. Then he would fake a new geo showing there was *no* oil, and that's the one I was to file.'

Magill grunted. 'Pretty damned stupid. Any one of your juniors might have talked.'

'That's why Mahmoud blew up the plane. Killed everybody who knew.'

'Except you. How did Mahmoud know you were still alive?'

'I've got an idea. Last time I was in Beirut I bought myself a phony passport, so I could cut out. Then I had my face made over. Maybe the surgeon talked to Mahmoud's boys or even the Jews. Anyway, somebody was watching me closer than I thought.'

'Uh-huh. Some people hate to be double-crossed.'

Farren snickered. 'But it worked! And now you and me are going to be instant millionaires.'

'You're forgetting. *I* have the microfilm. Not you.'

'But *I've* got the contacts.'

'You sure look it.'

'Jesus, do I have to rub your nose in everything? I mean, *the* contacts! I've already talked to guys with three companies right in Beirut. They're peeing their pants for the Anglo-Tex concession!' Farren paused. Even in the dim glow from the instrument panel, Magill could see the glower on Farren's face. 'I've fed you enough. Let's hear you do some talking. Are you with me?'

Farren was incurable. One minute weeping gratitude for his life; the next, issuing commands and demands.

'No.'

'No what?'

'I'm turning you in. And the microfilm.' Magill brought his automatic up for emphasis. 'All I care about is a clean name.'

'Christ Almighty! Right out of the hymnbook. Where's your tambourine?'

They drove in silence now. In the distance, the lights of the Casino blurred dimly. Farren squinted at the rear-view mirror.

'I wonder if that car is following us.'

Magill smiled tightly. 'There isn't any car.'

'Take a look.'

'Oh, sure.'

'It's that fucking colonel.'

'Naturally.'

Magill saw Farren lick his lips. He was bracing himself for something.

'Dave, maybe you ought to hide that pillbox somewhere. Just in case.'

Farren's concern sounded genuine. There was a flash of light in the rear-view. He had not been lying. Magill turned in the seat, to look back. He was off guard for a bare instant. The instant in which Farren struck the gun from his hand and smashed his head against the windshield. Magill felt the car swerve crazily as Farren's fist came down at the base of his neck.

He groaned. The sound he made seemed to come from somewhere far away. Nearer, there was a mushy throbbing sound. The pounding of his own pulse. His eyes wavered open. The light—sun? fire? searchlight?—felt as if it were scorching his eyeballs. His eyes closed again. Blessed darkness. He shifted his body and moaned. The pains were centered in his neck and jaw. Wherever he was, he was flat on his back. Then he sensed something above his face. He forced his eyes open again. A hazy image wavered into focus. A woman's face. She was breathing down on him. Alcohol breath. The face retreated. He pulled himself up painfully onto one elbow and stared around. He seemed to be in some sort of tunnel. A metal tunnel with windows. The face which had hovered over him was now attached to a body. That face. Where had he seen it before? Flushed, red-eyed, gray hair hanging limply. She moved farther away, and he saw that she was wearing a silk robe. That she had a bottle of scotch in one hand. That part of the robe was trailing behind her on the floor. That two gray tomcats rode happily on the tail of the robe.

Magill coughed and fell back onto the berth. He knew where he was now. In a private airplane. And that Mrs Preston Buck was very drunk.

15

'I thought you'd go for a cup of good old American coffee. That damned Lebanese stuff is pure puke.'

Magill was propped on the sofa bed in the plane's main cabin. A breakfast tray was on his lap. Preston Buck slumped casually in a lounge chair across from Magill. Mrs Buck, haggard and dull-eyed, occupied another chair at the foot of the sofa. It was dawn. Magill could see, through the opposite window, a huge Air France jet trundling along the landing strip. Beyond, in the distance, the great houses on Sursock Hill were catching the first sun of the day. He wondered if Passacougli and Chantal were up or had even gone to bed. Surely they must be in a ferment over his disappearance. Magill drained the last of his coffee and glanced at Preston Buck. He had made no reference to the happenings of the past few hours beyond the simple statement that he had found Magill unconscious on the highway and had brought him back to Beirut. Buck, the talkative, was very unlike himself. Biding his time, undoubtedly. Until Buck showed the direction of his interest, Magill had no intention of volunteering conversation.

'How about some more coffee?'

'Please.'

Buck turned to his wife. 'Honey, would you go tell Miss Wilson?' It was an obvious device to get Mrs Buck out of the cabin. She nodded vaguely and struggled half out of her chair, then sagged back helplessly.

'I'm sorry, Preston.'

Buck frowned and said it was all right; he would attend to it. Mrs Buck watched her husband disappear into the galley. Then she pulled herself to her feet and dropped down beside Magill.

'May I call you David?'

'Certainly, Mrs Buck.'

'Well, David, you're not being considerate of my husband. He shouldn't be out all night worrying about you and bringing you home in such an awful condition.'

Magill stared. He wondered how she could sober up so suddenly, how much of her alcoholism was an act, and why she thought it necessary.

'You could be Mr Buck's own son,' she went on. 'That's why you must be considerate of him. A father doesn't like to put detectives on his own boy.'

'When was this, Mrs Buck?'

'Oh, ever since Paris. And all those radio messages back and forth—' She broke off. Her husband had reappeared with Miss Wilson and the coffee.

Mrs Buck lurched to her feet and excused herself. As the cabin door closed behind her, Buck gestured Miss Wilson to a chair. She settled into it like an obedient dog, and took out a note pad and pencil. Buck slid down into the seat opposite Magill and steepled his fingers.

'Yes, sir, you're a tough monkey,' he began. 'Tougher than I ever figured you for. I never guessed killing was your line.'

'Killing?'

'Those poor bastards in the car. Time bomb, wasn't it?'

'Had to be. But I didn't set it.'

'That so? Never killed anybody in your life, huh?'

'Never.'

'How about those people in the house, up at Byblos?'

Magill started. 'They were alive when I left them. But how did you—'

'Followed you, that's how. All the way. I saw that character drop on you from the roof. Then later, you and your friend come busting out of the house.'

Magill grinned. 'So it wasn't a pig eating fish-heads. It was you outside the house.'

'What I want to know is who was inside.'

'I didn't catch the names.'

'I'll bet.' Buck smiled down at his hands. 'Funny how things work out. I took the speedboat up to the casino. Got a rough case of sinus from the damp, so I phoned the airport to send a rented car up for me to drive back. When I go out to the parking area to get the car, I see you whiz by. Then a second Caddy starts up like it's going to follow you. So I play a hunch. I decide to tag along. Must say, I almost lost my enthusiasm when I saw that explosion up the road.'

'Glad you didn't.' Magill wondered how long it would be before Preston Buck would ask about Ward Farren. Buck ended that suspense immediately.

'About your friend. The one you and your gun escorted outside. Did he dump you on the road?'

'He did.'

'Lovers' quarrel?'

'You might call it that.' Magill decided to get him off the subject. 'There's something I don't understand. Where you found me was pretty far from Beirut. Yet I didn't come to until you got me here on the plane.'

'You came to, all right. I had to tap you out again. Twice.'

That explained Magill's sore jaw. It also might explain the gold pillbox missing from his pocket. But no. That was why Farren had slugged him; he had retrieved the microfilm for himself. The situation was as before; each had one half.

Buck was smiling. 'You see, I wanted us to have a little cozy. Just you and me.' He leaned forward; his voice dropped an octave. 'I've been adding up everything since London. First, Scotland Yard asks questions. Then you hop to Paris with Little Miss Pretty Tits. Then another skip-out. Next, you're the social lion of Beirut. Pal of Alex Passacougli. Bodyguards following you up the coast. Then boom! Then a midnight huddle in a spook house. Then you kidnapping somebody. Then, pow! You face down in the ditch. Boy, you ain't any commando for the Salvation Army.'

Magill had to smile at the recitation. 'So tell me.'

'First, I want to remind you of something. I was the one who picked you up on that roadside. You might have got yourself rolled. Even killed.'

'I know. I appreciate it.'

'You do?'

'Yes.'

Buck rubbed his chin thoughtfully. 'That's one thing I like. Gratitude. In fact, I'll pay you one-half-million dollars for it. Cash.'

Magill could not be hearing correctly. Buck must have hit him once too often.

'What makes you think I need money?'

'Told me yourself. In Paris. Your well out in California needed some fresh mullet money.'

'That was Paris. I've raised all I need.'

'As of when?'

Magill heard the cold intensity in Buck's question. 'As of yesterday.'

Buck smiled sweetly. 'You're busted.'

'The hell I am!'

The smile broadened. 'Flat, dead-assed busted. And as of yesterday, your well turned to saltwater.' Now the smile was almost a leer. 'If you don't believe me, Miss Wilson can bring us the radiogram from my man in California.'

Magill felt the blood drain from his face. Now he understood Mrs Buck's words: '*All those radio messages back and forth . . .*' No oil, only salt water. The game was over. Still, he would not concede.

'Let's get back to this gratitude you want to buy. How do you want me to deliver it?'

Buck's face softened. His voice cooed. 'I told you, boy, I always had a bone-feeling about you. You've got a pudding, a really big pudding. An oil concession. That's it, isn't it?' Buck paused and watched Magill's eyes. 'That's why you're in Beirut. Oil. Arab oil, Egyptian oil, Turkish oil, Iranian, Libyan—I don't care where it is. I want it.'

Magill sagged deeper into the sofa. So Buck had guessed it. Why fight him off any longer? Tell him the whole thing. Be done with it. These were Magill's urgings. But they were countered by an intuitive feeling. Not yet. An idea, a scheme, a strategem, was beginning to form in his mind. It was inspired by something that Buck himself had said. Magill had to get away from him long enough to think it out.

'Half a million, cash.' Buck dangled the temptation in front of him again.

'Today?'

'As soon as the banks open.'

'I'll have to talk it over.'

'Talk?'

'With my partners.' Any lie would do that got him off that damned plane.

'You're not alone?'

'No. Too big for one man.'

For the first time since Magill had met Preston Buck, he looked ill. Finally, he got out the words: 'These partners, they're here in Beirut?'

'Sure.'

'Well then, suppose I invite them out here for lunch. I'll send a car—'

Magill got to his feet. 'Thanks for the coffee.'

'You're leaving?'

'If you want me to talk to my partners.'

'When will you let me know?'

'Can't say. Maybe never.'

Alexander Passacougli threw his arms around him. 'It is so good! So good! Chantal and I, we say we shall never see him again!'

'A few hours late, and you write me off just like that?'

'With reason! Chantal tells me she has a very bad feeling. She cries. We come back to Beirut and, aha! the police are at my gate. They tell me one of my Cadillacs is wrecked. They tell me the license. I know it is the car you drive. Then I am very sad. And those men, that scum I sent to protect you!' He spat his disgust.

Magill frowned. 'Don't you know? Didn't the police tell you?'

'Yes! That, too. Stupid pigs! I warned there would be danger.

Did they inspect their auto? Did they look for a bomb? No! They earned their deaths!'

Finally Passacougli bankrupted himself of emotion. He took Magill's arm; they would go to the living-room and talk in comfort.

Magill described everything from the moment he had left the casino. When he finished, Passacougli shook his head glumly.

'Stolen microfilm is not a petty crime—but the key to an Israeli oil field, this is of international importance. Many lives will be spent.' Passacougli paused and chewed his lower lip in thought. 'It is significant, I think, that this Farren abandoned my Cadillac near the Bourj Centrale.'

'Why?'

'The location. In two minutes he could walk to the whorehouses. There a man can hide for weeks, months.'

'No. Only today.'

'Explain, please.'

'Farren has had the hell beaten out of him. He's shot. He's got to rest. Sleep it off.'

'As you must, too.'

Magill nodded. Actually, he was feeling better. He was stimulated by the ideas that linked together in his mind.

'Let's say Farren loses this whole day. But by tonight, he'll start making plans. How to put distance between himself and Colonel Mahmoud. And how to squeeze at least some money out of the microfilm.'

Passacougli pondered. 'But one-half of the microfilm is of no value.'

'Yes, it is. The film shows enough to clue an oil company into the right area. That's worth a good deal.'

'So Farren goes to America, perhaps, and sells it. He escapes you, after all.'

'No. Remember, he said he had contacts with three oil companies right here in Beirut.'

'If one may believe him.'

'I do. I think he started talking business with them. Then Mahmoud got on his tail. So he cuts for London. He figures he can sell the film to some company at the Petroleum Congress. Then Barakati shows up, and Colonel Mahmoud. So it's back to Beirut to pick up his first deal.'

'If that is true, he must move at once.'

'By tomorrow.'

Passacougli hummed thoughtfully. 'There are many oil companies in Beirut. If we knew which three were involved, we could warn the police . . .'

'A waste of time. Farren can't walk into anybody's office. He's got to stay holed up because of Colonel Mahmoud. But he will try to get to a telephone. That's how he'll make the deal. The oil company will have to come to him.'

'Then we talk in circles. There is no solution.'

Magill lit a cigarette. He blew a smoke ring and watched it drift and dissolve. He turned back to Passacougli.

'You say Beirut is a city of eyes and ears, that news gets around fast.'

'As quick as thought.'

'Even if the news isn't exactly the truth?'

'Still it goes.'

'In other words, stories can be planted.'

Passacougli pulled his nose. 'I do not see the connection. You wish to make a rumor?'

'I want to know if you have men who do that sort of thing.'

Passacougli smiled. 'I should be a much poorer man if I did not arrange certain states of mind.' He raised his eyebrows expectantly. 'What is this rumor to be?'

Magill grinned. The idea which had germinated aboard Preston Buck's plane was now in full flower. 'Not a rumor. A letter. A letter that drops out of a briefcase or falls out of a pocket.'

'Hmm. That is very imaginative. And this letter?'

'It will say something that will interest every single oil company in Beirut. Each one will think the letter is intended for a competitor.'

Passacougli sighed with admiration. 'Most artistic! Yes, this is very Lebanese!' He paused to savor the idea further. 'This letter will say—'

'That I have a microfilm, the geophysical of an Israeli oil discovery. That I'm going to auction it to the highest bidder.'

Passacougli's face went blank. 'This is what you Americans call a practice joke?'

'Practical joke.'

'I do not see the amusement.'

'Neither will the oil companies. Three of them have talked to Ward Farren about the same deal.'

'Ah-h-h! So when this Farren telephones them, they will tell him he is a cheat, that *you* have the film. That it is from *you* they will buy!' Passacougli rubbed his hands in satisfaction. 'Yes! If Farren is to sell his film, he must come to you! Let you be his selling agent. And then the police!'

'Right. Now, where can we hold this auction?'

'But there is no need. This is pretend.'

'We've got to make it look good. Farren has to believe that I'm going to sell my own half of the microfilm.'

Magill braced himself for what must come. There was no easy way, no softening of the blow.

Passacougli's cheeks reddened, his jaw set.

'When we first met, I put that question to you. I asked if you had such film.'

'I lied.'

'You gave me your word.'

'I'm sorry.'

'You did not trust me.'

'I had to get to know you. I didn't want to show all my cards until the right time.'

Passacougli looked at him morosely. The excuse was too thin. 'You propose an auction that looks to be true, but is not?'

'Exactly. But Farren's got to think it's for real. That means some place to rig up a screen and a movie projector, like I'm going to show off the goods. It's got to be some place that Farren feels safe in visiting. Where he thinks he can duck out, in case he's spotted by the police or Mahmoud.'

Passacougli was silent. He tugged his earlobe and sighed and hummed to himself. Then he brightened.

'Moumeili!'

'What's that?'

'A village. It is in the mountains. There is a cinema. I own it. It is one of my outdoor operations.'

'You mean, a drive-in movie?'

'Ha! Peasants do not possess automobiles! These are poor people. Farmers, shepherds. There is a bean field. There are two tall trees. A screen is pulled up between the trees. The people sit on the hard earth.'

'Is there a road in from Beirut?'

'Of course! Everything you wish. A movie screen. A projector. An audience. Farren will come and hide himself among farmers and shepherds. He will think himself safe until farmers and shepherds become police!'

Magill bobbed his head. 'Why not? Why not?'

With the decision made, he relaxed, and the strain of the long night asserted itself. His mind went dull; his arms and legs grew heavy with fatigue. He had to sleep. But not yet. First, he had to bait the trap. He seated himself at Passacougli's desk and wrote the letter which would be delivered to Preston Buck. He read it to Passacougli, who pronounced it perfect and—seeing Magill's exhaustion—volunteered to write the necessary copies which were to slip from certain briefcases as certain men visited certain offices in downtown Beirut.

It was eight-thirty A.M. when Magill finally fell into bed. It was past three-thirty P.M. when he awakened. His sore jaw was gone, as was the ache at the back of the skull where Farren had slugged him. He went to the bathroom for a long, cold shower, which revived him further. He was toweling himself when he heard the bedroom door close. He wrapped the towel around his hips and went to the bedroom. For a moment, he did not see Chantal. She was seated on the edge of his bed, smoking a cigarette. Yellow silk dressing-robe, black hair falling loose to her shoulders, bare feet. Her eyes were puffed, as if she, too, had just risen from a long nap.

'You are refreshed?'

'Yes. Thanks.' Magill tightened the towel around his hips.

'Last night was very bad. For all of us.'

'Yes. Wasn't it?'

She crossed her knees casually and the robe fell away from her tan legs. It was obvious to Magill that she was naked under the robe. He glanced nervously at the hall door as if it would instantly fly open.

She smiled. 'Mr Passacougli is at the warehouse.'

'Oh?'

'He wishes you to know that he has spoken to various gentlemen.'

'Good. Fine.' Was it possible she had come to deliver that message? No. She still sat there. Waiting. This was a complication Magill did not need, no matter how tempting.

'I'm just getting ready to go downtown,' he said. The idea came as a surprise even to him.

'Ah?'

'I want to just spin my wheels for a few hours. Maybe take in a movie. Eat dinner out.'

Her eyes hardened. 'I see.' She rose from the bed and padded stiffly to the hall door. It closed behind her with an eloquent slam.

Magill sighed. Chantal had laid her pride on the line and he had spurned her. She would not forget that. Nor must he.

He dismissed the taxi on the east side of the Bourj Centrale. While Magill intended a few hours of forgetfulness, it would do no harm for him to familiarize himself with the area where Farren had abandoned the Cadillac. As he strolled, he was conscious of two impressions: heat and noise. The pavement scorched up through the soles of his shoes. Every doorway was an assault by radio or record. Autos honked, streetcars clanged, donkeys brayed. A gaggle of boys lugging brass shoeshine boxes trotted beside him, each shouting for his patronage. Finally, he escaped into a side street. He saw a group of chairs and tables ranged along the front of a bakery. Wrinkled men in fezzes were playing backgammon and smoking water pipes. Magill slumped down at one of the empty tables. A waiter—dirty turban, baggy red pantaloons, black vest—shuffled to the table. Magill pantomimed the act of drinking. He hoped for a cold lemonade or a cola drink. Instead, the waiter brought a cup of coffee. The damned Lebanese hot syrup. Magill sighed and tossed out some piastres.

At least it was a change of pace. To sit, do nothing, plan nothing, while Passacougli's men went about with their letters. He stared along the sidewalk and saw a small black dog limping on three legs. A few feet ahead of it was the mashed remains of a watermelon, covered with flies. A buck says he pees on it. Two bucks says it eats it first, then pees on it. Two bucks won. He watched the dog hobble across the street. It paused in front of a parked car and raised its leg against the bumper. Poor kidneys.

Then Magill noted the make of the car. It was a Cadillac. Black. The driver was dozing behind the wheel. Or was he? If he opened his eyes, he would be looking straight at Magill. One of Passacougli's men, undoubtedly. Chantal had reported Magill's excursion, and Mother Hen was taking care of the wayward chick.

Magill rose from the table and started down the street, away from the Cadillac. He paused to light a cigarette in front of a bookstore and glanced back. The Cadillac was pulling away from the curb. He started walking again. He cast another glance behind him. As he did, he saw a man duck into a doorway. A young Arab in a turban. A coincidence? He decided to find out. A streetcar was ricketing toward him. Magill stepped out and swung himself aboard. He saw the Arab dash after the streetcar. He was too late. Magill paid his fare to the operator, then stooped and peered out the rear window. The Arab had flagged down a taxi and was gesturing toward the streetcar. Behind the taxi was the black Cadillac.

Magill found an empty seat beside a fat black woman with a crate of live ducks on her lap. At that moment, he felt as helpless as one of her fowl. Every time that he had been followed, something happened. London and Barakati. Paris and Preston Buck. Beirut Airport and the gang of boys. Byblos and Passacougli's men bombed to shreds. Magill looked out the window behind the black woman. The taxi was pacing the streetcar, neither gaining nor falling behind.

The streetcar turned into Hamra Street, with its fashionable shops and theaters. A movie. That ought to work. Magill had seen the trick used in a dozen spy films. He would dash into the theater and lose himself in the darkness.

The maneuver went off brilliantly. Magill slumped down in the back row and waited for the young Arab to appear and pace up and down the aisles in futile search. But the aisles were empty; they remained empty. It was peculiar. When Magill had bought his ticket, he had seen the taxi skid to a halt and the Arab leap out. He must be waiting on the street or outside a fire exit. Very well, Magill would outwait him.

It was dark when he emerged onto the street. The young Arab was nowhere in sight. In fact, there was no one on the street. Then Magill saw the reason. An army tank was stationed in the alleyway beside the theater. In the next block there were three half-tracks bristling with soldiers. Somewhere beyond there was the rattle of a machine gun.

Hamra Street definitely was not for strolling. Magill trotted along the sidewalk, keeping close to the sides of the buildings. He hoped he was going in the direction of the Bourj Centrale. Luckily, he was, and there he found a taxi. He told the driver to take him to the Phoenicia Hotel.

He drank two scotches in the bar on the lobby floor, then went up to the rooftop restaurant, L'Age D'Or. It was a semicircular room with a view which swept the Corniche, Ain-Mreisse, and the entire bay. There were few diners, and of those, most spoke with British or French accents. Magill caught repeated references to Al Fatah, which, he concluded, explained the armor on Hamra Street.

After his dinner, Magill went down to the lobby again. He

went to the newsstand in hope of finding the local English and French newspapers. He wanted to see how the bombing of Passaçougli's Cadillac had been reported. He was in luck. Papers in both languages were on display and—surprise!—on the front pages there were photographs of Preston Buck. Magill tossed some piastres on the counter and carried the papers to a lounge chair near the front desk.

'Famed Independent Oilman Visits Beirut. Local Officials Predict Mr Preston Buck to Enter Near Eastern Oil.' Those were the captions of the English-language paper. Magill was halfway through the story when he heard a babble of voices behind him and the trundling of baggage carts. He glanced around. A group of travelers carrying Pan American flight bags was filing up to the registration desk. One stood out because of her youth and her brilliant red hair. Magill's throat tightened. It was Sandra Morgan.

16

He watched her sign the desk register and hand in her passport. A bellboy took her bags and she followed him to the elevator. The elevator door closed and she had not seen him.

Magill slumped down in his chair and thought rapidly. First, Ward Farren in Beirut. Then Preston Buck. Now Sandra Morgan. Coincidence? Not likely.

He got up and crossed to the concierge's desk and asked for a sheet of writing paper and an envelope. He puzzled what to write. Anything, really, would do. He smiled to himself. Of course.

What commotion
In the ocean
When whales
Get the notion!

He folded the note, inserted it in the envelope, and took it to the marble-topped counter of the room clerk.

'Would you put this note in Miss Morgan's box, please?' The clerk looked blank. 'Miss Sandra Morgan. The young lady who just checked in. American. Red hair. Blue eyes.'

'Red hair? Ah-h! To be sure, m'sieur.' The clerk turned and slid the note into the box numbered 478.

Magill smiled his thanks and walked briskly to the elevator. His eyes swept the lobby. No one was watching.

There was no answer to his knock. He repeated it. This time he heard the muffled flush of a toilet. He knocked again. Footsteps hurried toward the door. It opened.

'*Dave*! Oh, my God!' She flung herself at him. Her arms

circled his neck, her lips scattered kisses.

He guided her back into the room and closed the door. She still clung to him.

'Oh, what timing! I was just going to phone the American Embassy to find you!'

He put her at arm's length and looked at her. He had forgotten the intensity of her blue eyes, the fire of her hair. She had never looked prettier nor dressed more becomingly. Pale blue suit, pale blue blouse, knee-high boots of pale blue kid. Finally he spoke.

'Have you had dinner?'

'On the plane.'

'Then would you mind if I stayed and talked a while?'

'Would I mind!' She hugged him again.

'Sandy, how did you know I was here?'

She smiled guiltily. 'Don't ask.'

'I've got to know.'

She sighed. 'You won't like it.'

'Okay. So I won't.'

She slipped her hand into his and led him toward the balcony window. The lights of the harbor and the Lido, directly below, reflected up into their faces.

'Well?'

'All right. I'm a dirty little sneak. I overheard—no, I *listened*, on purpose—when you were on the phone. In Paris.'

Magill scowled. 'When?'

'In your room! At the Ritz. The morning after that lovely night. Somebody phoned. You took the receiver into the bathroom. To get away from me. But I was just outside the door.'

'I never said Beirut.'

'Yes, you did!'

It began to come back. The telephone call from Van Zordich saying that Ward Farren had been seen in Beirut.

'But I told you Munich. That's what I put in my note.'

'And I believed it! At first. I even told that friend of yours you'd gone there.'

'Preston Buck?'

'Yes. He came by the hotel. I remembered you said he was a

friend of yours. So when he asked where you were, I told him Munich.'

Magill opened the window and stepped out onto the balcony and stared down at the Lido. He placed himself so that his back would be to Sandra. It was a device which he had learned from his father. A man might be able to lie convincingly to your face; but if he cannot watch your eyes, cannot judge your expression—then his talk will falter, will become stilted. The lie will betray itself. But Sandra's voice showed no hesitation, no lack of assurance.

'Buck phoned me hours later. Absolutely furious. He called me every kind of bitch. He said you weren't in Munich, and I'd sent him sniping. That's when I started thinking. I remembered hearing you say Beirut.'

Yes. She was telling the truth. But why was she in Beirut? He fished into his pocket for his cigarettes. He lighted one, and then remembering Sandra, offered it to her. He lighted another for himself. He looked out to sea.

'Okay. Then what?'

'Then the police.'

He gave a start. 'The Sûreté?'

'They came to the Ritz. Two men. They asked me about you. Who you were. How long I'd known you. Where you'd gone. Lots of questions. They wouldn't tell me why.' She paused as if expecting him to finish her story for her. 'After they left, I got to thinking. They never showed me any identification. Maybe they weren't police, after all.'

'I'm sure they weren't.'

'That's what worried me. So many strange things had happened. That Arab in London who hired me for all that fake publicity about a murdered brother and a plane explosion. You following me to Paris and saying there *had* been an explosion and to watch out for whatever-his-name. Then the two men coming to the hotel and maybe following me as well as you. I just got scared spitless.'

He faced her and smiled. 'I can imagine. Why didn't you cut for home?'

'You don't know?' She looked hurt. She tossed her cigarette over the balcony railing and clasped her arms around Magill's neck once more. 'When I found you never went to Munich, I thought that was your way of breaking it off. I felt awful. How could it be? We'd been so good together. It just couldn't end there. And after the men came to the hotel, I knew you'd gone for another reason. Everything was all right.' She brought her face up to his and brushed the inside of her lower lip against his mouth. The tip of her tongue teased for entry.

'You shouldn't be here, Sandy.'

'But I am!'

'I want you to leave.'

'Just like that?'

'Yes.'

'Just go. Without explanation.'

What could he tell her? A confusion of happenings. Sandra had traveled from Paris, but he had been to the moon and back. No. He would tell her nothing. He would not involve her. That was why she must leave Beirut.

'Well?' she challenged.

'Suppose I order us up some drinks.'

She smiled. It was a concession. 'Would cognac do?'

'Anything.'

He followed her back into the room. He watched her go to her flight bag and rummage until she found the bottle. She had bought it at Orly, she told him, 'just in case'. She preferred liquor to sleeping pills. There was a thermos and two glasses on the nightstand. She poured three fingers into each glass. They clinked their glasses together, then swallowed and gasped in unison. He felt a sag of relief—not from the liquor, from the end of suspicion. It was good to be with her again; to be with an American girl, to hear American speech. He had had his fill of the foreign and exotic.

'How long—' she ventured. 'How long will you be in Beirut?'

He shrugged.

'Is it expensive here?'

'The hotel?'

'And food and things. Clothes.'

'It's expensive. More than you can afford.'

'I've still got those diamonds. I can sell them.'

'Sandy, don't try to make me responsible—'

'I'm not.' She took a sip of her cognac, then walked to the balcony window and sniffed the air. 'Sultry, isn't it?'

'Yes.'

'Like that night in Paris.'

'Except here there are soldiers and tanks and bombs.'

'I know. But it's still a sexy place.'

'Sandy—'

'Coming into town, I saw all those minarets. God, what a lot of marble erections.'

He had to laugh. That was her cue. She turned back into the room; she threw out her arms and pirouetted. 'It's going to be such fun! You'll teach me to ride a camel and I'll buy all sorts of crazy clothes. Caftans and djellabas. And a fez! Won't I be terrif in a fez?'

'With your red hair?'

She put her arms around his neck again and brushed her cheek against his. 'Okay. A turban. A white turban.'

'That's better.' He buried his face in her hair and inhaled her perfume.

'I'll learn to smoke one of those hubbly-bubbly things. And to belly dance!' She hummed a bar of cootch music and wriggled her loins against his. 'I'll madden you with desire!'

'Absolutely. And one night I'll sweep you up onto my Arab steed and carry you off to my desert tent.'

'Your love prisoner!'

'In chains of iron.' He bent her head back and fastened his mouth to her throat.

'Promise you'll teach me all the unspeakable wickedness of the wicked East. Promise?'

He raised his face to hers and their tongues fluttered together. He felt the warmth of her breasts against his chest, her mound rubbing insistently against his loins, and his own rising answer. He knew this was what he had wanted all along. He would fight it no longer.

He released her waist and, without breaking the kiss, peeled off her jacket. It dropped to the floor. His hands went behind her and unbuttoned her blouse. She wriggled it off. He unfastened the black net brassiere and tossed it aside. He gazed down at the rose nipples, already swelling, expectant of his mouth. He nursed them hungrily, impartially. He felt her tremble, heard her make little animal sounds of pleasure. When he returned to her lips, he felt her fingers at his zipper. They opened it and darted inside. They explored him, drew him out, stroked him. Then he heard her laugh. Not a titter, not a giggle. A convulsion of laughter. He pulled back to look at her face. Her mouth was wide, almost in anguish.

'What in Christ's name—' he began.

'I just saw . . . saw . . .'

'Yes?'

'There! *There! In the mirror!*'

He swiveled his head. He saw the reflection of Sandra, naked to the waist, clutching his penis, and somewhere behind them, a bellboy.

He was very young. And in shock. Round-eyed, jaw dropped, one arm extended, frozen. A stone statue. Lot's wife, male version. The hall door behind him was open. If he had knocked, Magill and Sandra had been past hearing Gabriel's own trumpet.

Sandra cleared her throat. 'I guess all we can do is act natural.'

'How natural can we get?' He glared at the bellboy. 'What the hell you want?'

The boy's jaw waggled, but no sound came.

Magill tried French. '*Qu'est-ce que c'est?*'

The boy gulped. He remembered. He dug into his pocket and brought out an envelope. He edged toward them and held out the envelope at arm's length. Sandra took it, the bellboy backed away—no tip wanted—to the hall door, backed through it, darted in again, grabbed the doorknob, backed out once more, closed the door.

Sandra tore open the envelope. She read the message aloud.

What commotion
In the ocean
When whales
Get the notion!

She stretched lazily beneath him. They were on the bed.

'Dave?'

'Hmmm?'

'How long will you be in Beirut?'

'I told you.'

'You don't know.'

'Right.'

'Hmmm. I don't like the place.'

'I thought you did.'

'I don't.'

'Why?'

'Because you won't leave it.'

'Spoken like a woman.'

She kissed the tip of his nose. Her arms and legs tightened around him. Then: 'Why do you want me to leave Beirut?'

'There's something I don't want you mixed up in.'

'He says.'

'Look. Didn't it strike you odd that the bellboy just walked in on us?'

'Kind of.'

'Exactly. He could have slipped the note under the door.'

'Well, he's just a kid. Didn't know any better.'

'I'm sure the hotel taught him the rules. I think somebody put him up to it.'

'Why?'

'To check up on us.'

'But who—'

'I don't know. That's why I want you out of Beirut.'

'All right.'

'You mean it? You'll go?'

'If you'll come with me.'

'I can't.'

'You *won't*!'

'That's right.'

'Oh, fuck!'

'Beg pardon?'

'Fuck, fuck, fuck!'

'I believe that describes this activity.'

'Like hell! Every time we talk about Beirut, you go limp!'

They lay side by side and watched the smoke from their cigarettes eddy overhead. The steaming air from the open balcony window sifted across their sweating bodies. At intervals, heat lightning flickered over the Bay of St George and illuminated the room with a brilliant glare.

He heard her sigh heavily. 'Something?'

'No.'

A few moments later she sighed again.

'Okay. What is it?'

'Nothing.'

She reached for the ashtray on the nightstand and stubbed out her cigarette.

'Yes. There is.'

'I thought so.'

'I'm frightened.'

'Of thunderstorms? Hell, this is nothing! Probably a cheap little export model from Egypt.'

'Egypt?'

'Uh-huh. About a hundred and fifty miles south of us.'

'That close?'

'You're not much on geography, are you?'

'No.'

'We're about halfway between Egypt and Turkey. And almost in spitting distance of big brother Russia.'

There was another flash of light, then an explosion of thunder almost overhead. The windows and doors rattled.

'Go on. Keep talking.'

'What do you want to hear?'

'Anything. Just talk.' Her voice sounded strangled.

He rose on one elbow and stared at her. Her face was still soft, childlike, from her last climax. Red hair spread out on the pillow, a crimson halo; eyes wide, the darkest blue. Another glare of light. He saw that her cheeks were wet.

'You *are* frightened.'

She pressed her face against his arm. 'It's not the storm.'

'Then what?'

'I should never have quit my job in London.'

'Why?'

'I just shouldn't.' She paused, as if groping for reasons. 'I'd never had any money before. When that Arab gave me some, it went to my head. Now I'm out of work.'

'That's the story of the theater, isn't it?'

'And what I hate about it.'

'Then try something else.'

'No. No, I love acting. Love it, and hate it. When I'm on, I'm alive. Really alive.' She thought for a moment. 'Unless you've acted, you can't know what I mean. When you've got a good part, and you're good in the part, and the audience is with you, it's—well, magic. It's what Sarah Bernhardt called "when the god comes."'

He chuckled. 'Comes, does he?'

'Yes. Really. Both meanings. It's possession and surrender. When you and the audience are both tuned in, it *is* like coming together. Most of the time, it isn't that way, but you're always fighting to make it. For that moment when everything works.'

'And when it doesn't?'

'Emptiness. Failure. Loneliness. Like a shadow stumbling around looking for a body to follow.'

'That's you now?'

'Yes.'

'Because you're no longer with the troupe. You're off the team.'

She sniffed back the tears. 'Oh, God, I'm scared!'

He smiled and touseled her hair. 'It'll pass.'

'Will it? Dave, I'm out of a job. Maybe I'll never get another.'

'You will. You're not exactly ugly, you know. And you've got talent.'

'How do you know? You've never seen me act.'

'The hell I haven't. The way you dramatize a screw . . .'

She giggled. 'A crotch thespian, huh?'

'—who is now suffering from withdrawal symptoms.'

She gave a relaxed yawn. 'Thank you, Dr Magill.'

The storm had faded to a mere grumble in the distance. He awakened with a start. He felt her hand on his shoulder.

'Darling?'

'Hmmm?'

'Talk to me.'

'Ummm. What about?'

'Us!'

'Us?'

'Yes!'

'For instance?'

'For instance, how do you feel?'

'Exhausted.'

'Nothing else?'

'Uh-huh. Bushed. Zonked. Zapped.'

'I mean, how do you really, really feel?'

'Okay. I guess.'

'A literal-minded bastard, aren't you?' She pulled herself upright and frowned down at him. 'You're feeling okay, you guess. Would it absolutely kill you to say: "I love you"?'

'No. But it might make me impotent for life.'

'Oh, shit!'

He sighed. 'Sandy, don't make so much of us. Enjoy the moment. That's all we've got.'

'The hell it is! I've been waiting hours for you to say something to me. In Paris, you weren't afraid to tell me things. Even frightening things. Here—*nothing!*'

'Paris was different.'

She shook her head. 'It's the same. I loved you there, I love you here.' She watched him a moment. 'You just won't say it, will you?'

'Words are easy, feelings aren't.'

'All right. Forget the words.' She laid her head on his shoulder. 'Just come home with me.'

'Where's home?'

'Anywhere! We can leave tonight. Tomorrow, at the latest.'

'You go. You've got to.'

She jerked her head up again. 'That's all you say! *Go!* But never *why!*'

'Because I'm involved in something that may get me killed.'

'I thought so!'

'And I don't want you included in that package.'

'Don't go noble on me! Dave, we can be out of here—'

He cut her off. 'All right. I've tried to make it easy, but you won't have it. I'll give it to you straight. But first tell me one thing.'

'Yes?'

'Who told you to get me out of Beirut?'

He watched her face. The lips puffed from too many kisses, eyes hollowed from too many orgasms, hair stringy from sweat and hanging limp about her face. A face that faded to a lifeless gray. She shook her head slowly, dazedly.

'No—no! Oh, *no!*'

'Yes! Who's paying you?'

'You—*dare* say that to me?'

'I do. Who is it?'

She slammed her fist into the mattress. 'God damn you lousy bastard! God damn your soul to hell! Yes! *You!* I didn't ask you into my life! *You* followed me onto that train! *You* had to see me in Paris! *You* had to screw me! *You* did this to me!'

Her bitterness scalded him. He reached out to touch her, but she swept his hand aside. 'Oh, I had it all figured out! I thought if I acted like a cock-crazy nympho, I'd have you! I thought if I made myself the greatest fuck you ever had, you'd be mine!

Every time you exploded in me, I thought, *We're together! Together always!* And now, now you say, "Get lost!"'

'That's right,' he agreed calmly. 'I got all I wanted out of you in Paris. That finished it.'

'And here? Tonight?'

'A free lay.'

'And your talk about me leaving, not getting involved in this terrible, awful danger—'

'The brush-off.'

Her eyes went dead. 'I was just ass.'

'Right.'

'Some place to shove it.'

'Exactly.'

'That was why you wouldn't say you loved me.'

'Because my real girl is flying in tomorrow. From New York.'

Her mouth went wide in a silent cry. Her body shuddered with sobs that made no sound. Her fingers clutched convulsively at the sheet still damp from their lovemaking.

He dressed quickly. She was still crying when he went to the hall door. He looked back at her, a naked tumble on the bed.

'Stay as long as you want in Beirut,' he said. 'But keep away from me.'

17

Magill slept late into the morning. When Yussef served him breakfast in bed, he reported that Passacougli had left the villa at an unusually early hour. Magill smiled to himself. He understood why.

He showered, shaved, and strolled downstairs. Yussef was bowing to him again. There was a telephone call; the effendi could take it at the master's desk.

It was Preston Buck, at the airport.

'Got your note, boy. Seems kind of a shitty thing for you to pull on me.'

'In what way, Mr Buck?'

'The auction. I'm willing to pay high, but I don't like competition.'

'But you'll be there?'

'Hell, yes. There's one thing, though. I don't hanker driving out in the country at night with a satchel of cash. You think a helicopter could land at this Moumeili?'

'A helicopter?'

'I can rent a big one here at the field. We could leave early and land beforc it's dark.'

Magill thought rapidly. He dared not discourage Buck. The auction must seem genuine until the last moment.

'Tell you what, Mr Buck. You drop by here for cocktails and dinner and we'll all go to the auction together.'

Buck fairly purred into the telephone. 'Sounds like you're giving me the inside track, boy. What time?'

'Five-thirty.'

'Okay. See you.'

Yes, it was kind of shitty, the way he was treating Preston

Buck. The man would go to some Beirut bank and arrange for possibly a million dollars in cash for an auction that would never occur. But that in itself was part of Magill's plan. The news would be all over Beirut: 'Preston Buck is bidding.'

He looked at his wristwatch. By now Sandra Morgan should have checked out of her hotel. If she believed his scene of the night before. It was worth checking. He picked up the telephone again. Yes, the operator said, Miss Sandra Morgan was still registered.

Magill swore to himself. The stubborn little fool. He'd have to throw a real scare into her. The operator came back. Miss Morgan did not answer in her room. Magill asked to have her paged in the lobby. But there was no answer to the page. He asked for the concierge. He would know if Sandy had space on a late plane. The concierge said to hold, please. In the background, there was a muddle of voices, telephones ringing, the pounding of a document-stamper. The concierge came back, speaking in French. He had picked up the wrong telephone.

Magill cut in. 'Look. I'm calling about Miss Sandra Morgan—'

The concierge switched languages. 'Oh, yes, sir. I have booked you on the tour. But you must hurry, sir. The bus is loading at the door.'

'Hold on. I said Miss Sandra Morgan—'

'Yes, sir. The Baalbeck tour.' The concierge hesitated; his voice changed. 'Sir, you *are* the gentleman who inquired—' Another pause. 'Please, may I ask your name? . . . Hello? . . . Hello, sir!'

Magill's stomach tightened. 'Look! Just tell me one thing—who asked you to put him on the same bus with Miss Morgan?'

'Sir, I cannot speak of matters concerning our guests.'

'Listen, you bastard! Get a boy out to that bus! Get Miss Morgan back into the hotel! It's urgent!'

'Sir, you have not given me your name. You must identify yourself. I cannot disturb Miss Morgan or the tour unless—' He broke off. There was rapid conversation in the background. The concierge returned. 'Sir, I have just learned. The bus has already gone.'

Magill slammed up the receiver. It was happening. The thing he had feared. But who was tailing Sandy and why? He debated if he should try to get hold of Passacougli. But what could he do? And there was no time. Magill would have to act himself.

He raced upstairs, got his pistol from the suitcase and dropped it into his pocket. Baalbeck. Where the hell was it? Some place east. Then he remembered the books which he had studied on the plane flight from Paris. He flipped through the pages until he found a map of Lebanon. There it was. East, over the mountains. On the Beirut–Damascus highway. He checked the scale of the map and estimated the distance. Something between fifty and sixty miles.

He ran down the stairs and almost collided with Yussef. Just the one he wanted to see. Would Yussef please tell Mr Passacougli that he was borrowing one of the cars? He wanted to do some sightseeing. He would be back in the afternoon. Oh, and which was the quickest way to the garage? Yussef was still explaining as Magill went out the front door.

He found two Cadillacs in the garage, as well as Chantal's red Maserati. He chose the Cadillac with the fuller tank.

He decided the best way to find the Damascus highway would be to drive down to the center of town, where he could pick up a road sign. He lost his way, of course. Each street he tried betrayed his sense of direction. Finally, by sheer accident, he found himself in the milling traffic of the Bourj Centrale. He hailed an officer and asked directions. The man spoke only Arabic. Then a second officer. Arabic again. The third understood French. Magill was on his way, forty minutes behind Sandra's bus.

The mountain road climbed and curled and looped back upon itself. The rooftops and minarets of Beirut receded into the morning mists. All that was visible to the west now was the Mediterranean itself, a brazen mirror dotted with occasional tankers. The Cadillac swept along dizzying precipices and flashed through canyons still vaporous with morning mists. Here and there, roosting on a lonely crag, Magill saw a summer villa of some Beirut millionaire, or the tumbling walls of a Crusader outpost. Road traffic was light and Magill pushed the car as fast as he dared, hoping at each turn he would see the tourist bus. After a while, he realized that it had too much of a head start. He could not overtake it short of Baalbeck itself.

He was near the summit when he heard a horn echo across the gorge to his left. There was no car in sight ahead. He eyed the rear-view mirror. Nothing. Yes, there was. On the last curve below him, a flash of red. Ridiculous. It couldn't be. There were a lot of red automobiles. Besides, nobody knew he was on this road. Still, damn few cars could eat up a mountain the way this one was doing.

The red Maserati pulled even with him. Chantal waved gaily. There was a man beside her, one of Passacougli's men. Magill saw a turnout ahead; he braked, swung onto it and stopped. The Maserati halted alongside.

'You will find this more exciting!' Chantal called, indicating her car.

Magill glowered and shook his head.

'Please! Mr Passacougli insists! You are not to be alone.'

Magill watched her get out and come toward him. She wore barefoot sandals and a sleeveless butter yellow dress. An officer's cap shielded her face.

'I shall be your guide,' she continued. 'I know all about Baalbeck.'

'You know all about a lot of things.'

She leaned her elbows on Magill's door and gave him her most disarming smile. A scent of citron perfume teased his nostrils. 'You may drive by yourself, if you wish. But we shall still follow you.'

They would. There was no way he could prevent it. He stared at the man in the Maserati. Magill had had his fill of double agents.

'Okay,' he said. 'But we go without *him*.'

She considered for a moment, then spoke to the man in

Arabic. They switched cars. Passacougli's man got into the Cadillac and headed it back toward Beirut. Magill slipped behind the wheel of the Maserati, ran through the gears experimentally, then gunned up the grade. Chantal slipped down comfortably in her seat and hummed to herself. After several miles of silence, she smiled shyly.

'You are angry with me?'

'I don't like people who listen into private telephone calls.' He watched her puzzle for a moment. 'That's how you knew about Baalbeck, isn't it?'

She shook her head. 'Mr Passacougli phoned me from his warehouse.'

'I see. Then he bugs his own line.'

'Bug?'

He did not bother to explain. Obviously, Yussef had reported Magill borrowing the Cadillac for the sight-seeing trip, and Passacougli had some means of recording telephone calls at the house. All he had to do was to push a button at the warehouse and listen to a playback of Magill's call to the Phoenicia Hotel.

Although Magill was not ready to admit it to Chantal, her company was a pleasant addition to the journey. True, she might be an encumbrance at Baalbeck. He had no idea what would happen there. He was confident that he could handle the man who was following Sandra, but less confident how to avoid a face-to-face between Sandra and Chantal. Then, as he thought about it, he saw a plus in the situation. If Sandra should see Chantal with Magill—from a distance, of course—it would prove that his 'real girl' was very much on the scene, and that Sandra might as well pack up and leave.

The Maserati attained the summit and began the long descent of the Anti-Lebanon. The pines and cedars of the rain-blessed western slopes gave way to low brush and long stretches of barren rock. In the eastern distance, beyond the Valley of Bekaa, across the border in Syria, Mount Hermon rose in hazy silhouette.

Chantal flicked on the car radio and tuned in Radio Damascus. A smoky contralto voice wavered above the static. It was Um Kalthoum, Star of the East. Her language was Arabic, her meaning universal. Behind the voice, drums thumped, reed instruments whined, cymbals and gongs and bells marked the end of every verse. Chantal opened her handbag, took out a cigarette, lighted it and placed it between Magill's lips. Then she lighted another for herself. All this while, her handbag lay open, allowing Magill to see the gleam of her silver-handled revolver.

He nodded toward the gun. 'That was how you planned to defend me?'

She laughed. 'That was duty of the man you sent back to Beirut.'

'There won't be any trouble. Nobody's tailing us.'

'True. But Mr Passacougli did not know that.'

'Do you always carry a revolver?'

'Yes.'

'Why?'

'Habit. One never knows.'

'That implies you've been in some tight spots.' She smiled at him enigmatically and let it pass. He tried another tack. 'You haven't always had the easy life of Beirut and Passacougli.'

'No. But interesting.'

'Where?'

'Cairo. Istanbul. Teheran. Other places.'

'And *who?*'

She held up one hand. 'This part, it is very beautiful.' The contralto voice soared, higher and still higher, then dropped abruptly to a growl, keening in quarter tones for a lost love.

The record ended and Chantal sighed. 'It is truth, what she sings. When one loves, one lives. While it is so, one must never turn away from the feast.'

Magill looked at her sharply. She laughed. 'You see. I really tell you nothing.'

'That's for sure.'

The road straightened and coasted down the last long slope of the Anti-Lebanon. The Maserati sped past bedouin camps, with their low-spreading black tents and troops of barking dogs. Then a camel caravan, plodding upward, laden with textiles for the *souks* of Beirut. Vineyards and groves of almond and apple trees flitted by. Then, rushing toward them, Magill saw the towering, gray-pink columns of Baalbeck.

He had supposed wrongly that Baalbeck was simply a collection of ruins thrusting out of the plain in isolated splendor. Now he saw that it was circled by a native village of shattering ugliness. Chantal directed him onto a side road which brought them to the main parking area for the ruins. Then Magill was surprised again. Where he had expected one tourist bus, there were half a dozen. Some bore Lebanese license plates, some Syrian. All were empty. Sandra was already somewhere among the ruins.

They bought their entrance tickets and pushed past hawkers of postcards, Pepsi-Cola boys, old men selling 'genuine' Roman coins, drivers of hire-cars who shouted their rates for the trip to Damascus and Zahlah and Beirut. They walked westward through the rubble of two thousand years toward the main ruins, situated on a rise which Chantal called the Acropolis. A hot dry wind gusted dust up into their faces. Lizards scurried ahead or studied them from atop great stone blocks. Finally, the Acropolis and the tourists. Straggling groups plodding behind spieling guides, posing for pictures in front of tumbled archways, collapsed pediments, fallen columns. Men in sweat-damp shirts, women in wrinkled cottons. Teen-agers with transistor radios growing from their ears. Magill's eyes went from face to face—no Sandra—while Chantal talked of the building of the great temples and of Baal worship and fertility rites and sacred prostitutes. They wandered past the six colossal columns of the Temple of Jupiter, and Chantal told of Baalbeck's surrender to Saladin and, later, to the Turks. More tourists, these speaking German. No Sandra. Then south toward the crowning glory of Baalbeck, the Temple of Bacchus. A base of solid stone towering almost twenty feet above their heads; atop that, a neck-craning peristyle of nineteen granite columns. More sightseers. This time Magill caught a flash of Sandra's red hair. A guide was leading the group directly toward him. Magill slumped down onto a broken pedestal. Why not rest the feet a few moments? Chantal frowned; it would be more interesting inside the Temple of Bacchus; the interior carvings were worth much study. Sure, fine. But first there was a pebble in his shoe; it was killing him. He fumbled with his shoelaces. The tourists were passing now. Sandra on the far side of the group. The shoe was off. Where the hell was the pebble? He glanced up casually. Sandra was passing not more than ten feet away. Had she spotted him? Would she look at him? No. At Chantal. A hard, unblinking, appraising stare. Well, that was the damndest; no pebble, after all. The shoe back on the foot. More fumbling with laces. The tour was rounding the corner of the temple: they were disappearing inside. Magill got to his feet. So there were interesting carvings in the temple? Chantal began a history of the great structure, of the earthquakes which had demolished its roof. Sandra paused outside the temple. She rested her camera on a block of granite and stared upward, making a show of admiring the huge ceremonial entrance. Then she walked toward it. Magill interrupted Chantal.

'That girl! She's forgotten her camera!'

He darted forward, snatched up the camera and dashed into the temple.

The Temple of Bacchus is divided into two parts. The forecourt, or *cella*, immediately inside leads to a series of broad steps which mount upward to the main interior. It was on the steps, halfway up, that Magill spotted Sandra, purposely dawdling behind the rest of the party. He sprang up the steps, brandishing the camera.

'Miss! Oh, miss!'

'Oh, good heavens! How could I forget?' She projected her voice in the best stage manner. Then, taking the camera, and *sotto voce:* 'Congratulations! She's everything I was afraid she'd be.'

'Sandy, I'm here for one reason—'

'Mmhmm. To show her off to me.'

'No! You're being followed.'

'Yes, it's nice for a change.'

'You *know?*'

'Certainly. He bought me drinks last night, and this morning flowers and candy—'

He wanted to shake her. 'And you think he's got a thing for you? God Almighty, don't you see? That's the smoothest act of all!'

She frowned uncertainly. 'You sure know how to build up a girl's ego.'

'Sandy, I want you alive. Can you get that through your skull?'

She shifted uneasily. She glanced up the great staircase. At the top the guide gestured and declaimed the beauties of engaged columns and arched niches and pedimented shrines. Not all his listeners were visible; and of those, only the heads and shoulders.

Magill's eyes followed hers. 'Which one?'

'You see the two Arabs on the far right?'

'Yes.'

'The one with the dark glasses and the big moustache.'

'Uh-huh. And the other guy?'

'No. Just a tourist. Dave, are you sure—'

'Positive. It might even be the same outfit that's on my tail. Two murders in forty-eight hours.'

'Oh, God!' She was more than convinced; she was near panic.

Magill thought for a moment. 'Here's what you do. You walk out of here and wander around outside. Make him follow you.'

'What are you going to do?'

'Never mind. And when you get back to Beirut, I want you on the first plane out. Promise?'

She nodded. 'I promise! I swear I will!' She put out her hand, as if to touch him. Then she dropped it helplessly. 'Be careful,' she whispered. 'Oh, please, please!'

He watched her start down the steps. She reached the sunlight and looked back. She called to him, mouthing the words silently. *Remember me!* Then she was gone.

He turned his attention to the man with the sunglasses and moustache. Yes, he was running down the steps. As the Arab came even with him, Magill caught his arm and spun him around. The man grunted, one hand darted toward a pocket, then froze as Magill's pistol rammed his stomach. Magill frisked him, found the revolver, tossed it behind him.

'I have a message for you,' he muttered. 'Forget the girl. No more drinks, no more candy, no more flowers. Got that?' The pistol prodded. The man swallowed and nodded. 'Good!' Go back to the parking area and get in one of those hire-cars and head out. Because if you don't, if you aren't gone in three minutes—I'll use *this*.' The pistol jabbed again. He released the man's arm and propelled him down the remaining steps.

Magill strolled out of the temple. He shaded his eyes. Yes, the Arab was kicking up dust on his way to the parking area. In the opposite direction, Sandra elaborately took photographs of the Temple of Jupiter. Chantal was sitting on the stone where Sandra had left her camera. She flipped away her cigarette and smiled coolly.

'She is very pretty.'

There it was. The damning compliment. He wondered how much she had seen; why she had not followed him into the temple.

'These tourists,' he muttered lamely. 'They're so absent-minded, they'd forget their heads if they weren't screwed on.'

He proposed that they go up into the temple and inspect the carvings. Chantal shook her head.

'There is no purpose.'

'Sure! You said they were good. I want to see.'

'You have done what you had to do.'

He flushed. 'What are you talking about?'

'You put something into her camera.'

'No!'

'Then you took something out.'

'I did not!'

She shrugged. 'No matter. You came to Baalbeck to see her. And *I* came to see her.'

He stared unhappily. So that was it.

'You slept with her before Beirut?'

'Why ask? You seem to have all the details.'

'Yes. Mr Passacougli's man was most thorough.'

'Thank you, Mr Passacougli.'

They walked back to the Maserati. Magill put the car into a fast reverse, swung out of the parking area along the connecting road, then onto the highway. He pushed the accelerator to the floor and kept it there. They drove in silence. Chantal chain-smoked and stared bitterly at the oncoming mountains. Why in hell, he wondered, did Passacougli tell her? A fit of jealousy? And double why-in-hell had Magill allowed Chantal to come along?

Just before the first switch-back they overtook the hired car from Baalbeck. The passenger stared back at the Maserati, saw Magill, and leaned forward to the driver. The car spurted ahead. Magill smiled to himself. Amazing how simple it was to make people follow your commands. But the motive for shadowing Sandra? Colonel Mahmoud would remember hiring her in London to find Farren. Now she had turned up in Beirut. The colonel would want to know why. And Magill, in turn, wanted to know *how*. He was afraid that he already knew the answer. He had been followed to the Hotel Phoenicia. Someone had watched him write that note in the lobby: the note which was placed in Sandy's box. Well, thank God, she would be soon out of the whole mess. Only a few hours more.

Magill slowed behind a procession of trucks which labored up the switchback. The car with the Arab was somewhere up ahead. That was where he wanted it, so there would be no chance of it doubling back to Baalbeck. Chantal stubbed her cigarette in the ashtray. Then, as if continuing a dialogue which had been going on in her mind:

'Her hair, it is truly red?'

He winced. 'It is.'

'You would know. Yes.' She leaned toward him and shouted over the noise of the trucks. 'Tell me about her ass!'

For a moment, he doubted that he had heard correctly. He shifted and shot past the trucks.

'It is a beautiful ass? It fits well? Oh, I am sure! It takes you with such joy!'

'Oh, for God's sake!'

'But I must know! I appreciate good things. Tell me what you do with her. I want to know what I have missed—since *my* body is not worthy of you!'

He swerved out from behind another truck. Directly ahead, a bus bore down on them. He tramped desperately on the accelerator, shot forward and swung in front of the truck. There was a screech of horns, the bus plummeted past . . . Christ, he had to get hold of himself. The bitch would get them both killed.

She returned to the attack. 'Her mouth! You have not told me about that! It is a madness? But of course! She is so thirsty for you!' Then, almost at his ear: 'And that heaven between her legs! It is so tight, yes? And delicious!'

His blow caught her on the cheek. She spat in his face.

His hands trembled on the steering wheel. He was furious. He was disgusted. How could she so lower herself? She was no longer beautiful. She was ugly, venomous.

He turned on the car radio. If he were back in the States, he could at least listen to cooking recipes. Radio Damascus faded in. And Um Kalthoum again. With the slow, suggestive beat of drums. There was the trouble, he decided. It was the whole damned atmosphere of the Near East. Everybody steaming in sensual dreams. Still worshiping Baal and his fertility rites. How about turning off the radio? No. Don't give Chantal the satisfaction. There *had* to be something else he could think about. Yes. He was hungry. No lunch. At Baalbeck he had seen boys selling candy and flat bread. They should have bought something. Another 'should have'. He was conscious of a movement by Chantal. Still smoking, still scowling at the road, she hooked her heels into the front of the bucket seat and propped up her knees. Her skirt slipped down her thighs and exposed the full length of her legs. Purposely, of course. Taunting him with those long, tapering tanned legs that led his eyes to one place. Converging on it. Damn the bitch. That did it. That really did it.

They were near the summit. Ahead, to one side of the road, he saw a cut in the embankment and a trail that climbed up a wooded slope. He braked sharply, downshifted, and sent the Maserati growling and grinding up the trail until it was hidden from the highway. He cut the engine and sprang out. He yanked open the door on Chantal's side, seized her arm, pulled her from the car. He dragged her up the trail. She stumbled, lost a sandal. He jerked her to her feet; she limped on. He turned off the trail, towing her behind him, plunged through brush and scrub pine. Branches whipped their faces. They broke out into a clearing and Chantal began tearing at her clothing. By the time they reached the base of the pine tree, she was naked. He kicked together a bed of pine needles and covered it with her dress. She dropped down onto her knees and clawed at his trousers.

When he entered her, he drove with the fury of a battering ram breaching an enemy fortress. She writhed, arched, ground against him. Two animals locked in silent combat. He flung her about in the pine needles, wrestled her onto hard shale, rolled with her into a thicket of ferns.

Afterwards, they dragged themselves back to the pine needles. Bodies bruised and scratched, mouths gritty with earth, lungs and ears ringing from the altitude. High above them, in the pine, Magill saw a squirrel peering down curiously. Some show, huh, boy? It was ironic, he thought. Sandy, who had known discomfort and poverty, had made love with him in luxury hotels. Chantal, the elegant, the pampered, had coupled in the dirt.

She was kissing his shoulders and murmuring over and over '*Ya habibi! Ya habibi!*'—Oh, my love, Oh, my love!

He plucked the pine needles from her matted hair and smoothed away the grit on her cheeks. 'Why me?'

She smiled. 'Because.'

'That's a reason?'

'I do not need reasons. I knew it would happen, from that first night.'

'When you brought me from the airport?'

She nodded. 'I felt you already inside me.'

She kissed his mouth for a long time. Then she lay down beside him. They closed their eyes.

18

Some forty-five minutes out of Beirut they turned off to the mountain resort of Broummana. It was, Magill thought, a delightful retreat, with magnificent views of the sea and mountains. They drove past several deluxe hotels and a scattering of small restaurants. One of them surely could provide them with a late lunch. Chantal decided on the Restaurant Regal because, she said, she remembered that its women's room was hidden from the dining area. Without being seen, she could slip in and make the much needed repairs to her makeup and hair.

It turned out that they were the only customers. All but one waiter had already gone off duty for the afternoon. Magill chose a table by one of the picture windows and ordered two scotches. By the time he was joined by Chantal—as beautiful as ever and positively radiant—he had already finished his drink and had ordered the specialty of the house, pizza, and Chianti.

They fell on the food with abandon. Neither paused for words until the coffee and cognac. Magill lighted Chantal's cigarette and watched her curious smile. Something was greatly amusing her. Then she gave a little laugh.

'Yes?' he prompted.

She let the smoke curl from her nostrils. 'I think . . . I think I made much worry for myself. There was no need.'

'How so?'

She inhaled again. 'You are not as I thought.'

'Probably not. Nobody is.'

'You do not love the American girl.'

She paused, waiting for his confirmation. But since he did not wished to debate it, he decided to turn the conversation to put her on the defensive.

'Passacougli didn't ask you to follow me this morning, did he?'

Her eyes slid past him. She, too, wanted to evade.

'How did you know I was going to Baalbeck?'

'Yussef told me.'

'I never said Baalbeck.'

Her eyes flitted back to him, then away again. 'Yussef said you left in much hurry.'

'And that's all he could say. You listened in on a telephone call I made to the Phoenicia Hotel.'

'No!' She hesitated guiltily. 'I was curious. I listened *after* you had gone. After Yussef told me.'

'That's what I said before. Passacougli has his telephone calls recorded.'

She nodded. 'When he is away. It is a box in his desk. One pushes a button and it is all there.'

'And you heard me talking to the concierge about the girl and the tour to Baalbeck.'

She ground out her cigarette. 'I am not ashamed! I called Mr Passacougli. He said, yes. You should not go alone. I am glad for what I did!'

He saw that he was pushing hard. 'I'm glad, too.'

'That I followed you?'

'Yes.'

Her smile returned. A moment later he felt her bare foot, under the table, pressing against his ankle. 'You do not love her. This afternoon was proof.' The toes wriggled happily up his shin. 'I will tell my man it was a mistake.'

'What man?'

'The man I pay to follow her.'

He stared. 'A detective?'

'Since Mr Passacougli told me there was a girl. I know everything she does. Last night, after you left her, my man reported she walked the Corniche. Today, he will telephone me about Baalbeck.'

He began to laugh. He tipped back in his chair and whooped. Oh, he had been so dramatic, so protective, so damned heroic. About nothing. Then he was conscious of

Chantal's look of irritation.

'Sorry. I couldn't help it.' A final chuckle. 'The poor bastard! I threatened to kill him!'

Chantal shook her head. 'He was not my man.'

He frowned. 'You saw?'

'Yes. There was my man. And the other two. They work together.'

Magill came forward in his chair. 'Your man told you?'

She nodded. 'Perhaps there is another woman you make jealous?'

He was no longer listening. No wonder the fellow chased off so easily. His partner was still with Sandy.

He persuaded Chantal to drop him off at the American Embassy, on Avenue du Paris au Corniche. There was a matter, he said, which he must take up with the commercial secretary. Better to lie than to renew Chantal's resentment of Sandy. Then, as soon as the Maserati disappeared into the traffic, he took a taxi to the Phoenicia Hotel.

The room clerk was quite certain. Miss Sandra Morgan, Room 478—yes, she had checked out at least an hour before. Magill suppressed a smile of relief, then went to the concierge's desk. Of course, the young lady with the red hair. The concierge had booked her on Air France, a through-ticket to London. Flight time? The concierge glanced at the clock on his desk. 'It is already past, m'sieur. Ten minutes ago.'

Magill lit a cigarette and wandered out of the hotel. One less worry. He strolled along Minet el-Hosn and stared out at the bay and the speedboats towing the water skiers. He wished that he were one of them. Nothing to do but enjoy an afternoon of mindless physical activity. That was what he needed; something to dissipate the day's tension. Why not a walk? A really long one. Say, the entire length of the Corniche. Which is what he did. He breathed in the bracing salt air, noted the surprising coolness of the afternoon, admired the soft clouds which drifted overhead. And completely closed his mind to the evening to come, the final test of wits with Ward Farren. He walked for almost an hour. Then he hailed a taxi and told the driver to take him back to the villa atop Sursock Hill.

Yussef opened the massive front door. When he saw Magill, he gave a sob, tears started down his cheeks. Then Magill saw heads peering from doorways all along the main hall. Servants, male and female, all staring at him. He turned to Yussef. What had happened? Yussef choked out something in Arabic. Magill seized his arms. English, damn it! English!

It was the master. The Effendi Passacougli. He was dying.

It was totally unreal, like all such moments. Magill, shaken, dazed, trying to piece it together. Yussef, in tears, stumbling between English and Arabic, interrupting himself with appeals to Allah for mercy. A car had come to the house. A man. Chantal met him at the door. He said the effendi had been in an auto accident. He was dying. He asked for the mistress. She had gone off with him. Half an hour ago.

Magill wanted to curse, to scream, to smash something. That fucking walk. He was wandering the Corniche when he should have been there, at the villa. He could have gone with Chantal. He left Yussef and started down the central hall. The servants watched him pass, eyed him somberly, expectantly. As if he could do something, make things right. Just what *was* he going to do? He would call the hospitals.

He hurried to the main living-room, intending to use the telephone on Passacougli's desk. No. He had better wait. Not tie up the line, in case Chantal called to report. She would do that. Efficient as hell, that girl. Yes. He would wait half an hour. If she did not call by then . . . He slumped down onto the sofa and tried to think things out. Everything was in ruins. He could not possibly go ahead with the auction tonight, not without Passacougli. All of his planning, all of his hopes, had gone smash. And all of it seemed so unimportant, now. Magill lit a cigarette. Damn it, he had not realized how fond he had grown of that character. He understood, for the first time, Chantal's feeling for him. She could sleep with a dozen men—a hundred men—and still belong to Passacougli, because he was vital. A force, an original. He was the glue that held things together. For Chantal. For Magill, so long as he was in Beirut.

He got up from the sofa and wandered around the room. Somewhere he had seen a decanter. Cognac or scotch or araq. He'd settle for anything, even cleaning fluid. Then he heard Saladin's thundering bark. Somewhere in the front of the house. And men and women shouting and crying.

He dashed through the rooms and out into the central hall. He saw the servants, down on their knees, wailing and weeping. He saw Yussef, prostrate, touching his forehead to the floor, kissing Passacougli's shoes.

Alexander Passacougli was unharmed. He had simply returned home.

Magill groaned. It was clear now. Chantal had been kidnapped.

19

Passacougli's face was, for once, totally without expression. Neither frown nor grimace, neither puff of cheeks nor cluck of tongue. He neither groaned nor cursed. Rather, as he listened to Magill's account, he seemed to shrivel, to collapse inward. Like a sleepwalker, he moved along the central hall, then through room after room, until finally he came into the great living-room. He sank down behind his desk and looked vacantly at the telephone. Then, as if summoning the last vestige of strength, he picked up the instrument.

Magill placed his hand over the telephone.

'Not yet. No police.'

Passacougli blinked uncertainly.

'Wait until we get word from the kidnappers. Let's hear their terms.'

Magill's words were instant adrenalin. '*Terms*!' Passacougli exploded. 'I know them! I help you tonight, or I never see Chantal again! Those are the terms you will send me!'

Magill recoiled. The poor guy. He was coming unstuck.

'Chantal is your guarantee! I understand everything. You and this Ward Farren are partners. Tonight you will rob those oilmen of millions!'

Magill laughed, out of sheer disbelief. 'Sure, that's it. Ward and I put guns on everybody. We hijack the cash and skip.'

'And I help you! All Beirut laughs at Passacougli the fool!'

Magill's surprise turned to cold anger. 'Okay, since I'm a crook, I'll tell you a crooked suspicion of my own. You faked this whole thing with Chantal. You rigged yourself an alibi so you won't have to go through with tonight.'

It was a standoff. Neither believed his accusation.

Passacougli's eyes filled. He swiveled his desk chair, turning his back to Magill's gaze. He moaned something in Arabic, perhaps a prayer, perhaps a curse. Then, in English Chantal, his Chantal. She was more than a woman. She was beauty and mystery and life itself. She was Astarte, the goddess descended. She had blessed Passacougli with her presence, had made him young again. It was as embarrassing to hear as any excess of emotion.

After the emotion came the silence which was even harder to bear. Then Yussef hurried into the room. He bowed and babbled apologies and dragged behind him a white-haired man with stooped shoulders. Magill recognized him as the head gardener. The man shuffled to the desk and presented a small package which was wrapped in newspapers. The gardener, Yussef explained, had heard an auto horn at the front gate. He saw a man get out of a car and throw the package over the gate. Passacougli picked up the package, hefted it, shook it, smelled it, turned it over and read the words which were written on one side in grease pencil:

FOR MR MAGILL AND MR PASSACOUGLI. OPEN AT ONCE.

They tore off the wrapping. Inside was a cardboard box. They opened it and ripped out wads of tissue paper which cushioned an object: a disc of recording tape.

Yussef brought the tape recorder to the desk and Passacougli, fingers trembling, fitted the disc into place. He flicked the switch. They watched the spinning spools and the tape glistening through the playback head. At first, there was no sound. Passacougli swore and turned up the volume control. Then the voice filled the room. It was unmistakably Sandra Morgan.

'I'm sorry, Dave. I tried to keep my promise. I really tried to get out of Beirut. Then I was told you were in an auto accident.'

She paused. There was a rustle of paper in the background. She was reading from notes.

'This is what you are to do. You are to go to the auction tonight. But you must not show your film. You must not show Ward Farren's film. You will take it from him. You will give the film—all of it—to a man who will be there. You will recognize him. He will bring you to where I am. If you do everything just as he says, I will be all right. You must not call the police. He says if anybody interferes—' She broke off with a gasp. There was muffled confusion in the background. Then, finally, a sob. 'I love you, Dave.'

The spools whirled on. The two men stared at the machine. Grim, swallowing hard. Then they stiffened. A new voice spoke. Chantal.

She spoke in Arabic. Calmly, stoically. Magill listened intently, trying to guess her meaning. He recognized isolated words and phrases that he had heard from Yussef and the servants. *Inshallah*—'If God wills.' *Bsmillah*—'With God's blessing.'

'She says all is well,' Passacougli translated. 'Now that she knows I am not hurt, she thanks me for the days we have shared. She hopes to see me again.'

Whatever else she said was not for Magill's ears. But the final words, almost whispered, he did understand. He had heard them before. *Baatrack seedie*—'Goodbye, my master.'

Passacougli turned off the machine. 'Now we know.'

Magill nodded. 'Colonel Mahmoud.'

Passacougli called the Beirut chief of police and told him there would be no need for his men at the auction. There had been a stupid mistake.

Then they played the tape through again. Magill closed his eyes and listened. When he heard Sandy's gasp of pain, it was as if he had actually seen what was being done to her. Sourness surged up into his throat. When Chantal spoke, Saladin came galloping into the room. He barked at his mistress' voice, circled frantically, then leaped up at the machine and whined his bewilderment.

Magill slammed his fist against the desk and shouted over Chantal's words. 'God damn you, Farren! All of this, because of you! Damn your lousy soul in hell!'

Passacougli shut off the tape. 'He will not come tonight.'

'He will! We've *got* to get his microfilm. That's Mahmoud's deal.'

'He may not even know there is an auction.'

'He does! If Mahmoud knows, Farren does.' Magill groped for justification. 'Your men planted those letters of mine all over Beirut. The oil companies got them, and when Farren called them . . .' He stopped. What was the use? Words were only words.

Then, in the silent room, they heard a muffled whooshing sound. The stained-glass skylight overhead began to vibrate, the glasses in the liquor cabinet rattled and danced. The sound overhead increased to a clattering roar. Then Magill remembered. He stared at his wristwatch. It was five-thirty. Preston Buck was dropping by for cocktails.

'I thought you gave up the helicopter idea,' Magill said in greeting to Buck. 'You were to drop by here and we'd all go to the auction together.'

'And we will,' Buck retorted. 'By helicopter. I told you, I don't like strange roads at night, when I got this with me.' He patted his attaché case. 'We can land there, can't we?'

Magill turned to Passacougli. 'How about it?'

'If the pilot knows Moumeili.'

'I already asked him,' Buck said. 'Jack says he's done aerial surveys all over the place. It's a cinch.' Then Buck noted the cheerless expressions of the two men. 'What's eating you, boy? This is your big night, isn't it?'

Magill forced a smile. 'It's a long story.'

They drank highballs around Passacougli's desk and ate sandwiches as dinner. Preston Buck listened carefully to the events of the afternoon and to Magill's account of how it had all begun. When he finished, Buck twisted his mouth skeptically.

'Then you've been chasing Farren ever since London?'

'Yes.'

'But of course you wouldn't tell me this in Paris. Or right here yesterday morning. If you'd told me about the stolen oil maps . . .'

'I thought I could handle it.'

'Sure! Like some snotnose who believes in Mother Goose!' Buck glowered at his drink. 'All the bugger wants to do is clear his precious name.' He glared at Magill. 'That what you're asking me to believe?'

Passacougli intervened. 'We have one purpose, sir. One desire. All else is forgotten. Two lives must be saved. Two women who mean much to us.'

'If it were your own wife—' Magill pressed. 'If Mrs Buck—'

'Spare me the violins.'

In reality, Buck did not wish to be spared. He asked to have the tape played. He slouched back on the sofa and listened intently to the two voices. When the tape finished, Buck coughed to cover his emotion. He massaged his chin with his fist and pondered. 'Let's hear some more about this Colonel Mahmoud. You think all the killing and kidnapping is on orders from his boss?'

Passacougli shrugged. 'One must assume. Sheikh Ali Muhammid is known for his feelings against the Israelis.'

'This is what I'm getting at. Let's say the colonel has got carried away with his orneriness. Suppose this gets out, and his boss is unhappy with the publicity—the colonel may just be looking for a new job.'

'Christ, who cares?' Magill snapped. 'By then the girls will be dead.'

Buck grunted. 'Stop jumping ahead. I'm saying, maybe this colonel is already kind of uneasy about his future. Maybe he can be reached.'

'Bribed?'

Buck caressed the attaché case beside him. 'I got a million and a half. U.S. currency. You take your microfilm to the colonel, he hands over the girls. I give him the cash, he hands the microfilm to me. Next thing we know, the colonel is swinging it in Rio de Janeiro.'

Magill and Passacougli exchanged looks. Buck saw it and chuckled. 'Look. Legally, the microfilm belongs to Anglo-Tex, which has the concession. Israel's got a claim on it, too. So I go to everybody and I say, "Okay, boys. I just ransomed your property for a million and a half. That earns me a slice of the pudding. A nice big juicy slice."'

Magill was the first to recover from the surprise. 'Then you're with us tonight? The whole way?'

Buck grinned. 'Boy, I've tailed you all the way from London. It's a habit now.'

It was dark. The outdoor movie at Moumeili was already well into the second reel of an ancient western made without soundtrack. The villagers and farm folk squatted on the earth and stared up at the screen—strung between two giant oaks—and listened to the storyteller chant his interpretation of silent love scenes and noiseless battles. A troop of scruffy dogs snuffled through the audience in search of food leavings.

Preston Buck's helicopter had already landed behind a screen of cypress a quarter-mile downhill from the movie. Two of Passacougli's Cadillacs were parked along the dirt road bordering the movie area. They had brought Passacougli's most trusted men, who were now scattered through the audience.

Magill, Passacougli, and Preston Buck leaned against the side of one of the Cadillacs and stared down the road at the string of approaching headlights. It was ten minutes till eight. The oilmen were arriving.

One by one, the taxis discharged their passengers. American, British, French, Italian, Dutch, Japanese—all had chosen to disguise themselves. Robed, pantalooned, burnoosed and fezzed, they advanced into the village audience and plumped down onto the ground. The effect was as if members of a fancy dress ball had wandered into a meeting of a Kansas 4-H Club.

Passacougli nudged Magill. Another pair of headlights. This time it was not a taxi; it was a Land Rover. The man who got out from behind the wheel had not bothered with a disguise. He was plainly Arabic, his head was bald and there was an ugly scar on his forehead.

'It's him!' Magill hissed. 'One of the guys from Byblos.'

The Arab strode toward Magill. He nodded curtly and held out his hand, palm upward, as if demanding the microfilm. Magill turned to Passacougli.

'Tell him I'll give it to him when Ward Farren gets here.'

Passacougli translated into Arabic. The man scowled and growled a reply.

'He says if Colonel Mahmoud does not receive the film within one hour, he will know there is treachery.'

They watched the Arab stalk toward the audience and squat down where he could survey the whole area. Preston Buck checked his watch and squinted down the dirt road. There were no more headlights.

'Boy, it looks like your friend is going to be late.'

Magill glanced grimly at Passacougli. 'You sure your men checked everybody?'

Passacougli was certain. His men had required the storyteller and the movie projectionist to identify each male member of the audience. Farmers, shepherds, drovers, timber cutters, blacksmiths—each was accounted for.

Magill stared at the farmhouses in the distance. 'He could have got here early. He could be hiding in one of those houses or barns. We should have checked.'

It was ten past eight. The voice of the storyteller quavered with excitement as the Indians on screen shot their fire arrows into the beleaguered fort. The oilmen in the audience stirred restlessly. What was holding up the auction? Colonel Mahmoud's man got to his feet.

Preston Buck whispered, 'Do something, boy! Stall them!'

But how? Was it possible that Farren didn't know of the auction? Or was afraid to come? No. He *had* to. The plan *had* to work. The moment Magill saw him, he was to signal with a flashlight. Magill's men would converge from all sides. Pin him to the ground; seize his microfilm. But if Farren did not come . . .

Magill's stomach growled from tension. His feet hurt. His neck ached. His crotch itched. He could no longer think constructively. He could only remember Sandy's arms around him; Sandy crying during the thunderstorm; Sandy at Baalbeck, begging him to be careful; Sandy's gasp of pain, on that tape: *I love you, Dave.* Then—Chantal swimming beside him; Chantal moaning her ecstasy under the big pine; Chantal's moving farewell to Passacougli . . .

Preston Buck muttered again. 'The Arab's gonna walk out. Do something!'

Magill nodded dazedly. He moved toward the bench where the projectionist stood beside his machine. He signalled him to switch it off. The screen went black. Magill's voice cut through the darkness. Patience, please! The auction would begin in another minute or two. It was necessary to reload the film projector. There was a buzz of bewilderment from the villagers, who did not understand English; the oilmen clapped approval. Magill whispered to the projectionist to continue the movie. Unless the screen was lighted, he might not see Farren.

The screen brightened again. Magill swung his eyes over the audience. Mahmoud's man was still standing, undecided. Passacougli and Buck were to one side.

To the rear, in the open field, appeared the dark outline of a man. He was hurrying forward across the field. Magill stared hard. He was coming from the direction of the farmhouses.

It was Ward Farren.

Magill dared make no movement. He must wait. Farren had to get close enough to the audience for Passacougli's men to seize him. He was still coming. He was very near now. Magill looked sideways and saw Mahmoud's man start toward Farren. Magill blinked his flashlight. Then, as close together as two heartbeats, Farren recognized the Arab. He cried out 'No!' He flung out his right arm and fired.

It was almost instantaneous, and yet dreamlike, a nightmare in slow motion. Magill saw three spits of flame, saw the Arab pitch forward, saw Passacougli's men racing toward Farren, saw himself pushing through the audience, heard himself screaming curses at Farren.

Magill dropped down onto his knees beside the Arab. He thrust his hand inside the man's shirt. There was a great deal of blood. But no heartbeat.

20

Taxi doors slammed, engines gunned, gears ground. The oilmen were gone. Everyone wished distance between himself and the body sprawled on the ground. The projectionist packed his equipment and disappeared. The villagers melted into the night.

Two of Passacougli's men held Ward Farren between them while Passacougli wearied himself with spitting on the prisoner, slapping him, cursing him, kicking him. Magill looked on somberly. He could understand Farren killing the Arab who had tortured him in that house at Byblos. Farren had reacted out of fear.

Finally, Passacougli had vented all his frustration. He walked away.

Blood trickled from Farren's nostrils. His eyes were already puffing. Yet he managed a rueful smile at Magill.

'It would have worked, Davy. We could have pulled it off.'

Magill nodded wearily. 'We could have. We should have.'

Anything would have been better than this, Magill thought. His morbid determination to clear himself had brought only tragedy. He had dangled a bright shiny abstraction called 'Integrity' in front of his own eyes until he was hypnotized, and he did not know it for an abstraction. He was as sick as Farren because Magill had been dishonest with himself. Yes, sick. Sick with the hero syndrome. A terminal illness.

Preston Buck caught Magill's elbow and led him to one side. 'You got his microfilm?'

'For what it's worth.' The gold pillbox containing the film was safely in Magill's pocket.

Buck dropped his voice. 'What happens to the girls?'

'You heard the tape.'

'You sure the dead guy is the only one who could lead you to them?' He saw the answer in Magill's face. Buck shook his head and sighed. 'Jesus. I'm sorry, boy.'

They saw Passacougli walking toward them. He was nodding and smiling to himself. Unbelievably smiling.

'Chantal has escaped.'

Magill and Buck answered in unison, 'How do you know?'

'She carries a gun. Always, everywhere.'

'I know,' Magill said. 'But that's no proof she's escaped.'

'She is free. She is home. She is waiting for me.'

'Passacougli—' Magill took his arm, but he pulled free.

'I must telephone her. I must tell her I am coming.'

They watched him go. A sleepwalker in a dream of happiness. 'Christ!' Buck muttered. 'What a time to shoot his marbles.'

'Why not, if it helps?'

Magill decided that the police should be notified. They would want to examine the scene of the killing. They could take Farren in. Buck said he would have his helicopter pilot radio the airport, which would contact the authorities. Magill agreed; then thought of the radiotelephone in Passacougli's limousine. It was much nearer than the helicopter.

They found Passacougli in the back seat of the car. He was staring at the receiver in his hand. He shook his head; Chantal was not yet home; the recording device which answered the calls was still in operation. Magill reached for the telephone, still intending to notify the police. Then, at that exact moment it came to him with the force of a blow.

'Passacougli! This afternoon! Was the recording machine working?'

Passacougli blinked at him uncertainly.

'When we were at the house! When we first knew of the kidnapping! Was the recording machine working?'

'I don't know.'

'Think!'

'So much, so many things, I do not remember.'

'You've *got* to!'

Passacougli's face grimaced with thought. At least it was

serving to bring him back to reality.

'It was not working.'

'You're sure?'

'I telephoned the police. You were there. You heard me. I asked them not to come here tonight.'

'Right! But was the machine working *before* that? Before you made that call?'

'Perhaps.'

Magill shook him. 'Not *perhaps!* Was it?'

'Yes! I remember. That is when I turned it off. I did it, from habit.'

'And afterwards, you turned it on again?'

'I must. It is working now.'

'Is there some way to find out if any messages have come in?'

Passacougli nodded. 'One dials the next higher number. Then it plays back.'

'Do it!'

He thrust the car telephone at Passacougli. They waited for Central Telephone to relay the call to the villa and Magill explained. Chantal, he said, had told him of a detective who was shadowing Sandy; Chantal received regular reports from him on Sandy's movements. Suppose the detective had seen the kidnapping of Sandy. Suppose he had called Chantal, had left a message on the recording machine.

Passacougli's face clouded. He did not believe it. Why should Chantal hire such a detective? Why should she care about the American girl?

Before Magill was forced to answer, Preston Buck clambered into the front seat and stared at them quizzically. Only a moment's diversion, but enough. Then the telephone connection was completed.

There were several messages, which Passacougli relayed to Magill. A party invitation from a banker friend. Someone reminding of a charity benefit. Preston Buck calling Magill about the auction, and Magill inviting him to cocktails. Suddenly Passacougli gesticulated. Yes! Here it was! The detective. Calling Mademoiselle Larrigues. Magill placed his ear alongside the receiver. Damn. The man was speaking French, spewing it out at top speed.

Passacougli translated the gist of it. The American girl had taken the morning bus tour to Baalbeck. The detective had sat behind her. At Baalbeck, she talked to the American gentleman who was known to his client. She had returned with the tour to Beirut, to the Phoenicia Hotel. The concierge informed him she was checking out. She would be on Air France to London. End of report.

Magill swore. Their last chance. A blank.

Passacougli snapped his fingers. There was a second report.

The American girl had come down to the lobby. Her bags had been loaded into the airport bus. Two men had followed her outside. They talked, then she went with them. They got into a Land Rover. The detective followed in his own car. They did not go to the airport. They drove across Beirut, then north on the road to the Grotto of the Djinn. At the parking area for the grotto, they got out of the Land Rover and into a rowboat. They went into the grotto. The detective did not understand this. The American girl would surely miss her plane. He was making this report from the telephone at the bus station a mile from Jeita. He would return to the grotto and watch the Land Rover. He would report again.

But there was no further report.

Magill turned to Passacougli. 'What's this grotto of the Djinn?'

'A great cave. An underground lake. There are boats for hire and guides.'

Buck snorted. 'Jesus! Didn't that detective suspect something? Could he *see* something was wrong?'

'How would he know?' Magill countered. 'The Arabs come up to Sandy, at the hotel. They say I've been hurt badly. They'll take her to me. The same routine pulled on Chantal. So she goes without a struggle. By the time she sees through it, they've got a gun on her.'

'He did suspect, that detective,' Passacougli added. 'He said the girl would miss her plane. He knew about that. He knew she would not do the sightseeing. That is why he said he would report again.'

'Then somebody stopped him. Maybe paid him off, or—' Magill interrupted himself. 'Look. Time is running out. All we care about is, Where is Sandy right now? Where is Chantal?'

'In the grotto.'

Both men stared at Passacougli as if he were slipping back into fantasies.

'There are many caves. Many hiding places.'

'That couldn't be seen by tour boats?'

Passacougli bobbed his head. 'No boats. They are late morning, early afternoon. Then the guides leave. There is no one until tomorrow.'

'How big is this grotto?'

'Very big.'

'Like the Blue Grotto at Capri?'

'That is nothing.'

'Then much bigger?'

'Very, very much. Within the grotto there are other grottos. There are caves and islands and reefs.'

'Would Mahmoud be able to see us coming in?'

'Perhaps.'

'If he's there,' Buck said.

'He will be. He's waiting for the microfilm.' Magill turned to Passacougli again. 'This parking area for the grotto—could a helicopter land there?' Passacougli was certain it could. Then, to Preston Buck: 'Think your pilot could find the place?'

Buck scowled. 'Sorry, boy. This is where I get off.'

'You said you were with us. You wanted to buy the microfilm from the colonel.'

'That was before his man got killed. That queers my deal.'

Magill saw he would have to try another approach. 'Okay. On your flight back to the airport, you could detour, drop us off at the grotto.'

'I wouldn't want just to go off and leave you there.'

'We'll manage.'

'No. This isn't my can of worms.'

Magill waited a mental count of ten. Then, to Passacougli: 'So we go by car. How long will it take?'

Passacougli sighed. 'Too long.'

'Yes. Mahmoud will know something has gone wrong. He'll move out. And Sandy and Chantal will be . . .' Magill did not have to finish the sentence.

Buck scratched his cheek. He looked at Passacougli. He looked at Magill.

'Oh, what the fuck!'

The lights of Beirut swung in an arc below and to the rear. Magill stared out the cabin windows at the lights of the ships far at sea. Inshore, he saw the distant glow of the Casino du Liban. Further up the coast, he made out the lights of Byblos, where he had last met Colonel Mahmoud. Would they be too late? Was it already over? He shuddered and felt sick.

Jack, the pilot, swiveled in his seat and shouted something at them. The clatter of the helicopter almost drowned his words. He gestured and shouted again. The road to the grotto. Couldn't find it. No landmarks, no moon, no traffic, no headlights. Passacougli cupped his hands and shouted back into the pilot's ear. Turn back. To Beirut. Pick up the road where it left town. Oh, God. More delay. And less time . . .

They crisscrossed the northern outskirts of the city. Finally, Passacougli jabbed a finger downward. He recognized the road. Jack dropped the helicopter to one hundred feet. He switched on the landing lights beneath the fuselage and illuminated the road below. They followed it easily now. Skimmed above it as it curved through the hills, dropped down with it into valleys and soared again through more hills. Then a last bank and a downward swoop. They were on the parking area for the grotto of the Djinn.

There was one car in the parking area. They approached it warily and played their flashlights over it. It was a black

Volkswagen. The door on the driver's side hung open. Beneath it, face down, was the body of a man. A revolver lay just beyond one outstretched hand. Magill turned him over. He had been shot in the neck and the chest. Magill searched his pockets. There was no identification. But in one outside coat pocket, there was a stub of paper. He held it under the flashlight. It was part of an admission ticket to the ruins of Baalbeck.

Magill straightened up. 'Now we know why he never phoned in that next report.'

Buck looked queasy. 'Shot by the man Farren killed?'

'Probably. Came out of the grotto and saw the guy.'

Magill checked the interior of the Volkswagen. If he could find the detective's notebook, it might record what happened after his last report. But no notebook. Either it had been taken, or the man had been an egotist who kept everything in his head. Passacougli climbed into the car on the pretext of helping with the search. He bent close to Magill and whispered, 'There may be a sentry at the grotto. Someone we could bribe.'

'Maybe, if we can get inside without any shooting. How much money you got?'

'Sssh! Mr Buck carries a million and a half.'

Magill grunted. There was such a thing as overtipping. 'Don't say anything,' he muttered. 'Let me handle him.'

They clambered out of the car. Preston Buck was already starting toward the helicopter. Magill caught up with him, held out his hand, and thanked him for the use of the helicopter. It was nothing, nothing at all, Buck assured him. But now what did they plan to do?

'Go into the grotto.'

'After what you've just seen? Boy, this place is death!'

Magill shrugged. 'When you get back to the airport, I think you ought to let the police know.'

'Sure will!'

'There's one other way you could help.'

'Yes?'

'If you could stay with us a couple of minutes while we scout around. We may find something else you should report.'

There was no way out—with dignity. They rejoined Passacougli.

It was decided not to use Magill's flashlight, to save the batteries for inside the grotto. There was still no moon, but the night was clear and the faint starshine allowed them to make out shapes and to follow each other. They went along the edge of the parking area until Passacougli found the flight of wooden steps which angled down a steep bluff. They trod slowly, held onto the handrail, felt for each step. They heard bullfrogs and the murmur of a stream below them. There was a flap of wings, and a night-bird screamed. Then they were at the bottom, standing on a wooden landing. They made out the dim shapes of moored rowboats. At the end of the landing was a dark hulk which Passacougli said was the ticket booth for the boat tours.

'So now what?' Buck grumbled to Magill.

'Now we see if there's another body.'

'Jesus! Whose?'

Magill had set up the motive, now he gave the excuse. 'We'll need more than one flashlight. You two stay here.'

He started back up the wooden steps. When he reached the helicopter, he asked Jack to lend him the powerful worklight which he had seen in the cabin. Then he relayed 'Mr Buck's orders'. The pilot was to take the helicopter up and maintain a holding pattern over the area. At the end of thirty minutes, he was to land again. If they had not returned from the grotto by that time, Jack was to radio for the police.

The pilot was uncertain. He really should have such instructions from his employer in person. On the other hand . . .

On the other hand, Magill completed. Somebody might be out there in the darkness waiting to hijack the helicopter.

The pilot was a man of discretion.

Magill had just returned to the boat landing when they heard the clatter of the helicopter. The running lights of the helicopter rose into the night and curved away from them. Buck gave a panicky groan. 'God in Heaven! He's leaving!'

'Looks that way, doesn't it?'

'He's finking out on me!'

'Maybe he saw something. Or somebody.'

Magill turned casually to Passacougli and handed him the worklight. Passacougli switched on the powerful beam and swept it along the water. Beyond the boats, looking to the right, Magill saw the stream winding between sandbars. Then, still farther to the right, the abrupt rise of a rocky cliff. At its base the stream issued out of a jagged blackness. It was the entrance to the grotto.

Buck thrust in front of the light, blocking its rays with his body. 'Christ! Don't! They may have a lookout!'

'If they have,' Magill said, 'he's already gone inside.'

'How do you know?'

'He would have heard the chopper. He'd go in to report.'

'And if he has? Then what?'

'We'll find out.'

Passacougli played the light along the row of boats. They saw that most of them were powered by outboard motors and were chained and padlocked to posts. Magill pointed to one farther away. It was a simple rowboat, with oars slung inboard. Magill and Passacougli walked to it, and Magill crouched to untie its line.

'Hey!' It was Buck again, catching up to them. 'What about me?'

Magill looked up at him. 'Why don't you go back and wait for us in the Volkswagen?'

'With that dead guy?'

'Okay. Then right here.'

Buck stared around. The moon was just breaking over the mountain, and the light created a new menace. Shadows.

'We'd ask you to come with us,' Magill said, 'but there's no percentage. You've got everything to live for. Nothing to gain and everything to lose.'

'Mr Magill is right,' Passacougli agreed. 'In our case, there is no choice. We are about to know the breath of the tiger.'

'Huh?'

Passacougli nodded gravely. 'The man who dares the breath of the tiger is a very brave man, or a fool, or a dead man. In that moment, the disguises of a lifetime drop away, he knows himself for what he truly is. It is a moment of great richness.'

Magill choked. Melodrama, hokum, put-on—whatever, the old coot knew what he was doing. Preston Buck glanced around at the shadows again, drummed his fingers on the side of his attaché case—then clambered down into the boat . . .

Magill rowed. The stream was not wide, but it was deep. The current was leisurely, for which Magill was thankful. The moon was clear of the mountain now, and it was no problem to navigate the sandbars. The rock cliff loomed higher and the black mouth of the grotto loomed nearer. Then, abruptly, Magill rested on the oars.

'I just thought of something. Mahmoud must have set up some sort of a double-check.'

'Like what?' Buck grunted.

'Well, to be sure it isn't the police coming into the grotto. A password.'

Passacougli spat over the side. 'Which we have no way of knowing. We must reach our women before we are challenged.'

Buck shifted uncomfortably. 'Suppose we don't?'

Magill reached into his pocket and laid his automatic on the seat beside him. Passacougli followed suit with his revolver. Buck stared at them for a moment. Then he opened his attaché case and took out a pistol.

They were very close to the mouth of the grotto. From now on there would be silence. They dared not risk the creak of the oarlocks, so they began to paddle canoe-fashion. Magill knelt on one side, Passacougli on the other. Preston Buck hunched in the bow.

They glided through the ragged arch of rock. Moonlight and starlight snuffed out. They were in absolute darkness. The entrance was like a tunnel, Passacougli whispered. He remembered that there was a bend to the right, then another to the left. Then they would come out onto the subterranean lake. But how soon, Magill wondered, before the first bend?

They found out. The boat smashed prow-on into invisible stone. Magill and Passacougli lurched with the impact and almost lost their oars. Magill swore to himself. Buck was in the bow—why hadn't he sensed the coming collision? He could have stretched out his arms and felt the wall. No, what a ridiculous idea. Extrasensory perception was what was needed. Or light.

Magill shipped his oar. He dug out a cigarette lighter, shielded it with his hand, and flicked the flint. He had to risk it. It was a brief flare, but enough. Directly forward, there was a wall of slimy limestone. Overhead, great stalactites dripped moisture from their dagger points. But there, off the left gunwale—clear water. Passacougli nudged and pointed. A few yards farther, on the left, was the other bend. Magill capped the lighter. They back-oared, swung the boat, and paddled again. They would try to carry the proper directions in their heads, as if this were possible. Oars dipped. Water swished and gurgled. Overhead, seepage dripped onto their heads, splashed into their faces—bitter tasting, foul smelling. Then another crunch, another backward lurch. They had over-corrected. They had rammed the opposite wall. God, this was worse than Magill had imagined. They would never get out of the tunnel.

But they did. They could sense the lifting of the oppression of encircling rock. The swirling sound of the oars in the water faded to a whisper. They had come out onto the lake.

Now it was even worse. Now they were floating in nothingness. Black, limitless nothingness. Were they right side up or upside down? Magill concentrated on the pressure of the invisible water against his oar. The boat was beneath him; he could feel the boards under his knees. Right side up. Yes. So forget about it. But he could not. Each time he raised the oar from the water, lost contact with it, the sensation returned. He was falling, floating, drifting in eternal space. In the black of unconsciousness. And yet still conscious. Row. Just row. Magill's face, hands, arms, his whole body, flowed with sweat. He felt as if each hair on his body were standing on end. Row. Keep rowing. His lungs wheezed. He wanted to cough. He wanted to sneeze. He wanted to urinate. He wanted out. God, if this was the way he was feeling—what about Preston Buck? Or Passacougli? Or Sandy and Chantal? Yes. Think about the girls. Think about Mahmoud. Every stroke of the oar brought him that much nearer.

They had to be in the middle of the lake. Magill was positive of it. Yet no faintest glimmer of light from some hiding place. No voices. No scuffling of feet on rock. Then he felt the nose of the boat shift and tilt. It was Buck, groping toward them. Hands flailed the darkness, seeking Magill and Passacougli. Then he was between them and they were hissing into each other's ears.

'There's nobody here! Nobody!'

'Shut up!'

'For God's sake, Passacougli, why didn't you tell us what it would be like?'

'Would you have come?'

'Turn around! Get us out of here!'

'We can't. We don't know which way is out.'

'The flashlight! Then row like crazy!'

'Sure! Faster than a bullet—because that's what we'd get.'

'There's nobody here, I tell you!'

'Buck, you want me to slug you?'

'You're sick, boy! Sick! Get us killed, fine! We don't count. The girls don't count. All you want is revenge!'

Magill's fist shot out. He missed. Buck was out of range. He was crawling along the floor of the boat. His hands flapped the boards until he found it. A flashlight. He snapped it. Magill and Passacougli grabbed. The flashlight spun out of Buck's hand. There was a splash.

The three stared over the side. They saw the flashlight sink straight down. At first the light glowed light green. Then blue. Then dark gray. Then it winked out. Water had leaked into the case and shorted it.

Buck whimpered. 'Jesus God! *There's no bottom*!'

'Sssh! Listen!'

It was overhead. A soft whirring sound. Then squeaking. Bats.

They clung to each other. Held their breath. Not moving. The bats had seen the flashlight. But had Mahmoud? They waited. They listened. Finally, silence again. The bats had quieted.

Magill thought carefully. In that moment when the flashlight had arced over the side, what had he seen? Something. It was almost subliminal. They were not in the center of the lake, as he had supposed. They were far to the left. He was sure of it. Magill was younger than Passacougli; he was stronger; his stroke of the oar had carried more power. He had swung them in a half-circle. They were near the left wall of the grotto. He had seen something else. Something directly ahead. He whispered this to Passacougli and to Buck. Yes. They, too. It was an island. But how far away? Buck guessed one hundred feet. Passacougli thought it was more. He remembered the island; the tourboats called it The Spaniard's Hat. It was triangular in shape, like the hat worn by Spanish policemen, a tricorne.

At that moment, all three heard it. Low, hushed, calling. 'Dave! Dave! Over here!'

It was Sandra.

Then a second voice. In Arabic. Chantal.

Passacougli moaned with joy. He seized his oar. Magill caught his arm. Wait. They had to determine the direction.

'The island!'

'*Where* on the island?'

The voices repeated. 'Dave! Hurry! Over here!' Then Chantal, in Arabic.

To the right. They all agreed.

'They're alone!' Buck crowed.

'*Sssh!*' Magill listened to the calls again. 'No. There's something fishy.'

'Like what?'

'Sandy doesn't sound too eager. Or Chantal. If they knew how close we were, they'd be more excited. They'd both be calling at once. Instead, each voice is separate.'

Passacougli got the point. 'The tape recorder!'

That had to be it. They were listening to a tape. Mahmoud and his men had devised something far better than a password. If the Arab had returned to the grotto, he would know where the girls were located. But the police, if they came, would be decoyed toward the voice.

Passacougli followed it up. 'Our women are at the other end of the island!'

'Maybe. If they're alive.'

'And if they're not?' Buck's voice trailed off.

'Then Mahmoud takes your money and kills us.'

Magill was already stripping off his clothes. He was going to swim to the island. He would find out about Sandy and Chantal. Then he would report back and they would decide their strategy.

Buck and Passacougli tried argument. In the darkness, he would lose his way. Maybe. How did he even know the direction of the island? The rowboat might have already swung around: the island could be at any point of the compass. Again, maybe. And, from the island, he could never find his way back. Yes, he would. They were to give him ten minutes. A slow count to six hundred, then flick on a cigarette lighter. Repeat it every thirty seconds.

He was down to his jockey shorts. He groped for the worklight which he had brought from the helicopter. He covered the lens with one hand, then switched it on. He spread two of his fingers just enough to permit a thin pencil of light. He aimed at the water, then up slightly. A swing to the right, a swing to the left. No island. They were right. The rowboat had broached. The island was in the exact opposite direction. But now he knew. He snapped off the light. He swung himself over the gunwale and slipped into the water. The last words he heard were from Preston Buck.

'What if you don't come back?'

He trod water for a moment. When he had oriented himself in relation to the boat, he took a deep breath and went under. He hoped that he was swimming just beneath the surface. With the grotto in darkness, it was difficult to know. The water was cold. More than cold, it was icy. And deep. He remembered the flashlight sinking down, down, down, changing all those colors. No, mustn't think, of that. He would make a game. Try to imagine himself in a backyard swimming pool. Only thirty feet long. And shallow. He would swim one length of the pool and surface. No point in taxing his lungs. Was it thirty feet yet? It had to be. He surfaced carefully. Gulped in air. Exhaled. Inhaled. Then under again. He thought he felt the water less cold now. The exertion was warming him, was good for him . . . To the surface. More fresh air. Then under. Was he still swimming in the right direction? Suppose that he had made a turn in the blackness without knowing it. It had all seemed so simple a thing when he was merely talking about it. But now that he was *doing* it . . . End of the pool. Another thirty feet. He hoped. The surface. Air. He tried to look around, without turning his body. Christ! What was that? A flare. Behind him. Then blackness again. The cigarette lighter. Damn! They weren't supposed to do that until he was swimming back to the boat. All the same, he was grateful. He was truly swimming away from the boat. Heading for the island. That was what they wanted him to know. Under again. The island should be near. Buck had guessed a hundred feet; Passacougli had said more. But surely not much. The water was suddenly colder again. Perhaps it was a current. Or was he tiring? Nothing like the water at Sidon, when he and Chantal had lazed in that wonderful warmth. He told himself, Pretend *now* is *then.* Pretend any second that her magnificient body will flash into sight; pretend those beautiful legs are beckoning just ahead . . . The surface again. Air. Under. There *was* a current. A strong one. Probably flowing around the island. God! What if there were underwater reefs? If he smashed his head into one. He would go down like that flashlight. Surface. Air. How much farther was that frigging island? He blinked the water from his eyes; he swiveled his head. There! *Behind* him! He had veered off course. He had swum past it.

He saw the island because it was no longer in darkness. There was a glow, a reflection of light which seemed to come from *within* the island. That was it. A cave or a hollow whose interior he could not discern. He trod water and attempted to form an idea of the rest of the island. The light was too faint to do more than guess. It seemed to be an accretion of limestone, a jumble of hummocks and hollows and stalagmites which thrust upward into the darkness. Possibly fifty or sixty feet in length, possibly twenty feet at the highest point. A perfect hiding place. Easy to defend, hell to attack. Especially that cave. Magill had to see inside it.

He allowed himself to sink. When he surfaced again, he was in shallow water. His feet found a submerged ledge of rock and he raised himself half out of the water. Now he recognized that one of the shapes, which he had assumed was a promontory of the island was in fact a rowboat. It was drawn up onto a slanting shelf of rock. Good. It must be the most direct landing spot for the cave itself. Magill waded cautiously toward the boat. He would use the hull as a screen for himself. He reached it; his hands slid along the gunwale. He felt the end of an oar. Then, farther along, a second oar. They were worth remembering. He raised himself completely out of the water and peered over the top of the boat. Yes. The light on shore was brighter now. Better still, with the extra elevation, he was able to see over a hummock of limestone. To see, beyond the hummock, something round and moving. A mass of red hair. Sandy.

He raised himself still higher. Yes. There was Chantal. Just beyond Sandy. Her profile was silhouetted against the light. From the position of their heads, which was all that he could see, they must be side by side. Now to locate whomever was guarding them. There must be some sort of a route from the rowboat to the cave. But if his feet dislodged one stone, caused one pebble to roll . . .

He edged around the nose of the boat. Half crawling, he reached the hummock of limestone. His hands explored the slimy, slippery surface. He needed to find pockets that would serve as footholds. He found them. He pulled himself up, slowly, laboriously. He winced as the stone cut into his hands, his knees, the soles of his feet. He shivered as the water evaporated from his skin. Then he was on top. Flat on his belly. Staring straight into the hiding place. It was not a cave, after all. It was a deep hollow under an overhanging ledge of limestone. It was flanked on both sides by stalagmites and great knobs of limestone. In the deepest part of the hollow, in a clear level space, there was an oil lamp. Sandy and Chantal sat hunched beside it. Arms tied behind their backs, ankles roped, mouths taped. Chantal's yellow sport dress, Sandy's blue suit, were half ripped from their bodies. They must have put up a fight when they had been forced to record those decoy messages. Poor as the light was, Magill could see the defeated expressions on their faces. If only he dared call out encouragement . . .

But where in hell were the guards? Then, as if in answer, the women raised their heads and stared off into the gloom. Magill saw a form materialize from behind one of the stalagmites. He was going toward the women. The rays of the oil lamp reached his face and Magill recognized him. The Arab with the broken nose. The one who had held the gun on him at Byblos. This time, Broken Nose was unarmed. He was carrying a boxlike object that Magill identified as a tape recorder. He crouched down beside Chantal and whispered something. Was he asking her to record something else? Then Broken Nose stared upward, toward the ridge of the island. So that was it. Relaying a command from the man up there. Someone who could look down and spot Magill.

It was time to get back to the safety of the water. To report to Passacougli and Buck. Magill slipped down the side of the hummock. As he reached the beached rowboat, there was a brilliant flare of light. He ducked down below the gunwale. No. The light was not aimed at him. It was reflected off the ceiling of the grotto. Its source was on the other side of the island. Then he heard the creak of oarlocks. Christ, it was Passacougli and Buck. The fools were coming straight for the island. Flashing that worklight. The idiots! Had they given Magill up? He should have known he couldn't trust Passacougli; the man would risk anything for Chantal.

Magill peered over the gunwale. High up on the ridge of the island, he saw the outline of a man watching the oncoming boat. Magill saw him raise his right arm. The man on the ridge was aiming a gun.

'Colonel! This is Passacougli.' His voice boomed and echoed through the grotto. 'We bring the microfilm!'

The voice that answered belonged unmistakably to Colonel

Mahmoud. 'I want to hear it from Hassan!'

The man Farren had killed.

'He cannot talk! There is a bullet in his jaw!'

'Police?'

'No. Mr Magill! Your man killed David Magill!'

Now Magill understood. His announced death was a hint that he should work this side of the island while they occupied Mahmoud's attention.

'Show us the women!' Passacougli shouted.

'The microfilm first!'

There was a new voice. 'This is Preston Buck! Give us the girls, let us keep the film, and you've got yourself a million and a half dollars, cash money!'

'It is with you?'

'Right here!'

For one wild moment, Magill thought Buck would win. Buck's voice called out again:

'The girls and the microfilm—and the money's yours!'

The colonel laughed. 'It is mine, yes!'

The light from the rowboat swung and targeted on Colonel Mahmoud. He fired. The light snuffed out. There was a yell of fright or pain.

Magill saw the Arab who was guarding the women pick up the oil lamp, as if he was going to smash it. He changed his mind, put it down, and shouted up into the dark. A moment later a revolver hit the ground at his feet. He picked it up and turned toward Sandy and Chantal.

In that same instant, Magill reached over the gunwale of the boat and seized an oar. He hurled it at the man's back. It hit hard, in the kidneys. He sprawled forward. There were two quick shots from above. The bullets shattered the gunwale beside Magill. Slivers of wood stung his bare chest. The colonel had seen him. Magill grabbed the second oar; he leaped ashore and reached the shelter of the overhanging rock. Broken Nose was already on his knees. He aimed his revolver at Magill. The oar smashed down the Arab's arm. The gun skittered across the rocky floor. They both dived for it. Then the Arab had it again.

He backed away from Magill, panting, grinning, enjoying the moment.

There was no escape. Nothing Magill could do. He heard the revolver cock. He saw Sandy and Chantal, struggle to their knees behind the Arab. As the gun fired, their bodies smashed against his legs. The bullet went wild. Then Magill was on him, pounding his head against the stone, until he went limp. Until he was dead.

The whole grotto roared with gunfire. Shouts and curses echoed, answered by more shots. How many bullets did Mahmoud have? How often could he reload? Magill could see him clearly. He was still high on the ridge, barricaded behind a great stalagmite. He aimed his flashlight down the opposite side of the island, and fired again. There was a scream.

Magill searched wildly for the dead man's revolver. God, where did it go? Somewhere in the rocks, or into the water. He seized one of the oars. It would have to do. He started climbing between the stalagmites, over the rocks, cutting his knees, gashing his feet, trailing blood behind him. Praying that Buck and Passacougli would not mistake him and shoot.

He was almost to the top, coming up behind Colonel Mahmoud. Then the colonel heard Magill. He swung his flashlight. He fired. Magill's right arm flamed and went limp. He sank to his knees. His left hand closed on the fallen oar. He threw. It caught Mahmoud full in the face. Gun and flashlight slid from his hands. He toppled backwards. Magill heard the splash in the water below, then a bubbling sound. Then silence.

Magill pressed his fingers against the pulsing wound in his arm and began the downward climb. Below, he could see Buck holding the oil lamp while Passacougli knelt beside Sandy and Chantal, untying hands and feet, untaping mouths. Mouths which, moments later, covered Magill's face with kisses.

21

They stood at the foot of the steps leading to the forward cabin of Preston Buck's plane. Magill, Passacougli and Chantal. They talked aimlessly in the manner of all people saying goodbyes. As he looked at Passacougli, his face smiling with the old animation, and Chantal, never more beautiful in a white suit and white toque—Magill realized that they were already a memory. Even as they talked, he missed them.

The aircraft engines whined and came to life. It was time to go. Passacougli arranged a spasm of coughing and turned away discreetly. Magill held out his hand to Chantal.

'I remember something you once told me.'

'Yes?'

'You said a woman always leaves her mark on a man.'

'Has she?'

'She has.'

Chantal smiled quietly. 'Also, a man leaves his mark on a woman.'

'Has he?'

'He has.'

'I'm glad.'

She raised up and kissed him on the lips. Slowly, tenderly. Then she moved away and Passacougli came forward. As he embraced Magill he spoke into his ear.

'She did love me. She will again.'

They smiled at each other understandingly, then Magill turned and ran up the metal steps. He did not look back. The steward locked the door. The aircraft trembled and began to move.

Miss Wilson brought him a scotch and soda, which he took in his left hand. Even after two days, his bandaged right arm was awkward and his hand uncertain of grasp. He sipped the drink and glanced around the cabin. Preston Buck was forward, standing in the doorway talking to his radio officer. Far aft, Sandra Morgan was nodding agreement to something that Mrs Buck was telling her. After those two days of official investigation by the Beirut police, after so many questions asked, so much testimony given—everyone connected with that night in the grotto now avoided each other. They were emotionally spent, perhaps even tired of each other. They wanted to forget what could not be forgotten.

The official investigation had been a marvel of tact, the newspaper coverage most sympathetic. It was Beirut's own Alexander Passacougli who had led the rescue of the two beautiful young ladies. As for the dead kidnappers, they were unidentified gangsters of uncertain nationality. There was some mystery as to the motive for the kidnappings. Certainly, none of the newspapers made connection with another story—a very small item—about one W. Farren, American, who had been handed over to the Israeli authorities for trial on unspecified charges. Nor was any link made to an announcement in the business news that Anglo-Tex Corporation was to commence large-scale drilling on its concession in Israel.

Magill finished his drink and immediately felt thirsty again. He got up and went forward to the bar and poured himself three fingers. He glanced into the mirror behind the bar and saw that Sandy was watching him. She caught his look and turned back to Mrs Buck.

He kept his eyes on the mirror. He noted the way the sunlight streaming through the window set her hair aflame. He noted the subdued taupe of her suit. He noted the almost prim way she held her legs. Subdued, that was the word for her. It was strange, he thought. She had helped save his life when the Arab had fired that gun; and certainly, he had saved her own life. Yet now they were wary of each other. Avoiding each other, as if afraid of what might follow. Was it, he wondered, an unconscious reaction to that Chinese idea—that if one saved another's life, one was then responsible for that person? What the hell, that was only a superstition.

The cloud cover broke and the Aegean Sea gleamed below like a great shield of silver blue. Magill, seated alone, saw Preston Buck bearing down on him. He waved two sheets of paper.

'I couldn't help reading these,' Buck said. 'They were sent care of me at Beirut Airport. They just relayed them.'

The first radiogram read:

BARAKATI CASE CLOSED. ALL GOOD WISHES YOU PERSONALLY. BROMLEY

Magill grinned up at Buck. 'News travels fast, doesn't it?'

'Yeah. All kinds.' Buck nodded toward the second radiogram.

WELL SHUT DOWN. ALL SALT WATER. WHERE IS THE MONEY? WHAT DO I TELL EVERYBODY? REPLY URGENT. BARNEY

It was like a message found in a bottle washed ashore. Words written by a stranger in another century. Poor Barney. Sitting it out in that California wasteland. Fretting about a hole in the ground that Magill had all but forgotten.

Buck sat down in the opposite chair.

'I can send your reply, if you like the wording I got in mind.'

'How would it go?'

'"Money tomorrow. Buck Oil & Gas Corp. just bought half-interest in lease."'

Magill pursed his lips. 'After all that's happened?'

'*Because* of all that's happened. I told Mrs Buck from the start, "That boy has got a pudding." A big pudding. Only I thought it was something in the ground. Instead, it's *you*. You're it. Brains plus guts. That's what I need to head up my next big play.'

Magill shook his head. 'I had a wife who wanted me to go broke so I'd have to work for one of the majors. I'm not about to prove her right.'

'Who said I'm a major? I'm an independent. One of the biggest.'

'No jazz about salary and stock options and fringe benefits?'

'Hell, that's for chicken-shits. You and me, we call 'em, we roll 'em and take what comes. We let your friend Barney try a few more holes in California—but you and me, we'll concentrate on the North Slope.'

'Alaska?'

'I got acreage down there all over the place. It's gonna come in big. So now, about an answer to that radiogram . . .'

Magill smiled slowly. 'Send it.'

He looked down the length of the cabin. Sandy and Mrs Buck had been playing cards, but now the girl was alone. He got up and walked forward and dropped into the chair which had been occupied by Mrs Buck. Sandy gave him a startled smile, then suddenly bent forward and busied herself with laying out the cards again. It made her lipstick too bright, the freckles on her cheeks and the bridge of her nose stand out as distinctly as the dots on dice.

He cleared his throat. 'I suppose stage people play a lot of cards.' Now *that* was a brilliant opener.

She nodded. 'Puts in time between entrances.'

They both stared at the progression of the cards, as if the fate of nations depended on it.

'When you get to London, you'll be looking around for another part?'

She shook her head. 'New York.'

'Oh, I see.'

'And you?'

'Buck has been talking to me about a deal.'

'Alaska?'

It was his turn to look startled. 'Christ, is this cabin bugged?'

'Mrs Buck told me. At least, she said she hoped—'

'Uh-huh.' He reached out and swept up the cards which she had laid out so carefully. He shuffled the deck and cut it. Then cut again. 'The bottom card is the ace of spades.'

She looked. 'Right.'

He shuffled again. Cut. Showed her the cards. Still the ace of spades.

'Can you do that every time?'

He nodded. 'I play a lot of solitaire, too.' Another shuffle. 'I was thinking: in case you don't find yourself a play right away—'

'Nothing is ever right away.'

'I've noticed that myself.'

'You were saying?'

'Well, if you've got some spare time on your hands, you might give New York a miss.'

'Oh?'

'Kind of take a look around. See a little more of the world. Unless you're tired of traveling.'

She dove into her handbag for a cigarette. He lit it for her and noted that her fingers were trembling. The color was rushing back into her cheeks. Her eyes were now a deep electric blue.

'Think you might?'

She let the smoke curl slowly from her nostrils. 'I might.'

Another cut. The ace of spades. 'Of course, Alaska might be a little out of your way.'

'A little.'

'And it's kind of primitive.'

'But full of opportunities.'

'The land of the future.'

She examined the cigarette between her fingers. 'It just might be my kind of place. Isn't Alaska where . . . where the nights . . .?'

He grinned. 'Uh-huh. They last for months and months and months.'

Also in Magnum Books

J. F. BURKE

Location Shots

A Sam Kelly thriller

Private eye Sam Kelly is flash, snappy and tough. Officially he's hotel detective at the Castlereagh, but other business takes him round most of the bars, card-rooms and bordellos of New York's Upper West Side. He likes to keep his 'patch' peaceful and that's how it stays – until one fine May morning he wakes up to find the hotel has been the scene of some very nasty murders.

'Don't miss this . . . Hyper-readable'

Observer

'The murders are ingenious'

Financial Times

'bursting out of its covers with vitality'

Irish Press

Death Trick

Sam Kelly is in the sack with Madam Bobbie when one of her 'girls' phones in urgently. The trouble is the hooker's client – he's lying on her bed, strangled with piano wire. When Sam starts investigating the dead man's business colleagues he discovers some interesting facts that spark off a tense and dangerous gamc of hunt-the-killer.

'It's a good fast-moving yarn'

Western Daily Press

'*Death Trick* is a very good thriller indeed . . . the action is fast and furious'

Irish Independent

ERLE STANLEY GARDNER

THE CASE OF
The Musical Cow

Rob Trenton is holidaying in Europe when he meets the lovely and mysterious Linda Carroll. Arriving back in America he readily agrees to take charge of her car. The problems begin with a puncture, when he discovers $40,000 worth of heroin concealed under the chassis. From that instant he is sucked into an international narcotics racket that lands him in the dock – charged with murder.

THE CASE OF
The Fabulous Fake

Diana Douglas is convinced that her brother is being blackmailed – she has discovered a blackmail note, a contact code 36-24-36 and $5000 in cash at his flat. Despite Perry Mason's advice, she is determined to pay off the blackmailer. But when she makes contact she finds him dead, and at his side is her brother's gun.

ERLE STANLEY GARDNER

THE CASE OF
The Hesitant Hostess

The woman on the witness stand was deadly clever. Unless he could shake her testimony the defendant was going to be found guilty. Mason had one surprise, and only one surprise. He hoped it would be a bombshell.

There was hardly time to spring that surprise and capitalise on the confusion it would cause before five o'clock, yet if he floundered around for twenty minutes with an aimless cross-examination the jury would retire for the weekend firmly convinced that the woman's testimony should be taken at face value.

Mason reached a decision.

'Mrs Lavina,' he said, smiling courteously . . .

THE CASE OF
The Worried Waitress

Waitress Katherine Ellis was young, orphaned and beautiful – she was also desperately worried. With growing interest Perry Mason listened to her account of eccentric Aunt Sophia, who skimped on housekeeping but would take taxis from shop to shop in search of bargain buys. More curious still, it seemed she had a fortune stowed away in hat-boxes. But when he heard of the strange noises at night, Mason was convinced that Katherine was in greater danger than she realized.

'When you get off at nine o'clock, go home. Pack up your things. Get out of that house.' This was his urgent advice.

JOHN D. MACDONALD

Soft Touch

Jerry Jamison had married a beautiful, spoiled child, and she had stayed that way. He had joined his own small business to her father's, and found frustration. After eight years the marriage had gone sour, the business become boring. Jerry was ripe for temptation.

It came from Vince, a war-time buddy. He arrived suddenly from South America, with a proposition. Millions of dollars were being smuggled out to buy arms. Vince intended to intercept the next cash delivery, and he needed a partner he could trust . . .

That was the first temptation, and there were more to come . . .

Dead Low Tide

Her name was Mary Eleanor – the boss' wife. She was one of those dark-haired Alabama girls and had on a sort of blue denim play suit. She slouched in the chair and crossed her brown legs. 'Will you find out something for me?' she asked. 'Will you find out what's wrong with John?'

Andy McClintock had no wish to start spying on his employer, and said so firmly. Nevertheless he became involved, and still further involved. The clincher was the body on the sand with a harpoon barb through the throat.

COLIN WATSON

The Flaxborough Crab

'I'm a bee,' said the voice in the darkness. 'I want to pollinate you. I'd like to lift your petals.'

The startled Mrs Pasquith was the latest victim of the Flaxborough sex-fiend, though her ordeal was vocal rather than physical. There had been three incidents, all at night and with one common factor. In each case the attacker was described as 'running sideways', almost like a crab. The virtue of Flaxborough's womanhood is in peril. Inspector Purbright and Sergeant Love get to work – and soon find themselves dealing with a certain Miss Luscilla Teatime.

Coffin Scarcely Used

Who would have thought that one of the mourners at Councillor Carobleat's funeral in May would be following him to the cemetery six months later – and from the very next house too? And what was one to make of the very curious circumstances of this new death?

Mr Marcus Gwill, proprietor of the '*Flaxborough Citizen*', had been found electrocuted at the foot of a pylon, his mouth full of marshmallows. This unfortunate occurrence lays an exciting and dramatic trail for Inspector Purbright.